DON'T COME LOOKING

AJ CAMPBELL

Code Grey Publishing

JOIN MY READERS CLUB

As a member of The AJ Campbell Readers Club, you will always be the first to know about my upcoming book launch promotions, get sneak previews of my book covers and receive free downloads of my work. Upon joining, all new members will receive a copy of *Choices* – a FREE short story, exclusive to club members.

See the back of the book for details on how to join. I look forward to welcoming you personally.

AJx

For Andy

PART 1

ONE

DAY 1

The day Marc disappears, I'm running up the steps back into work when I see him barge out of the automatic double doors like a prisoner trying to escape. I don't recognise him at first. The hood of his parka covers his head as if protecting him from a storm. My first thought is that the man must be baking in this June afternoon sunshine. I stop abruptly and do a double take. 'Marc! What're you doing here?'

His eyes are fixed firmly on his feet as if scared that he'll fall if he dares to look elsewhere. He rushes past me, and his small holdall, thrown over his shoulder, bashes against my arm. It knocks me off balance. I'm carrying a Costa, and coffee spills out over the lid and dribbles down my shirt sleeve. Damn, it's hot. I turn and watch as his urgency launches him down the steps two at a time. He marches off left towards the main road, turning the corner at the funeral directors.

Puzzled, I carry on into the police station, delivering the latte to Leo, one of my colleagues who works the front desk. 'Happy birthday,' I sing over the hum of officers talking on phones and tapping away on keyboards.

He looks up from his screen and laughs. 'My favourite afternoon treat,' he says, picking up his present. 'You're going to heaven, Eva Barnes.'

I grin at how fitting his friendly expression and stocky frame are for facing the increasing numbers of crime victims we encounter every day. Leo's like the station's guard dog. An Alsatian – courageous and loyal, but boy, don't get on the wrong side of him. I wipe small beads of sweat from my forehead. 'It's a scorcher out there again this afternoon.'

'You are coming for birthday drinks with us all later, aren't you?' he asks. 'My shout.'

'Busy, sorry. I'm off home soon.'

His bottom lip droops like the dog who didn't get the bone. 'You're always busy.' He shouts across at the other workers, 'Eva's not coming for birthday drinks.' Several heads look over at me, directing a roll of eyes or down-turned lips my way.

'What was that man doing in here? The one with the holdall,' I ask.

'Parka boy?'

'Marc O'Sullivan?'

'Correct.'

'What did he want?'

'Fancy this. He came in here and said he's leaving home, and when his family report him missing, he doesn't want to be found.'

'What?'

'Turner spoke to him but reported that the guy seemed the full ticket, so logged the incident and off he went. Adamant, he was. Married with three kids too. Can you believe that?'

'No, I can't,' I say, tapping the desk with my fingers, 'because he and his wife are our close friends. And as far as I'm aware, they are very happily married.'

I charge back outside, following the direction Marc took in the vain hope that I can catch up with him. It's the beginning of rush hour, and the usual surge of commuters heading towards the Underground packs the streets. I guess that's where he's aiming. Or maybe he's thinking of taking British Rail somewhere? I zigzag my way through the crowds, searching, trying to spot him through the flow of hurrying bodies. There he is, by a bin, searching through his holdall. Stepping sideways onto the road, I follow the double red lines, quickening my pace. I cough on the exhaust fumes from the heavy traffic as black cabs and red buses sweep past. I see him zip up the holdall and dart into the Tube station.

Breaking into a jog, I follow him, hindered by the

swarms of people desperate to get home. There he is, heading towards an escalator. I hop on too, sliding into the left-hand line so I can get to the bottom as fast as the crowds will allow. My shirt is sticking to my back like a second skin, the intense late-afternoon heat rare for this time of year. As I step off, I cough again with the potent smell of rush hour chaos and grinding train brakes. I can no longer see him. Am I too late? Has he taken the Victoria line north or south?

I try the north. Bingo. There he is, waiting to board the next Tube heading to Walthamstow Central. I work my way through the wilting commuters, apologising, ignoring the tuts and scowls directed my way. The parka has gone, revealing a smartly-dressed Marc in a suit. Why so smart? The train approaches, clattering and screeching as it decelerates. I reach for his arm and gently squeeze it. He spins around. He's wearing a tie too, as if he's off somewhere important.

'Marc, are you OK?'

His normally friendly tone spits fire at me. 'You've followed me.'

'I don't understand. What's going on?' My hand brushes his shoulder.

'Go and speak to your colleagues. Leave me alone.' There is no doubt that he means it. He thrusts his hand out towards the exit. 'Go away.' The train doors squeak and hiss open. He pushes me out of the way and jumps into the carriage, turning his back as the doors clunk closed.

This is not the Marc I know. Kind and generous Marc, the committed husband and father who possesses the ability to continually roll limericks off his tongue like a professional comedian. The guy who promotes moral excellence in all aspects of his life. He's the type you see helping old ladies to their cars with their shopping, and crouching down to hand notes to the homeless. Flummoxed, I watch as the packed train picks up speed and disappears into the dark tunnel.

What the hell is going on?

I glance at my watch, turn around and retrace my steps back to the station with equal urgency.

Damn, I'm going to be late home. Again.

Marc and Sasha are happy, aren't they? She's never let on otherwise. I've only known them three years, but when I visit them with Jim, for his weekly physio sessions with Sasha, their busy, loving household has always led me to believe nothing but.

'Tell me what that man said again,' I say to Leo when I arrive back at the station. I walk behind the desk.

'Best ask Turner for a full rundown. He took him into a room and had a chat with him, then logged the incident.' He lifts his takeaway cup. 'The best birthday present I've had.' He continues talking while he taps away on his computer.

I keep quiet. Leo's a trooper but talks far too much, and now's not the time for idle conversation. He points to an entry on the screen. 'Here you go; this is the discussion.'

I read the details but learn nothing more than what Leo already briefed me on earlier. It's all there, clearly stated. Marc O'Sullivan is leaving home, and if anyone reports him missing, he doesn't want to be found. He's not at risk, no mental health issues, no previous reports of disappearing.

It doesn't make sense.

'Have a good evening,' I say. 'And have a beer for me.'

'You haven't changed your mind, then? I've reserved an outside table at the Elders.'

I shake my head.

'Won't be the same without you, Barnes.'

I wink at him and leave to hurry to my car, praying the traffic has eased. Taking my phone out of my bag, I start to text Jim that something has come up, and I'm going to be late, as a text arrives from Sasha.

I need your help. Please call me as soon as you can. X

She knows.

I insert the key in the ignition and sit for a few seconds, deciding what to do. Sasha's house is on the way home. I could be there in ten minutes, twenty maybe with the traffic. Should I get involved? I could pretend I never saw Marc and let events unfold as they will, but Sasha doesn't deserve that from me. I can't lie to her. She's like the sister I never had.

I finish my text to Jim, telling him that his physio session is cancelled tonight and that I'll be home soon. Then I drop a text to Paula, who babysits on a Monday evening while I take Jim for his physio, to say we won't be needing her tonight. I start the engine and turn the air conditioning to max.

Turning out of the station, I join the queues of exasperated drivers swearing along with me that London's congestion is getting worse by the day. My phone beeps – another text from Sasha asking me to call her. The day is going from difficult to downright impossible. I can't talk to her because I'll have to lie. And that's something I can't do – not to people who matter anyway.

I divert my route to Sasha's, stopping off at the super-market to pick up a few items we need at home. Sasha lives in a small, private development – Napier Close, comprising of six moderate-sized detached houses, each fronted by well-pruned eucalyptus trees. On a good day, it's less than a ten-minute journey from home. Attached to the side of each house is a studio annexe some of the resi-dents use for small business purposes. Sasha runs her phys-iotherapy practice from hers. An attractive complex, especially for the area, it was built on an old factory site about twenty years ago. The new-millennium developer clearly had the foresight to understand children would be unable to afford to fly the nest and that there would be an increase in people working from home. A paved, double parking space fronts each studio, and at the rear of each property is a small courtyard garden.

Fake calmness fails to conceal the panic in her voice as Sasha appears from her studio. Her slender, athletic frame, dressed in white gym shoes, Lycra leggings and a white T-shirt with *The Body and Back Clinic* logo embossed across the back in emerald green, appears before I've switched off the engine. She's such a pretty woman. Two soft dimples usually light up her face when she smiles, but today they are lost in the darkness of her troubles. I climb out of the car.

'You got my texts then?' she says, her voice shaking. Her

long, shiny dark hair is dishevelled, and her face, filled with a nervous vulnerability, has lost its usual healthy glow. I've always been in awe of that glow. The way she always looks like she's just finished an hour of yoga and eaten a kilo of spinach. 'Marc has gone.'

'Let's go inside,' I say, dreading what's to come. After ten hours poking around into the life of suspected criminals, I'm done in. Actually, suspected isn't the right word. We know the two brothers we've had under surveillance for the past four months for their unabating involvement in crime are as guilty as the Krays. We've just got to nail the scum.

'We can't. The kids are there. I can't talk about this with them around.' She gulps down tears. 'Come with me.'

When she turns her back, I close my eyes and take a deep breath, preparing myself for the deep water I'm about to dive into. I follow her into her clinic. It's a spacious room with a skylight roof. Soothing music plays from a wireless speaker filling the room with a sense of relaxation. Not for long, I guess.

Anatomy pictures cover the whitewashed walls. The human body illustrated in every form – the skeleton, muscular system, nervous system, internal organs, joints and ligaments. I've seen her refer to them regularly during Jim's physio session to reinforce a point she's trying to make. One of them explains the working of the digestive system, the guts displayed raw and twisted like hers must be at the moment. She sits on her saddle stool and passes me a scrap of paper.

It doesn't take long to read the single paragraph

scrawled upon a folded piece of paper informing her that he's had enough. He's sorry, but he wants out of his life, and she mustn't come looking for him. The chill in his words snowballs all kinds of thoughts through my mind. What happened to the respect that twenty-plus years of marriage and three kids should reward? Was he really so unhappy? Is there another woman?

'If I didn't know his handwriting so well, I would say someone else wrote this,' Sasha says.

The torture on her face is killing me. I reread the note, before handing it back to her.

'OK. Let's start at the beginning. Tell me what's happened these past few days?'

Her legs bounce furiously. 'He went out last night. I don't know where. He wouldn't tell me.' She shrugs. 'He never goes out without telling me where. And never on a Sunday. I tried calling him, but he didn't pick up. God, it's hot in here. My fan has broken.' She stands and reaches to open a window. The catch jams. 'Blasted thing,' she says. 'Marc was meant to have fixed this.' She tugs at it until it opens. A police siren wails in the background.

She paces the room. 'He got home after midnight. I was in bed. When I questioned him about what he'd been up to, he said something about a potential business connection, and that he was tired and would tell me in the morning. But when I woke up, he'd already gone out again.'

'What time was that?'

'Around six. And let me tell you, my husband's a night owl. Only an emergency would get him out of bed that early.'

9

'Where did he go?'

She throws her arms around as she strides up and down the studio. 'No idea. I never got to ask him. I had back-to-back appointments all day. One client texted me to say they were running late, so I went to grab a sandwich, but he still wasn't back. I tried calling him between clients, but it kept going to voicemail. Then this afternoon, after I finished my last client, I went to look for him, but he was gone. Like, gone, gone.' She shakes her head, continuing to pace the room. 'The holdall he uses for work trips isn't in his wardrobe. He's taken a handful of clothes and his wallet, and, from what I can tell, that's it.'

It takes a lot to make me speechless. I guess this is a lot.

'He's left his phone. I heard it ringing in the bedroom when I tried to call him again this afternoon. I don't understand it. He wouldn't do this to Harry in the middle of his A levels. He adores his kids. They are everything to him.' Her hand slaps against her forehead. 'Oh, God, and it's Harry's eighteenth on Saturday. We're meant to be having a get-together. You are still coming, aren't you?'

Is she thinking this will still go ahead? I nod and make a mental note to source a gift.

'It was meant to be family and family friends only, but Harry's invited a few of his school mates now.' She stops pacing and slumps in her seat. Her elbows drop to her knees and her head into her hands. Her troubled eyes look up at me. 'You don't think he's found someone else, do you?' Her arms circle her middle as if she's trying to contain her pain as she sways backwards and forwards. 'He wouldn't, would he?'

'Don't jump to conclusions. It's not helpful.'

'Eva, you have to help me find out where he's gone.'

I inwardly sigh. I should be used to delivering news people don't want to hear. Many times, I've had to convey brutal accounts to suffering families, but this one's up there on the difficulty scale. 'I can't,' I say, clenching the corners of the bench. 'He came into the station earlier.'

'What! You saw him? What was he doing there?'

'I bumped into him on his way out and followed him to the Tube.' I pause and bite my lip. 'He doesn't want to be found.'

'What's that meant to mean?'

'He was interviewed, and he clearly stated that he doesn't want to be found. The police can't do anything, not against his wishes. So, my job won't allow me to help you.' I explain some more, but she's not listening.

'The police have to find him. He's gone missing.'

I shake my head. 'They don't. He's not deemed a missing person. If you try and file a missing person's report, they'll tell you what I've just told you. I'm sorry, but they won't look for him.'

'But this can't be right. He wouldn't leave us. He wouldn't. I'm begging you. You have to help me find him.'

'Take one day at a time. You should tell the children.'

She shakes her head, forcefully. 'No, I can't. Not until Harry has finished his A levels. I can't ruin his future. Hannah will be devastated. You know her, she's such a daddy's girl.' She pauses, deep in thought. 'That's what I can't understand about all this. Harry has to get his grades, or he won't get his place at uni. Marc knows this.

11

He wouldn't walk out at such a delicate time. He wouldn't.'

'When do Harry's exams finish?'

'Friday week.'

'There's only one thing for it, then.'

She looks at me, questioningly.

'We've got eleven days to find Marc.'

TWO

'So, you can help me find him?' Sasha says.

'Not officially, no.'

'But you know him, Eva. You know he wouldn't do anything like this.'

It doesn't make sense to me either. I've seen Marc with their kids numerous times. Aside from Sasha being Jim's physio, we are like family. We've spent birthdays with them, last New Year's Eve too. And the whole family regularly come over to ours for a barbecue which Marc always cooks. He has always appeared the devoted husband and father. The type who attends parents' evenings and stands, cheering, on the rugby pitch sidelines – even when he's drenched in torrential rain. They are both always helping us out in one way or another.

'Have you noticed any change in him these last few weeks?'

'He's been up and down. Very up and down. He's been having some dreadful mood swings. Today marked six months since he was made redundant. He always said he'd be in work again within a month. You know Marc, forever the optimist, but he's not even had one offer despite more than two dozen or so interviews. He's tried so hard. He's had a few temporary offers, but nothing permanent. I can't understand it. He's so good at what he does.' She shrugs. 'Perhaps it's his interview technique. He's taken it badly.' She shakes her head. 'But not enough to run away, surely?'

'I didn't know he'd been for so many interviews.'

'He doesn't like me to tell anyone. Sharing the disappointment when he gets the rejection emails has got too much to bear for him. The agencies don't even call him anymore. He's even attended a few interviews below his pay grade.'

'Apart from disappearing in the evening, was there anything else odd about his behaviour yesterday?'

'Not to start with. We had a typical family Sunday. Harry was revising, so Marc took Hannah and George to see a film while I did some housework and caught up on my patient files. He cooked dinner. I washed up, and he dried as normal. Luke came over, Harry's friend, who lives next door. Marc tested the two of them on some maths for their exam today. We watched some telly. A usual Sunday until he got a call and went out.' She pauses and thinks. 'Before he went to sleep last night, he hugged me really tight.'

'Do you know who called him?'

She shrugs. 'I checked his phone earlier – No caller ID.'

'Can I look at his phone?'

'Why?'

'To see if I can find anything suspicious.'

'I need to text the kids from it first.'

'What?'

'I'm going to pretend to be him and send them all a quick text to say everything is OK.'

What is she thinking? 'Anything else you've noticed strange about him lately?'

'He hasn't been sleeping properly. Not since he was made redundant. He wakes up in the early hours and goes into his study and works, which explains why he can't get up in the morning.'

'What, job-searching?'

'Yeah. And faffing about on this project he's been working on for ages. Some security device for the clothing industry. "It's going to make us millionaires," he always says.' She laughs, but only briefly. 'And he plays those stupid computer games the kids are addicted to. I keep telling him that mucking about on technology will only keep him awake, but he doesn't listen. I've given him books to help him, but you know what blokes are like.' She gestures to a shelf behind her stacked with books on muscles and stretches, sports injury prevention and reha-bilitation, pilates and relaxation. Leaning back, she picks up a paperback from the small desk behind her: *The Effort-less Sleep Method*. She waves it at me before hurling it across the room. 'He didn't even open the blasted thing.'

As five years in the police have taught me, certain emotions are best to ignore. 'Anything else?'

'He's had dreadful mood swings. Some real highs, but mostly lows. Terrible. But look, he lost his job. What can I expect? He's taken it hard. The redundancy money has run out, so we've had to dip into our savings which weren't that big to start with. That hasn't helped. I've upped my hours to full-time.' She throws her hands up towards the house. 'But with three kids' school fees and a mortgage, we're struggling.' She does that – talks with her hands. It's more apparent today than usual. 'He was so confident he would be in work again by the end of January that we didn't curb our spending for the first few months after the redundancy.' She pauses before adding, 'Do you think he's had some kind of breakdown? How was he when you saw him?'

'He was angry with me for following him. And serious. I've never seen him like that before.'

'Because he's not the serious type.'

George's sudden burst through the door interrupts our conversation. 'What time's dinner, Mum?' he asks as if he hasn't eaten all day. He stops in his tracks. 'What's wrong?'

Sasha jumps up, magicking a smile. A trick only a mother could perform in these circumstances. 'Nothing, we were discussing Jim's treatment plan. I'm coming in now.' She turns to me. 'Stay for dinner? I made a salad earlier and put some jackets in the oven.'

'Oh, not salad,' George says. 'We always have salad.'

'Stop whining and go lay the table.' She shoos her fifteen-year-old towards the door.

'Thanks for the offer, but I must get home. I'm already late.'

'I can't treat Jim this evening. You understand, don't you? I'll rearrange for later in the week.'

Does she think I'd expect her to work tonight? 'Of

course. I texted him earlier and told him his session is cancelled.'

'So, Marc's not really missing?' she asks as we plod towards the house.

'Not technically, no.'

'What would the police do if he was?'

'What do you mean?'

'If he hadn't reported that he didn't want to be found.'

'Has he ever disappeared or done anything like this before?' I doubted it, but I had to ask.

'Never.'

'Then, we'd probably not do much at this stage. We'd carry out a risk assessment, determine his vulnerability and state of mind. But he's a grown man with no history, and he hasn't been gone long, so we wouldn't class him as high risk. Plus, he wrote you a note. Most people who go missing in these circumstances return within forty-eight hours.'

'Do they?' A glimmer of hope lights her eyes.

I nod and link my arm through hers.

'And if they don't?'

'We'd begin conducting search-based enquires. Speak to family and friends – that kind of thing – known associates, who they have spent time with recently. Check CCTV, conduct house-to-house enquiries.'

'And?'

'If nothing comes from that, things may progress to financial enquiries, looking at telephone call histories, searching their homes and places of work, where they were last seen.'

'Can you do that for me?'

'Not formally.'

'But you will help me, won't you?' Her voice quivers. 'Please, Eva. I have no one I can trust like you. I'm begging you.'

'I'll see what I can do. Not now, though. I have to get home. Mel will want to go, and she can't leave until I get there. The kids will still be up.'

'This is real, isn't it?'

'Focus on the positives. It's early days, and you know he's alive. Can I pop inside to the loo before I go?'

'Do you think he will?' The desperation in her voice saddens me. 'Return in the next forty-eight hours?'

'Let's hope so.'

'You go ahead. I've realised I've forgotten to reply to a client email. I'll be with you in a sec. Remember, watch what you say in front of the kids.'

After I've used the toilet, I stand at the kitchen door observing the children, who are so acutely unaware of the turmoil their family is in. It's buzzing with teenage banter in there. Some rap song blares out from the TV, and Hannah and George, both still in their school uniforms, are preparing drinks and laying the table. They are twins – not that you would ever think so. As opposite as war and peace, George is tall, dark and argumentative and Hannah is short, fair and calm. The only similarity is the pattern in which light-coloured freckles powder the area below their expressive blue eyes. Harry and George are mocking the salad situation and bickering about who has the highest ranking in their favourite Xbox game. 'Fancy a quick game?' George asks Harry as he lays the final knife.

'You'll only get stroppy when I beat you,' Harry says.

'No chance, come on, a quick one,' George says, juggling with the controllers.

'Mum'll kill us. She doesn't look happy today either. Turn that fricking telly down, will you?'

'You turned it up.'

'No, I didn't.'

'You did.'

Hannah is discussing effective policies to reduce climate change – phasing out fossil fuels and improvements to transport links – with Luke, Harry's friend, who is lying on one of three beanbags under the TV, at the end of the room. He's texting without even looking at the screen. 'If you're really serious about doing your bit,' he tells her, 'you need to sell the car, stop taking flights, become a vegan and have your tubes tied.'

'Be easier for you guys to stick a condom on it.'

'But that's using more plastic.' He gets up, walks over to the kitchen area and takes a handful of crisps from the bag of Walkers on the side.

'I hate you,' she says and snatches the packet away from him. She doesn't, though, hate him. There's a teenage crush going on for her brother's mate. I can tell from the coy smiles she keeps directing his way along with her feigned apathetic attitude. Luke is tall with dark hair and eyes, and thick lips – an appealing diversion for any fifteen-year-old. She turns away from him and fills glasses with water.

'No, you don't hate me.' He grabs her waist and tickles her. He knows, as much as I do, that she fancies him.

She shoves him in the belly, and he theatrically doubles over in pain. Staggering back to the beanbag, he flops down as if seriously wounded. Hannah turns her back to him and sits at the breakfast bar. 'Where's Dad?' she asks her squabbling brothers.

George shrugs. 'Not seen him today.'

'Me neither,' says Harry. 'Did he go uptown for an interview?'

The family's furry cocker spaniel, Ralph, is hanging about somewhere. I can smell his something's-dead-in-there breath. There he is. Drooling by Hannah's feet, his tail thumping against the floor as he patiently waits for her to bung him another crisp.

An ordinary family going about their daily existence but, today, acutely unaware of hidden secrets.

There are so many like them out there.

'I'll need you to report him missing, you know. That's what you'd do if I hadn't told you about him coming into the station,' I tell Sasha as she walks me to my car.

She nods, but not convincingly.

'What's his date of birth?'

'Why?'

'I'll look into what I can.'

'Twelfth of February nineteen seventy-three.'

'Does he have a middle name?'

'Anthony. Marc Anthony O'Sullivan.'

I mentally note these details. When we reach my car, I grasp her forearm. 'You should tell the kids the truth.'

She shivers, releasing her arm from my grip. She jiggles her index finger in my direction. 'I'm going to tell them that he's had a temporary job offer up north and so has to stay over.'

'And you're convinced they'll buy into that?'

'They know he's desperate to work again.'

'What happens if he doesn't return for Harry's party at the weekend?'

'I'll send texts to them all from his phone later on. They'll be fine.'

She's deluding herself. I've dealt with the toughest of kids. Cases involving drug possession, abduction, rape, murder; the real dregs of humanity. And it doesn't matter where they've come from, or where they're going. Wealthy, poor, privileged or deprived, kids all share a common characteristic. When life really matters, none of them are stupid.

THREE

As I pull into our gravelled driveway, Arthur calls. If there's one annoying thing about my boss, it's his ability to phone me when I could do without it.

'I've got to go out early tomorrow. Can you and Sharpe pop in and see me first thing?'

'Sure. What's happening?' I ask, staring at the weeds smothering the flower beds, and even more aggravating, sprouting up through the gravel. I must tackle the garden when I'm off work next week.

'I'll explain tomorrow. Get hold of Sharpe, can you, please?' he says before hanging up.

I sit staring at our home, mentally preparing myself for round two of the day. I adore our Georgian, red-bricked house with its symmetrical sash windows, reminiscent of a former rectory, but on extra challenging days like this, I need a moment before I go inside. It's larger than we need, and I remember Jim insisting we buy it. I hadn't been so sure. The price tag had made me wince. 'Ignore the price.

I've been watching the housing market for years. The only way is up for the right property,' he told me all those years ago, when I was pregnant with our first child. Back when he was a high-flying director in a private equity firm, and we failed to appreciate money didn't magically appear in our bank account on the last Friday of every month. 'We'll make a fortune on this one when the time comes to sell it in a few years,' he added. 'Leave it with me.' And without me knowing, that's what he did. He bought it and started doing it up for our future together.

We didn't move in for quite a while because he had a bad car accident, and everything changed. We've reconfigured the downstairs – knocked down walls to make the ground floor more open plan, converted the dining room to a bedroom and added a small extension to provide a wet room. All steps have been removed, and we've ramped the garden, so it's now entirely accessible. That's because for the months after Jim had battled the spectre of death, we were told that he would probably never walk again. But three years of intense therapy, numerous trips to the States and a dogged determination proved the medics wrong.

As soon as the front door closes, the kids come bouncing up the hallway. 'Mummy, Mummy, you're home.' They each grab a leg and cling to me tightly as if they're afraid I'll run back out if they let go.

I ruffle their mops of curly hair, inhaling the smell of apple shampoo. That smell! 'I sure am. How was school today?'

'Great,' Joe says. 'I got all my sums right.'

'Mel took us to the lido,' Isabella says.

They are all smiles and joy as I prise them off me and bend down to lift handfuls of brightly coloured dinosaurs and sparkling princesses onto each hip. Joe has put on weight. When did that happen? I alternately kiss their angelic faces, revelling in their infectious giggles and silky skin tingling my lips.

'She made us a picnic,' says Isabella, yanking at my heartstrings. Another special time I've missed to add to the ever-growing list. Work versus motherhood, a never-ending tug of war that neither side can effectively win. 'And she bought us ice creams.'

I hear the squeak of Jim pushing himself along the floorboards. I've been meaning to get some oil on those bearings for months, but he's not had to use his chair much until the last few weeks. His pain levels must be bad today.

'Evening, darling,' he says.

'Pain bad?' I perch Joe on the hall table and slip today's pile of post into my bag to deal with later. I bend to kiss Jim. Joe throws his arms out at me, kicking his legs against the table. I slide him back into my arms.

'Dreadful,' Jim says. 'You're late. I was getting worried.'

'I'm sorry, something came up. I did text you.' He needs a haircut, I notice. His floppy hair is hanging over the tops of his glasses; and his usual olive-toned skin looks pale.

'We're going to be late for my physio,' Jim says. Isabella climbs on his lap, beaming like she has won a precious prize.

'We're not going.'

'Why?'

'It was in my text. Long story.' I glance from Joe to Isabella and back at him as if to say, let's discuss this later.

Mel appears, scuttling towards us, carrying her carpet bag like Mary Poppins. I apologise for my irresponsible tardiness like it's *Groundhog Day*. 'Not a problem. For you lovely lot, anything.' She kisses the top of Isabella's head then Joe's. 'See you in the morning, my smarties,' she says, and they chorus their heartfelt goodbyes to her.

'Bye, Mel,' I say, and she tells me she'll see me tomorrow, before disappearing out of the door like our family's fairy godmother. I'm sure one day, if we peep out of the window, we'll see her take an umbrella out of that bag and launch herself towards the sky and fly away.

'Time for bed,' I tell the kids, and they respond with their usual tirade of guilt-tripping words and questions to add to my already stricken conscience. 'It's not fair. We haven't seen you all day.' 'You'll be gone before we wake up.' 'Why can't you pick us up from school like our friends' mummies do?'

I guide them upstairs with promises of not one, but two stories for whoever's first in bed. Barefooted, they chase each other up, tripping and laughing, knowing as well as I do they will both get two.

'Lay with me, Mummy,' Joe says after I've finished his second story.

I smile, casting my mind back to that terrible period in my life when he was born. He came early with a serious heart defect, and we nearly lost him. Mercifully, he's OK now. 'Just five minutes,' I say, sliding my arm around him. 'Your sister's waiting for me.'

After I've read to Isabella, I sit at the top of the stairs, where they can both still see me from their beds. I cross my legs and close my eyes, ready to attempt my daily dosage of mindfulness – five minutes of focused breathing to keep me balanced and calm, and all such claimed benefits. Years ago, I used to count things randomly all the time to keep me calm, a habit which motherhood knocked out of me, and then Sasha taught me about this technique. Some evenings I manage it, others not. On the days I do succeed, I've yet to determine if it makes a difference other than the relief it brings to know the kids fall asleep straight away if I'm there outside their bedroom doors.

Taking a deep breath, I drop my head and try to banish the intrusive thoughts invading my concentration. I rake my fingers through my hair, wincing at how dry the ends feel. I must book a trim. It's grown past my breasts. But, it's no surprise. I haven't been to the hair-dressers since Christmas. Strands shed away in my hands. Opening my eyes, I see ten or so curls land on my trousers. I gasp as I pick out a grey lock amongst the wisps of blonde. I thought they were a treat for your forties, not your early thirties. Perhaps I need to change my shampoo? An image of Sasha's forlorn face from earlier flashes into my mind and my thoughts turn to her husband's disappearance.

Tonight, it's not happening. Marc has taken the space reserved for meditation.

Once I hear the kid's delicate snores, I creep downstairs and, after dimming the kitchen lights, head straight to the fridge. 'It's only Monday,' Jim reminds me with raised eyebrows and a teasing smile, to which I reply, 'You'll want a glass too when I tell you about my day.'

My stomach rumbles as I hand Jim the bottle of chilled white. 'Sounds like you skipped lunch again,' he says. He fetches two glasses and wheels himself to the table and half-fills them both.

I lower the lights of the ruby red chandelier that hangs above the table and dish up what's remaining from Mel's daily culinary delights. Sticky chicken and roast potatoes she would have prepared while the kids were at school. There are sides of buttery peas and honey-glazed carrots. She's even set the table. What would I do without that woman?

I switch over the radio station before sitting down on the wooden bench opposite him. *Classic FM* treats us to a Beethoven piano concerto. Number four, I think. I move aside the glazed ceramic bowl piled with fresh fruit from the middle of the table. Marc and Sasha brought us this bowl back from their holiday in Thailand a couple of years ago. Marc had chosen it, Sasha told me, because he knew turquoise was my favourite colour. 'The sea was exactly that shade of blue,' Marc said. 'I knew you'd love it.'

'I wonder why the pain is so bad again,' I say.

'I needed to keep alert today as I had a deadline for Chrissie, remember? So I skipped the painkillers this morning. I took some when you were upstairs with the kids. I'll be fine soon.'

'I'll give you a massage later.'

He air-kisses me. 'I'll never say no to that.'

'Did you get the first draft off to Chrissie?'

27

'Yep. All done. I feel confident about this one. More so than book one and two. I'll wait to see what Chrissie has to say.'

'You know her. She won't hold back if she doesn't agree.'

'Rightly so. That's an editor's job.'

I relay the Sasha and Marc drama as we tuck into dinner.

'For Christ's sake, Eva. You can't get involved.'

'I can't not, either.'

'You could get yourself into deep water.'

'Not sure it'd go that far.'

'You certainly won't get promoted if they discover you're helping to find someone who has clearly stated they don't want to be found. You've worked yourself to the bone to get where you are.' He adds with a little too much emphasis, 'And sacrificed loads.'

'She's my friend. And Marc. Yours too. Think about how much they've done for us.'

He reaches out and squeezes my hand. 'I know. But still.'

'She needs my help. She's desperate. You know she's like a sister to me.'

'Don't you think it's weird that he went into your station? Did he not consider he might bump into you?'

'He couldn't have been thinking rationally. I suppose it's his local.'

'Where do you reckon he's gone?'

'Haven't a clue, but I tell you what, I've got a dreadful feeling he's not coming home anytime soon.'

'What makes you say that?'

'The way he was with me at the Tube station. He got a bit nasty. Actually, not just a bit. He shouted at me to get lost in so many words. He meant it too.' I shove a carrot into my mouth.

Jim arches a brow. 'That doesn't sound like the Marc we know.'

'That's what I mean. Has he said anything out of character to you lately?' Over the past couple of months, since Jim started having intensive physio with Sasha again, we'd often go into their house after the session for half an hour or so. Sasha and I would chat over a coffee, or sometimes something more substantial, while Marc and Jim would squash into Marc's office, a tiny room opposite the front door that barely has space for Jim's wheels when he's using them.

He shakes his head. 'Nothing that springs to mind.'

'What do you two talk about when you're alone?'

'I don't know. Stuff.'

'What kind of stuff?'

He stabs a roasty with his fork and pauses for a second to think. 'Everyday stuff. I don't know – the news, politics, the kids. He talks about the kids a lot. He shows me funny things he's seen on the Internet. Music. My writing. I run plot twists by him.' He lifts the bottle of wine from the cooler, looking at me questioningly.

I slide my glass towards him. 'And?'

'He tells me about the jobs he's applied for.' Jim goes to pour me a glass of wine but pauses. 'Actually, he hasn't spoken about the job situation lately.' He resumes filling my glass. 'Sometimes, not often, we play that online poker game. And he talks a bit about his magic pen.'

'Magic pen?'

'Yep. He's been developing this pen idea. *Marc O's Magic Marker*, he calls it.'

'Sasha did mention something about that.'

'He reckons it's going to revolutionalise security in the clothing industry.'

'How?'

'I don't fully understand how it works, but instead of using security tags, shop owners mark clothing with this pen. It engrains a code into the fabric undetectable to the naked eye. If someone tries to steal the item, they set the shop alarms off. It's early days. Actually, he used to talk about it a lot, but not lately.'

I find a space in my crowded head to park this information. 'Answer me something. From a guy's point of view, is Marc the type to cheat?'

He throws me a look that says what a stupid question. 'Marc, a cheater? No. No way.' He thinks for a second as if wondering if he could be wrong. 'He's never given me that impression anyway. Why? Do you think there's a woman involved?'

'I never would've thought that before today – not of him. I agree, he's not the type. But now I don't know. He had a suit on when he came to the station. As if he was going somewhere important or somewhere special. Maybe he was going for a job interview?' I take a sip of wine and another. 'I didn't tell Sasha that, of course.'

'What're you planning on doing about it?'

'Missing people often return after a couple of days. Saying that, it's rare for someone to officially declare they don't want to be found. Not that it's a first, though.' I think for a moment. 'Do you remember me telling you about that girl from Herne Hill? She was young, barely eighteen. She didn't want to go through with an arranged marriage. I was there the day she came into the station and declared she was going to run away from home and didn't want to be found. There was that man, too, a few years ago – the one with curly hair. I remember him because he reminded me of Ben. Both cases were pretty much the same as Marc. I wonder what happened to them?'

'Why don't the police encourage them to go home?'

'We'd encourage them to leave contact details and for them to keep in contact. And get their permission to pass such messages on to the family, so they know they're OK. Everyone has rights, though. We don't know what goes on behind closed doors.' I sip more wine. 'I'll give it a few days, and if he doesn't appear, I'll make some enquiries.'

'Look, I know they are our friends and, believe me, I think a lot of them, but you're a heartbeat away from promotion. What's that line Arthur always tells you?'

'I know. I know.' I repeat Arthur's precise words: '"Don't get involved in their story. It's not your problem."'

'You're a hotshot rising star.' He squeezes my hand again. 'I love you too much to see you ruin your career. Think about this carefully.'

I push away my half-eaten plate of food and drain my glass. He offers me another.

'I've got some work to do.' I pick up his plate and stack it on top of mine.

'But it's nearly nine. You look tired, darling. Take a break.'

'I'll only be half an hour, honestly.'

I load the dishwasher, and we take ourselves to the lounge but go our separate ways. Him towards the telly where he transfers himself to the L-shaped sofa and me to the corner that houses my improvised study. It's a small area but with enough space for a desk for my laptop and printer and a cupboard for files. I can work from here while I watch the kids. And be on hand to help them, and Jim, when they need me. I hear Jim swear.

'For Christ's sake, where've the kids put it now?'

After locating the remote control down the back of the sofa, along with some Lego bricks and a doll's hairbrush, I text Rob, a colleague who I've been working closely with for the past few years.

We have a meeting with Arthur at eight in the morning. E

He replies with a middle finger emoji. I chuckle as I fire up my laptop. He sends another text.

Car broken. Can you pick me up?

I tell him OK before attempting to tackle my out-of-control inbox. But I can't fully concentrate. Marc's tormented face at the Tube station today won't let me. I dig into my bag for today's post to add to the jumbled pile that I haven't got around to opening from last week. I open each envelope and sort the contents into piles of bills and rubbish for recycling.

'Eva,' Jim calls out. What now? 'It's been over an hour. I'm going to bed.'

I look at my watch. He's right. 'I'll join you in five.'

He wheels himself off while I finish what I'm doing and click my laptop shut. I clear up the lounge and empty the dishwasher then join him in the bedroom where I slip into a skimpy nightie. Tonight's heat won't allow anything more. He turns out the light when I get into bed, and I snuggle into the comfort of his open arms. He falls asleep straight away but an hour later, I'm still staring at the faint moonlight outlining the window shutters, thinking of Marc. His disappearance has unnerved me. I think back to when I last saw him before our clash at the Tube station today. Two weeks ago, he and Sasha came over for an impromptu barbecue, minus the kids. They were off doing their own thing. As teenagers do, Marc rightly pointed out when Sasha had a moan. Thinking back, Marc was quiet to start with that day, but after a couple of beers he livened up when Joe and Isabella begged him to play hide and seek. They are as fond of him as we are.

Where have you gone, Marc?

I spend the night agitated, hot and harassed by images of Marc's face. Around three, I pick up a book. I've got a great Val McDermid on the go, but I can't concentrate. Jim wakes and needs more pain medication, apologising for leaving his pills in the kitchen. I throw on my dressing gown and traipse out of the bedroom to fetch him some. After swallowing a couple of tablets, he lays back down. 'What's bothering you?' he asks.

'I can't stop thinking about Sasha.' I cuddle up to him

and share all the possible scenarios of Marc's disappearance that I have conjured up in my mind.

He strokes my hair, concern crinkling his brow. 'I'm worried about you.'

'I'm fine.'

'But you won't be if you find yourself out of a job. As far as this Marc situation is concerned, I really think you should stay out of it.'

FOUR

DAY 2

I'm up at six and in the shower.

'No run this morning?' Jim asks as I deliver his morning cup of tea. He grabs my arm and pulls me towards him for a kiss.

'I didn't sleep well.' This is an understatement. After telling me to keep out of Marc and Sasha's affairs, only minutes passed before I was counting his slow rhythmic breaths. For me, it wasn't until the birds started their early morning concert that I finally nodded off.

As soon as Mel arrives, and I make it to the car, I call Sasha. She answers on the first ring, sounding as if she didn't sleep much more than me. I start the engine and pull out of the drive. 'He's not back yet,' she says, which doesn't surprise me. Not that Marc hasn't returned, but that she's still hoping he might. It often takes a few days for the reality of someone's fate to fully register. I've witnessed it several times in differing situations. The shock blocks rational thinking with denial until the anger sets in. Next, she'll tread the bargaining and depression stages before reaching the moment when she can fully accept what's happening in her crumbling world. She might even skip a step, or go backwards, depending on how complex the investigation and the progression it takes. Rarely, but it does happen, some never truly accept.

'I went down to the police station.' Her voice breaks. 'They repeated what you told me.'

'You didn't mention that I'd already told you, did you?'

'Of course not.'

'How are the kids?'

'Fine. I told them he got a last-minute job offer yesterday. In Scotland, revamping some computer systems for lots of money we couldn't refuse. I said he'd be gone for a couple of weeks.'

I inwardly sigh. Heavily. Oh, Sasha. What's going to happen when they realise he doesn't phone? When Harry doesn't receive a birthday hug from his dad on Saturday? 'I have some visits to make today, out and about. I'll call in on you at some point.'

'I'm busy all morning,' says Sasha. 'Free after two.'

'I'll try this afternoon. All depends on how my day pans out.'

I stop in Clapham to pick up Rob. He rents a basement flat near to the common with two other officers: Phil, who works for the British Transport Police, and Kit, from the Territorial Support Group. I don't go in. The undefinable waft of untidy bachelors will be too much for me this morning. After ten minutes and two texts asking, *Where the hell are you?* Rob comes running out with wet hair and his tie swinging in his hand.

I wind down the window to the acrid scent of summer floating in the London fumes. 'Any time today.'

'Sorry.'

'Next time you can take a cab.'

'Morning to you, too.'

'We're going to be late. I'm always late when you're involved.'

'You love me, though, don't you? Go on, say it.' He leans his ear towards me. 'Let me hear it.'

Shoving him away, I stick up two fingers and carry on driving. Although I'd never admit it to anyone, I'm fond of Rob. We've worked together for three years now. At thirty-three, he's a couple of years older than me but still a DC which irritates the hell out of him in a funny kind of way – especially since Arthur told us he was considering both of us for promotion. 'I thought I'd at least get a year of being a higher grade than you. That would've been so much fun,' Rob said, a fake grin concealing his amusement.

Pulling down the sun visor, he looks in the mirror and swings his head from side to side, combing his hands through his hair. Once done, he stares at himself for a moment.

'Don't break my mirror,' I say.

He laughs. 'Who had a bowl of sarcasm for breakfast?'

I laugh, as I mostly do when I'm around him.

'What does Arthur want to speak to us about?' he asks.

I shrug, and we discuss our latest case until we get to our desks. Arthur beckons us over, tapping his watch.

'Sorry, sir, my fault. Car has broken down, and I had to call Eva to come and pick me up,' Rob says.

'Give the bullshit a rest,' Arthur replies, hitching up his trousers. He slaps a file on the table. 'You're going to make *me* late now.' He tuts in that way we're used to. As if to say, I'm too old for this. He opens the file and launches into detail about a new lead in a case we've been working on, instructing us to make some inquiries. He hands the file to me. 'Any questions?'

'Nope, we'll get straight on it, sir.'

'Also, I need you two to look into a Jason Harper. That name ring a bell for either of you?'

Rob and I glance at each other, and we both shake our heads.

'Possible links to Shane Baker.'

Interesting. We've had Shane Baker on our radar for some time as part of a larger drugs gang we are trying to infiltrate.

Arthur rolls up his shirt sleeves with his pudgy hands. 'Jason Harper. Twenty-five. Non-custodial sentence for theft in 2017. Got caught with a boot full of designer shoes and similar crap. Lives at seventeen Pineland Avenue with his parents. Neighbours have reported strange comings and goings, claiming he's dealing drugs, but there's no proof. This is the second time they've called about it. Stokes visited them. They said they've seen Harper with a gun too, but when Stokes called next door, Harper wasn't there. Stokes spoke to the parents who claimed the neighbours were a couple of busybodies. Follow up, will you? They don't want uniform, so get down there sometime. Not urgent. In the next day or so will do.'

'Which neighbours?' Rob asks. 'Fifteen or nineteen?'

'Nineteen. First, Operation Carlisle.' Arthur looks at me. 'Where's this report you've been promising me for the last week?'

'Actually, sir, you only gave it to me last Friday, and you said I had until the end of this week to complete,' I say, with confidence. Despite being the office Rottweiler, his growl is far worse than his bite.

'You'd better get on with it, then,' he says, ushering us away like we're a couple of annoyances he could do without.

I catch up on endless admin and manage to finish the Operation Carlisle report by midday. Rob and I head off to carry out some witness interviews, popping into Tesco Express for a meal deal on the way. On the drive back, we stop off at Pineland Avenue. Mr and Mrs Shirley, a retired couple, are sweet enough, but give us nothing to go on other than a hunch their neighbour's son is friends with the "wrong sort".

'It's only when his parents are out,' Mrs Shirley says, twitching her net curtains. 'All strange kinds of men and women appear. Would you like some tea, dear?' She gestures to Rob. 'And your friend?'

I politely decline her offer. I don't want to spend more time here than I have to. Annoyingly Rob accepts, so I say I've changed my mind. 'No problem, everything's already prepared.' She wanders off to the kitchen, returning less than five minutes later with a tray of cups and saucers and a teapot covered in country roses. There is a plate of chocolate digestives on there too. She pours the tea and tops up each cup with milk from a small crystal jug.

'Can you describe these men and women to me?' I ask.

Mr and Mrs Shirley exchange shrugs. 'Some are tall and big,' says Mrs Shirley, handing around the biscuits, prompting Rob to take two. Not that he needs the encouragement, I laugh to myself.

'Young. Around your age,' Mr Shirley says. He's sitting in a recliner by the fireplace; a newspaper and the TV remote rest on the arm of the chair.

'The policemen who visited you before asked you to keep a record of your observations.'

'That's right,' says Mr Shirley, peering over the top of his spectacles.

'Can I see it?' I ask.

'Oh, no, you can't,' says Mrs Shirley, perching on the edge of the sofa beside me. She places her cup and saucer on the table and gathers the folds in her pleated skirt like a fan, letting them spring free before repeating this action. Gather, fold, repeat. 'We were too worried.'

'What about?'

'We're too old for any trouble.'

'I can assure you, Mr and Mrs Shirley, that anything you tell us will be dealt with in the strictest of confidence. We need help catching criminals, and it's only the local community – people like you – who can help us do that.'

Mrs Shirley wiggles herself up straight, fiddling with the chain on her thick-rimmed spectacles.

'Do you think they are criminals?'

'I never said that. What I mean is the police can't be everywhere all the time. We need the public's help in spotting anything they think isn't quite right.'

'What do you need us to do, dear?'

'Do you have a notebook?'

'You could use that one Jane bought me for Christmas,' Mrs Shirley says to her husband, her eyes gleaming like the well-polished carriage clock on the mantelpiece. 'I knew we'd find a use for it.'

'Jot down a brief description of who knocks and how long they spend there. Make sure you note dates and times. And if they come by car, write down their number plate too.'

'I don't suppose you have any CCTV installed at the property?' Rob asks.

They both shake their heads. 'Our son, Philip, he's been saying for a long time that we should,' Mrs Shirley says, 'but we've never got around to it. Seems a lot of bother.'

'Your son is right. It could substantiate your suspicions. It's a good deterrent, if anything.'

'He hasn't worked for a while.'

'Who, your son?'

'No, Jason Harper. He used to drive off every morning about seven. Dressed in a suit and tie, real smart like. Gone right downhill, he has – lost a lot of weight, wears scruffy clothes. His mum told me he lost his job.'

'Do you know his mum well?'

'Not really. She keeps herself to herself. She's polite enough, says good morning and that, but whenever I try and start a conversation, she always says, "I must dash." I sometimes see her up at Asda. She works there, behind the cold meat counter, but she always says she's too busy to talk then, too. Even when she's not serving customers, she has all sorts to do out the back.'

'I understand you saw him with a firearm?' I say.

'What do you mean, dear?' Mrs Shirley asks.

'A gun. There are reports that you saw Jason Harper with a gun.'

Mr and Mrs Shirley eye each other. 'I think so,' says Mrs Shirley.

'Can you tell us about it?'

'Well, it was dark, so I'm not completely sure.'

'When was this?'

'Last week.'

'When last week? Can you be more specific?'

'I can't, dear. Sorry.'

I probe some more, but they don't give us anything further to go on. Rob hands them our number. They wish us goodbye, vowing to start the notebook and call their son to enhance their security arrangements.

'Sweet couple, but they really should've sold up and moved to a seaside bungalow years ago,' Rob comments as we knock next door with a story of routine enquiries. Nobody answers.

'Nosy neighbours, or do you think they're right about this Jason Harper?' I ask.

Rob shrugs. 'Nice car for this part of town.' He nods at the Audi TT in the driveway.

'2018 plates too,' I say as we head back to the car.

· · ·

It's approaching four before we are en route back to the station. When I pull up outside Sasha's, I tell Rob, 'I'll be back in five.'

'What's happening here? Looks interesting. I want to come,' he says; just like Joe does when Jim and I are going out for the night, and he has to stay with his sister and a sitter.

'You can't. Do some revision for your exams or catch up on paperwork. Whatever.' There's no good involving him in this.

Sasha opens the door. Her face is pale. A mobile phone occupies each of her hands like a pair of walkie-talkies. She shakes one of them in my face. 'Look. Look. You have to see this.'

As I step inside her hallway, I take the phone from her.

'It's Marc's,' she says.

A text message, sent this morning, fills the top of the screen.

See you later. P xx

'Whose number is this?'

Sasha's hands are shaking. 'That's Pen's number.'

'Pen?'

She takes the phone back, grabs my hand and drags me into the lounge. It's cold in here despite the sunny day. Several empty mugs and a book, *How to be Emotionally Strong and Have Thick Skin*, litter the floor. The sofa is messy with saggy cushions and a screwed up faux fur blanket. The curtains are still drawn, and judging by the musty smell, I guess she slept in here last night.

Over at the window, she rips the curtains apart and

points to the house diagonally opposite to the left. 'Penelope Price. She lives in that house on the end. The one with the hanging baskets. She's a dog groomer. Why are she and Marc meeting today? Tell me.' Her voice is forceful, aggressive almost. As if I really should be able to give her an answer.

I shrug. 'There could be several reasons.'

'Do you think they're having an affair?' Her voice is brittle. 'Pen is unhappily married. She hates her husband. Pete the Prick she calls him. She's meant to be my friend. We often walk the dogs together.'

'Why don't you ask her why she sent the text?'

'And let on that he's gone?'

'People are going to find out. That's why I think you need to tell the kids the truth.'

'I'm meant to be seeing her this afternoon. Ralph's booked in for a groom.'

'Then you can ask her.'

She shakes her head. 'I'd have to tell her about Marc leaving.'

'You've never told me about the other people who live around here,' I say, to distract her. I peer out of the window at the other five houses in the development, arranged to form a horseshoe shape. Sasha and Marc's house sits at the base alongside another.

She gestures to the neighbouring house to the right. 'That's Art and Annie Walker's house. Luke's parents. Art's a personal trainer. It's great because he often sends new clients my way. He trains a few wealthy people in his home studio, and he owns a bigger gym on that small industrial estate up by the park. Do you know it?'

'Stokes Hill?'

'That's the one.'

'I went there on an investigation once.'

'What, Art's place?'

'No. There's a plumbing shop up there.'

'What happened?'

'Let's just say, plastic pipes and tubes of sealant were not all we found in the stock room.'

'Bit of a rough old place, I know, but he has a good number of local clients. By the way, what time can you bring Jim along tomorrow for his physio appointment?'

'I'll have to check. I'm on a late shift, so we could do the morning if you're free. What time were you thinking?'

'I've got a slot at ten.'

'Sounds good. Don't want to make you feel bad, but he's been in a lot of pain again these last couple of weeks. I don't want him to miss a session if we can help it. He always feels so much better after he's seen you.'

'We need to strengthen him up. I've been meaning to have a word with Art, actually. Be good for Jim to get some core strength training sessions in with him. I'll pop over and speak to Art later and see if I can sort something out. Apart from that, how is he?'

'The pain gets him down. He finds it hard to concentrate on his writing when it's bad, and that frustrates him.' I tense up. 'He's been down too, this past month, about his parents.'

'What's happened to them?' She frowns. 'You know, I don't think I've ever heard you talk about them – not in any detail.'

I sigh heavily. 'It's a very long story for another time.' I debate how much to tell her. Marc is the focus at the moment, not some despicable criminal about to be released from prison. 'Let's just say, his father is an evil, worthless piece of trash but his mother still loves him. I'm really fond of her. I can't help feeling sorry for her, but she infuriates the hell out of Jim. He calls her his father's doormat; we only still see her for the sake of the kids. God knows what's going to happen when he comes out of prison.'

'Sounds like an interesting story. What did he go to prison for?'

'I promise to tell you one day.'

'Is Jim still on about having another baby and moving out of London?'

I nod, sighing again.

'He hasn't given up, then?'

'Not at all.'

'And you're still against it?'

'Not against it, as such. I don't know how I'd fit it all in. I'm torn. Work is going so well at the moment. I'm hoping for promotion soon. But Joe and Isabella are growing so fast, I don't want to leave the gap too big. Then some days I think, why put us all under the stress of having a third?'

'You'd find a way to cope. You're that kind of person.'

'As for moving out of London. Not a chance. We've got too much going on here. There's the money situation too. We're just about doing OK as we are. We'd be stretched expanding the family at the moment.'

'Doesn't that worry Jim?'

'He doesn't know. I look after the finances.'

Jim used to take care of all our admin and finances before his car accident. He was so much better at it than me. But life changed, and I had to learn to master the intricacies of everyday life. I sigh and turn back to the window. There's an estate agent's board erected in the garden to the left with a SOLD sign pinned across the middle. 'Where were we? Looks like new neighbours next to Pete and Penelope?'

'Not sure. No one's moved in yet. Hope they're as nice as the previous people. Over there,' she points to the house diagonally right, 'Tom and Alisha Davies. Tom's a graphic designer and Alisha a lawyer. She works up in the city for some high-class law firm. Goes out early every morning, comes back late. Tom uses their studio as his office. Big office, eh? Not sure what he does with all that space. I've never been in there. And the family next to them have gone abroad for a year for the mother's job, so it's vacant too at the moment.' She rubs her temple. 'Like this one will be if Marc doesn't come back.' Anxiety cracks her voice. 'I hope he hasn't been having an affair. It'd kill me.'

I place a hand on her shoulder. 'Let's go and get a cuppa.'

The kitchen is unusually untidy, the sink choked with unwashed cups and dishes and the worktop cluttered with stuff that didn't make it to the sink. 'Shall I make some tea?' I ask.

'I should be making you some.'

I reach for the kettle and wash some cups as her phone beeps. She snatches it and sighs. 'A client trying to rearrange. They do that all the time. It's so annoying.' Her mouth turns upside down. 'I thought it might be Marc.' She sighs again. 'I've got another problem.'

'What?'

'Marc was meant to do the music for Harry's party. We cancelled the DJ to save money. Marc said he'd put together a playlist and plug it into his speakers which will work well outside. Who can do that now? I don't want to ask the kids otherwise we'll get all that rap crap. This is meant to be more of a family affair.'

'Leave it with me.'

'You've enough to do. How're you going to find time to do that by Saturday?'

'Jim will do it. He loves his music, doesn't he? It's one of the things that has kept him sane since the accident. He'll know all the up-to-date tracks to include. What else needs doing?'

'Do you know anyone who could make an eighteenth cake at short notice? I can't face it.'

'Leave that with me, too. What kind of cake were you thinking of?'

'Doesn't have to be anything spectacular as long as it's chocolate.'

'Done. Tick it off your list.'

'If you're sure,' she says, then continues debating why Pen would have sent her husband that text.

'Does Marc keep a diary?' I ask, topping the cups with milk.

'He does on his computer, but I haven't looked at it. Do

you still want to look at his phone? I spent hours searching through it last night, but there are no clues.'

'I'll give it a go. You never know what I might find. Do you know the password to his computer?'

She nods. 'I think so. Being the security-conscious freak that he is, he rotates it each month. So it's always one of our dates of birth.'

'Can we take a look? We might be able to see his diary on there.' It intrigues me how much people differ. If I were her, Marc's diary is one of the first things I would have looked at, but maybe that's the detective in me.

We walk along the hallway to Marc's office opposite the front door. A compact room with two planks of mahogany fixed to two of the walls. They join together in the far corner to form a desk which houses the typical paraphernalia – a computer screen, a printer, a pair of speakers, pens and a jotter. Above sit three shelves storing books and files. Sasha turns on the light to a loud bang, frightening us both. 'I keep telling him to look at that fixing. Bulbs keep blowing, and they cost a fortune to replace.' She switches on a lamp positioned next to a pile of computing magazines on top of a grey filing cabinet. 'So, the password should be 7June2001 for Harry's birthday this month. If he didn't get around to changing it, that is. If not, it will be 1May1980 for mine.'

Attached to the opposite wall is a floor-to-ceiling whiteboard with a small ledge for pens and a wiper. The room is so small, if Marc were sitting at the desk, he could swing round to write on the board without leaving his seat. So, this is where he and Jim talk about all their "stuff".

It's dark without the main light on. There's a window, but bushes growing in the neighbour's garden hamper the sunlight. Sasha picks up a shabby tie-dyed covered cushion from the chair and holds it to her pallid cheek. 'Marc made this in his first year at secondary school, all those years ago.'

I pick up a red marker. Twiddling it with my fingers, I gesture to the whiteboard. 'What does he use this for?'

Her head jerks around. She raises her eyebrows. 'That's usually full of his scribbles: computer code and all his gobbledygook. Stuff I don't understand. Where's all that gone?'

'When did it last get wiped?'

She thinks for a moment. 'I usually only come in here to hoover. I did the housework on Sunday morning. I can't remember if it was clean then or not.'

'Try and think. Can we log into his computer?'

'Go ahead.' She pulls out the desk chair. 'You know more about these things than me. I wouldn't know what to look for.'

I power up the Dell. The tower hard drive whirs at my feet. I wait hopefully, despite sensing what I'm about to find. I shiver with that chilly suspicion I often get when I start an investigation and a suspect leaves me cold.

'What's that face for?' she asks.

'This computer has been restored to factory settings.'

FIVE

'What does that mean?' she asks.

'All the data – personal files, programs, profile – has been wiped.'

'What, everything?'

'Every single thing. Looks like the drives have been cleared too.'

'Why would Marc have done that?' She's thinking the same as me, I'm sure. It's as if he has tried to destroy all evidence of his previous existence.

I shrug. 'Where would he keep a USB stick if he had one?'

'No idea.'

I look around. A desk organiser occupies the corner, similar to the one I have at home. It has several sections. In mine, I keep our USB. I use the Cloud these days but keep ours for old times' sake. It stores Jim's and my chequered history. I rummage around the safety pins and treasury tags but fail to find what I'm looking for.

'I've often seen him with a laptop when he's sitting with the kids in the kitchen. Where's that?' I ask.

She scans the top of the desk and the shelves. 'It's not here.' She looks underneath the desk and pulls open the bottom drawer of the filing cabinet, searching fruitlessly inside. 'He usually keeps it on the bottom shelf. He must've taken it.'

'I don't think he had it with him when I saw him come out of the station. It wouldn't have fitted into the holdall he had with him, and he wasn't carrying anything else.'

'You're right. It wouldn't fit into that holdall he took.' She looks me directly in the eyes. 'Where is it then?'

'He could've left it somewhere.'

'Wait a minute. It was here on Monday. I think. No, actually, I'm sure of it. I'll ask Harry. He sometimes borrows it.'

My phone beeps. It's Rob.

Do you need rescuing?

I text him back telling him to carry on with the revision.

Sasha glances at her watch. 'Ralph's appointment. I need to get going. Will you come with me? Please. Have you got time?'

I don't, but I'll find it.

She grabs her keys and phone, and I follow her and Ralph over to the house diagonally opposite hers, mouthing to Rob, I'll be five minutes. A discreet sign saying, *Pen's Parlour* hangs above the door to the studio, and to the side sits a family of concrete dog statues. Sasha presses the buzzer, and a bell chimes the theme tune to

Lassie. I throw her a look. At least she manages a quick chuckle with me.

'Hiya. You're early. I wasn't expecting you until five,' Penelope says, flustered, as she opens the door, treating us to the strong smell of coconut.

'Oh, I thought I was due at four-thirty. We changed it, remember?'

A bearded ginger-haired man steps out. 'Sasha,' the man says.

'Tom, not seen you for a while.' Sasha introduces me to the pair of them. 'Tom lives in the house over there, remember me saying? The graphic designer. He's one of Marc's jogging partners.'

Tom nods at me before abruptly disappearing. I'm not sure if Sasha notices he doesn't have a dog with him.

'Who else does Marc go jogging with?' I ask Sasha.

'Pete, sometimes – Pen's husband – and Art too. They all try to be a bit healthy around here.'

'Tell her what we call them,' Pen says to Sasha.

Sasha smiles despite the effort. 'The MCB. The Midlife Crisis Brigade.'

Pen crouches down to make a fuss of Ralph. Her fake gold, giant earrings swing like pendulums with each move of her head. 'How's my beautiful baby boy?' She ruffles his fluffy coat. 'Who's overdue a visit with aunty Pen-Pen?'

Pen's parlour is something else. Triangular bunting, crafted with pictures of different breeds of dog, runs from corner to corner across the ceiling. At the end of the room, a pink picket fence sections off an area with *Groom Room*, stencilled in pink, on the wall. It's divided into three gated areas from which a cacophony of barking dogs fills the room. Pen is something else too. She wears her hair in an immaculate bun, and she's dressed in black trousers and a shocking pink tunic and trainers. They perfectly coordinate with everything else in the room – the walls, chairs, towels, even the black and pink striped appointments book sitting on the small reception desk.

'You OK, honey?' Pen asks, straightening her uniform. The first few buttons are undone, exposing the top of her thick cleavage. 'You don't look your normal zesty self.' She prepares to tackle Ralph's overgrown coat.

Sasha's tears surprise me. Pen too. They appear to spring out of her eyes before she can stop them. 'Give me a sec,' Pen says and whisks Ralph off to the Groom Room. 'Now, now you little beauties, settle down.'

I snatch a tissue from a box on the desk and hand it to Sasha.

Pen returns and squirts some antibacterial gel into her hands, rubbing them together. 'Tell Pen all about it.'

'Marc's gone.'

'Gone? Where?' Pen asks, frowning.

'He's left us.'

Pen's jaw drops. 'Dear Lord. That I would never have guessed in a million years. When?'

Sasha relays her acute pain of the last twenty-four hours.

'How are the kids coping?' Pen asks.

'They don't know.'

'Why ever not? He's their dad.'

'Harry's in the middle of his A levels. He doesn't finish until next Friday. If Marc's not back by then, I'll tell them.'

'Where do they think he's gone?'

'Work assignment in Scotland.'

'Do you think that's a good idea?'

A brain does exist somewhere behind those eyelash extensions and slug eyebrows.

'Men,' says Pen. 'They're a law unto themselves, the useless pricks. I should know. I married one. Why do you think I call mine The Prick? Pete the Prick. I wish he would bleeding disappear too.' She's trying to lighten the mood, but it's too heavy.

Sasha glances at her watch. 'I need to go. Art referred a new client to me this morning. I could do without it, but she'll go elsewhere if I turn her down.' She pulls a phone out of her pocket. 'I need to ask you something, Pen.'

'Sure, honey, anything.'

Sasha pauses, as if preparing herself for an answer she doesn't want to hear. 'Why did you send Marc this text this morning?'

Pen takes the phone and holds it at a distance, squinting. 'Oh, did I send that to Marc? Silly me, I meant to send it to you.' She points to the end of the room. 'I was referring to Ralph's appointment.'

I step out of the door, overdosed on tweeness.

Pen shouts out. 'I'll drop Ralph back when he's finished.'

Sasha turns and waves to her. 'She's a character, isn't she?'

'You can say that again.'

'Do you believe her?' she asks.

'Are you crazy? If you think she and Marc are having an affair, you really are barking up the wrong tree.' I laugh, relieved I've managed to make her chuckle too.

That said, I've seen more unlikely-matched characters indulging in extramarital liaisons. Only recently, I was involved in a case where a seventy-something-year-old was having an affair with his niece's husband. But Sasha doesn't need to know that. 'Is her husband really that bad?'

'No. He works up in the City. A trader of some sort. He does loads of fundraising runs for Kids with Cancer. Bit of a sad story. Their only child died of leukaemia. He was only six. It was before we moved here.' She sighs heavily. 'So, you believe that she texted Marc instead of me by mistake?'

'One hundred per cent. I think she was telling the truth.'

Harry and Luke are in the kitchen when we arrive back. Bacon fries on the hob as Harry butters bread. 'Boys! How did the exam go?' Sasha asks.

Harry chucks the knife in the sink, his expression as depressing as the pile of washing-up that has crept further along the worktop. 'Crap.' He yanks open a kitchen drawer and roots around. Removing a pair of tongs, he transfers the bacon to the bread.

Sasha looks at Luke, who shrugs his shoulders.

'Don't bother asking him,' Harry says. 'You know what the answer will be.'

'I'm guessing that means you found it easy,' Sasha says to Luke.

'He walked it like he always does,' Harry says, sticking his head in the fridge. 'When're you going shopping, Mum?

56

It's pretty sad in here.' He takes out a can of Coke and holds it up to Luke. 'We'll have to share.'

Luke gives Sasha an apologetic look and follows Harry to the beanbags where they plonk themselves down with doorstop sandwiches and start comparing notes on exponentials and logarithms.

My phone beeps with another text from Rob. 'I must go,' I say, and Sasha walks me to the door.

'I'll see you tomorrow morning with Jim.'

'Any developments on Marc, let me know straight away. Even if it's the middle of the night. I'm here for you.'

Someone knocks on the door as I reach for the handle. Sasha opens it to Pen standing with her hands behind her back, frowning. 'I'm not sure if this has any relevance, but I remembered something that I think I should mention.'

Sasha thrusts a finger to her lips. 'Harry's in there.'

Pen pulls her outside. I follow. 'Last Friday morning, when I was walking the dogs, I saw Marc up on the common, next to the railway bridge. He got into Art's car, and they drove off past the little corner store. Bit weird, I thought to myself, I wonder where they're going. Usually, I wouldn't think anything of it, but given what you told me earlier, I thought I should bring it up. Do you know where they were going?'

'No,' says Sasha, frowning. 'He never mentioned anything to me. I thought he went for an interview last Friday morning.'

SIX

DAY 3

'What time did you get home last night?' Jim asks when I place his morning tea on the bedside cabinet.

'It was a late one. Past two.' I yawn, still fuzzy from lack of sleep. 'An interview with a suspect started later than planned as we had to wait for the duty solicitor. It went on longer than we thought. I couldn't get away. How are you this morning?'

'A bit better than in the night. Sorry to get you up again. I didn't realise I'd run out of painkillers. Come back to bed for five.'

'I haven't got time.' I kiss him. 'What time did Mel leave?'

'Around eight. After the kids went to sleep.'

I hate leaving him with the kids when there's no help around. Just in case. "Just in case of what?" he used to ask when I told him this. But I could never admit the truth – that there are too many what ifs.

What if they play him up?

What if the bathroom floods?

What if there is a fire?

I shudder. What if… what if… what if?

'I'll drop them at school, then I need to come back here to send a couple of emails. Can you be ready for nine-thirty to head to Sasha's?' He struggles to get moving on pain days. And this is a pain day. I can tell by his face which is a murky shade of grey, and the lines troubling his fore-head which make him look a decade older than his forty years.

Joe comes running into the room. 'Mummy, you're here. Where's Mel?'

I scoop him into my arms. 'I'm on a late shift today.'

'Does that mean you're taking us to school?'

'It sure does.'

'Daddy, Daddy, Mummy's taking us to school for a change,' Joe says. Here we go. The whistle has blown for the daily game of tug of war they innocently force me to play. The kids are already ahead. 'Don't get up yet,' Joe says, jumping on the bed and diving between the two of us. Jim yelps and turns to get up.

'Be careful of Daddy, Joe.'

'Pull your silky blanket over us,' Joe says.

I cover us with our chenille throw. It's too hot, but it's our morning ritual on days that allow. 'Keep still while I sip my tea.'

'Why do you have to go to work?' he asks.

'Because we need to pay bills and buy food.'

'Why doesn't Daddy go to work like other daddies? Then you could take us to school every day.'

'Daddy does work, but he works from home.'

'Why?'

'Because it's easier for us if I work full-time and he works part-time.'

'But why?'

The complexity of the kids and their never-ending questions. I feel like the suspects I regularly interview. Well aware that if I give the wrong answer, it could get me into serious trouble. I sometimes wish I could mutter, "No comment", too.

'Because it is.'

'Why don't Daddy's legs work properly like other daddies?'

'I've told you before. Daddy had a bad car accident.'

'Why?'

I jump up. 'Come on. Chop-chop. Go and get your sister up. Time to get dressed.'

I update Jim on the journey to Sasha's.

'You know that whiteboard in Marc's office? What does he use it for?'

'The one with all the drawing and computer code on it?'

'I'm not sure. There was nothing on there when I went into his office yesterday.'

'I thought you weren't going to get involved?'

'I can't not.'

He tuts and rearranges his position, trying to get comfortable. 'You can, Eva. They're not another work case.'

'What kind of computer code?'

He rolls his eyes. 'For that security system he's been working on. He sketched the outline of how the pen would work on it. And ideas for the computer code. I didn't understand any of it if I'm honest.'

'You went in there last week. Did the board have all that stuff on then?'

'Why all the questions?'

'Because Marc's computer has been wiped to factory settings, and someone wiped that board too, at some point.'

He tuts and rolls his eyes. 'You know what I hate most?'

'What?'

He tells me how much he hates seeing me playing with fire, knowing I'm in for third-degree burns when he can't get close enough to save me.

'By the way, I've offered you up for something.'

He gives me that dubious expression that says he knows he's not going to like what I'm going to say.

'We need you to put together a playlist for Harry's party on Saturday.'

'What did you do that for? I don't know what eighteen-year-olds like.'

'It's mainly a family party, only a few of his friends are going, so it can be a right old mix of tunes. I'll help you.'

'You're going to need to.'

'If you think putting a playlist together is hard, get this. I've offered to make the cake.'

'But you can't even bake.'

I giggle. 'I don't know what I was thinking. I meant to call around a few cake shops yesterday but got sidetracked. I'll do it today.'

'You're leaving it a bit late, don't you think? What's the backup plan?'

'Me.'

'You don't have the time.' He gives me a quizzical look I know I deserve. 'Or the ability. It's the boy's eighteenth for Christ's sake.'

We arrive at Napier Close with only minutes to spare. I get Jim's chair out of the boot and check my phone while I wait for him to sort himself out.

Luke and Harry emerge from next door in a hurry. 'Hi, Jim,' Harry calls out. 'Strange to see you here this time of day. I thought you usually came at night.'

'Couldn't make Monday evening, so we rearranged for this morning,' Jim says. He's struggling with the footplate on his chair. Luke bends down to help him, but Jim brushes him away. 'I'm fine, thanks. Where are you two off to?' Jim asks.

'Exam,' Harry says. 'Maths. Dad usually helps me revise, but of all the times, he's had to go away for work.'

Jim blushes and turns to Luke. 'You got an exam too?'

Luke nods.

'Good luck to you both.'

'Gotta go,' Harry says. 'Or we'll be late.'

'Want a lift to the Tube?' I ask.

Harry looks at his watch, then at Luke who nods. 'Thanks,' they chorus.

'Let me see Jim in. You can wait in the car if you want.'

'I hate lying to them,' Jim whispers.

'You didn't lie.'

'Indirectly, I did. I know damn well why his dad couldn't help him revise.'

Sasha is standing waving me in as if she has something to tell me that can't wait. 'I need to talk to you. Quickly, before Jim comes in,' she says as I take Jim's bag in while he takes a call. Her face holds the expression of both pain and fear. It's a familiar look. I've seen it on so many people before – the pain of loss and the fear of the unknown.

'He knows about Marc,' I say.

'Why?'

'I couldn't not tell him, Sasha. He knew something was up when you cancelled on Monday. I've offered the boys a lift to the Tube. You can talk about the situation in front of him when I get back.'

'I spoke to Art about Pen seeing Marc getting into his car last Friday.'

'What did he say?'

'He denied it at first. I couldn't believe it. We're meant to be colleagues and friends, I thought. I had to practically break down before he'd tell me the truth. I got it out of him in the end.' Her voice chokes. 'He gave Marc a lift to the doctors.'

'Why?'

'Apparently, Marc was suffering from depression.' She shakes her head, her bottom lip quivering. 'Why didn't he tell me? I'm his wife. He should've asked me to drive him.'

'Why didn't he drive himself?

'Long story. And a few reasons.' She sighs heavily. 'I

suppose I might as well tell you everything. Marc had an accident last Christmas. Only a small one, but he collided with another car which had a toddler in it. The whole incident scared him, and he lost his confidence. He stopped driving in the New Year.'

'Were you in the car too?'

'No. And I never told you about it because he asked me not to discuss it with anyone. I drive everywhere now, and he takes the Tube when he has to. So now I can't understand why he didn't ask me to drive him to the doctors. And why didn't he tell me he was depressed?'

'He gave you no clues?'

She looks at me like she's depressed too. 'With hindsight, maybe he did. He had mood swings and wasn't sleeping, but I put that down to the stress of the redundancy. Being laid off can't be easy. He was upbeat and optimistic most of the time.' She thought for a moment before adding, 'Or maybe that was the face he showed me.'

Jim knocks at the already open door. 'Alright to come in?'

'Don't let him underestimate the pain he's been in,' I say to Sasha, pointing to Jim. 'The sleepless nights are killing us both.' I jangle the car keys. 'I'll be back soon,' I say, kissing Jim on the way out.

Harry is sitting in the passenger seat and Luke in the back, both of them on their phones. 'What time's the exam?' I ask when I get in.

Harry manages to pull his face away from the screen for a brief second. 'Eleven.' He returns his focus to the screen and adds, as if a second thought. 'Thanks for doing this.'

'No problem.' I try to strike up a conversation, but that's hard when you're in fierce competition with a teenager's phone, so I have to keep trying. 'Looking forward to your party on Saturday?'

'Sort of. Would be better if my exams were over. Why can't I have been born in September like him?' He gestures to Luke with a nod. 'That's why he's way ahead of me. He's nearly a whole year older. Proper brainbox.'

'I wouldn't go that far,' Luke adds.

'His mum took him for an IQ test before he started secondary school.'

'You're embarrassing me, Haz.'

Harry laughs. 'One hundred and thirty-nine, he scored: very superior intelligence. Only one point off genius or near genius.'

'Hazza.'

'He's a member of Mensa.'

I look in the rear-view mirror to a blushing Luke. He looks much older than his eighteen years – confident, without being arrogant – and the way he holds himself in a crisp white shirt, suggests a man in his twenties. Other than a couple of stifled grunts, it's a struggle to get much more out of either of them.

Back at Sasha's, I stay in the car before going into the studio, catching up on chores I've been putting off – a call to HMRC about a payroll tax problem for Mel and an erroneous entry on my credit card last month. I update our online supermarket delivery order then click onto Amazon and order a princess fancy dress outfit for Isabella for an upcoming party.

As I enter the studio, scented oils are burning; jasmine I think, and Jim is lying face down on the bench. Sasha is performing myofascial release on him. An alternative therapy she once used on me after a fight I had to defuse between two reckless females outside a pub in Soho a few years ago. After one of them walked off, the other, a slight woman with bubble-gum pink hair and dozens of piercings, verbally abused me. She was angry at life, and I sympathised. I was once like that. I tried to placate her, which backfired on me as she lashed out and pushed me against the front of a coffee shop next door. Unfortunately, I fell hard against the glass frontage. She was charged with assaulting a police officer, and I ended up with a bad back and three months physiotherapy with Sasha. But let's look on the bright side; if it wasn't for Miss Pink Hair, Sasha and I would never have met.

'His hamstrings are extra tight this week. So are his glutes. This will be contributing towards the pain, I believe. I've concentrated on them this morning.'

'Why's that?' I ask.

'He needs to have regular breaks out of his chair. He's not stretching enough. Art is going to be able to help here.'

Jim waves a hand up. 'I am present, you know.'

Sasha profusely apologises then says to me. 'Marc's phone is over there if you still want to take a look.' She nods to her desk.

I pick it up.

'1066,' she says.

I enter the code and spend the next fifteen minutes flicking through the contents, but nothing stirs suspicion.

Sasha taps Jim on the shoulder. 'We're all done. Make sure you stretch your legs as much as possible.' She walks over to me. 'Find anything?'

I shake my head. 'Nothing untoward.'

'Art can see you next Monday, if that suits. Jim can have his usual session with me and afterwards go and have a chat with Art about the best way to proceed.'

'What time were you thinking?' I ask.

She picks up her diary. 'How about a session with me at two-thirty, then go and have a chat with Art at three-thirty. He's a nice guy, and so good at what he does. He has a waiting list, but he's agreed to fit you in as a favour. I'll introduce you to him at the party on Saturday. You can't help but like him.'

I pick up my phone and log on to my banking app. 'How much do I owe you?'

'Normal, please.'

'You've been more than an hour.'

She gives me a look as if to say, so what, I owe you ten times that.

Sasha and I step outside while Jim is getting dressed. 'I didn't finish telling you,' she says. 'The strange thing is, the doctor prescribed Marc some anti-depressants.' She claps her hands together and draws them to her lips as if she is about to pray. 'Art dropped him at the chemist to pick them up after the appointment. I found them at the back of his bathroom cabinet this morning. The seal is still intact, so wherever he's gone, he wasn't depressed enough to take them with him.'

SEVEN

'You were depressed and suicidal once. What did it feel like?' I ask Jim as we crawl back home. I'm edgy. We are stuck in a traffic jam. Mel needs the car today as Joe and Isabella have playdates after school, so I'll have to take the Tube into work. Arthur is going to be tapping his watch again.

'Where's this come from?'

'Just wondering about Marc's state of mind.'

'It's not a good place to be.'

'But what did it actually feel like? You've never really told me properly.'

'Before or after the accident?'

'Both.'

'They were different, I suppose. Different but inter-linked in my case. Before, I was more suicidal. A reaction to the situation. I mean, it was pretty dire, wasn't it?'

I scoff. 'You can say that again.' The car in front of us edges forward before its brake lights redden. 'Damn traffic,'

I say, straining to see what's holding things up. 'It's chocka out there.'

'I can still see myself sitting in that hotel room in New York, holding that bottle of pills. It was like I couldn't see clearly. I couldn't see a way out. With or without you.'

He turns his head, gazing out of the window. 'I emptied the whole bottle into my hand so many times. They were like little blue smarties.' He snorts. 'I could so easily have taken them.'

I place my hand on his knee and squeeze it. 'What stopped you?'

He turns to me. 'You. I couldn't bear the thought of never seeing you again. And what it would do to you. And Joe, of course. The thought of police officers knocking on our door to tell you I'd been found dead on a hotel room floor, that's what stopped me. I couldn't do it to you.' He put his hand on top of mine and squeezed it tightly. 'After the accident, when they told me I'd never walk again, I'd say that was more depression. I never thought about ending it all, though. I didn't know what to do, how the future would turn out. How I was going to look after you and the kids. I knew I'd never be capable of going back to my old job.' He paused. 'And I was scared you would leave me.'

'Jim!'

'I know, I know. That's what I mean. That's what depression does to you. You can't think clearly.' He taps his temple. 'You're confused all the time. Helpless, that's the word, you feel powerless, and you can't see anything positive. It's painful – mentally, as well as physically, harrowing.' He slaps his open hand against his chest. 'It hurt here. Like life had landed an anchor on my chest, and I couldn't find a way to break free. They were dark, dark times. I wouldn't wish it on anyone. You lose sight of what it feels like to be happy.'

I'm shocked. All the love I feel for him rushes to my heart, making it skip a beat. How distraught Sasha must have been to learn of Marc's depression. My voice breaks. 'You've never spoken like that before.'

'I guess I couldn't. It's been a long time now, though.'

'Do you ever feel like that now?'

He smiles and squeezes my hand again. 'Never.'

'You would tell me if you did, wouldn't you?'

'Don't worry. I may have legs that don't always work, but I have everything else I need in my life.'

'But you would tell me, wouldn't you?'

He nods.

I reach behind the driver's seat and fish in my bag for my phone. 'Do you think Marc was depressed?'

'What makes you ask?'

I relay what Sasha has told me while checking for traffic updates.

'If he was, he never let on to me. He was his normal self when I saw him last week. Perhaps he was a little down about not finding work, but he never came across as depressed.'

'That's what I can't understand.' I sigh heavily.

'It's hard to believe he was. Then again, people learn to disguise these things well. You know what? Looking back, however bad things were for me, I would never have walked out as Marc has. He must be in a bad place. Who knows what he's capable of?'

My fingers tap the steering wheel. 'I wish this traffic would get moving.'

'Chill out. There's nothing you can do about it.'

'I need to get to work.'

'Let's take the kids to the beach this weekend.'

I turn to him in surprise. 'Where did that come from?'

He shrugs. 'It's your weekend off, and the weather's going to be sunny. We haven't been to the beach since last summer. The kids'll love it. We need to have some fun.'

'For sure, I'm up for that.'

'Brighton?'

'Let's do it. Don't forget we have Harry's party on Saturday, so it'll have to be Sunday.'

'Gill's coming on Sunday for the week, remember? Mel is off on holiday.'

'How could I forget?' Gill has been like a mother to me. I've known her since I was sixteen when she fostered the unruly teenager I was back then. 'Let me check with Gill that she's happy to go to the beach.'

When we finally arrive home, I rush to get Jim's wheelchair out of the car. I might make it into work on time if I hurry. Mel comes out of the house, still in the PVC apron covered with dogs that the kids insisted on getting her for Christmas last year. I hand her the keys. 'Want a lift to the Tube?' she asks. I could kiss her.

I switch on the radio. A broadcast about depression and suicide catches my attention. Middle-aged men have the highest rate of suicide in the UK, and the rate for young females is now at its highest rate on record. 'What's the definition of middle-aged?' I ask Mel.

'I know this because my daughter told me on my last birthday that I am now officially middle-aged. Between forty-five and sixty-five.'

We celebrated Marc's forty-sixth birthday earlier this year at the local Chinese restaurant. My thoughts return to my conversation with Jim this morning.

I run to my desk, an hour late. Rob appears before I've managed to sit down. He's tapping his watch and smirking.

'Don't even go there. The Northern line came to a standstill. I had to get off and get a cab. I could've really done without the hold-up today.' And the cost! I remove my cardigan and wipe my forehead. 'I'm in court later, and I need to go through the papers.'

'I need to go up to the City. I'll give you a lift if you want.'

'What're you doing there?'

'I've got a lead on our Jason.'

'Jason Harper?'

He nods. 'A bloke he used to work with.'

'Tell me more.'

Before he can answer, Arthur hurries over. 'Late again, Barnes.'

'What can I do for you today, sir?'

'Some work would be good. A little treat has been delivered to our door. Shane Baker! I want you to come in on the interview.'

I tut. 'I'm due in court.' I would love to be in that interview. We've been trying to nab Shane Baker for so long. And, if what Arthur said yesterday about possible links to Jason Harper is right, it could be an interesting few hours.

'What about you?' Arthur asks Rob.

'I've got a lead on Jason Harper,' Rob says. 'I could rearrange.'

'You carry on. I'll get Peters to come in on this one.' Arthur returns to his desk.

When we pull away from the station, I ask Rob about his lead on Jason Harper.

'It seems the neighbours were right. He used to work for a software company up at Moorgate. He was a sales-man. I gather he got the boot at the end of last year. The bloke I'm going to see hinted at drug use.'

'Interesting. I wish I could come with you.'

'Nosy, nosy. Always want to be involved, don't you?'

I elbow his arm.

'I fancy a drive-through. You got time?' he asks.

'What is it with you and food?'

'I'm a growing lad?'

I pull a face at his gut. 'Exactly.'

'Be kind, DC Barnes, be kind.'

'I'm just trying to give back.'

'You're not trying too hard.'

'Cut the sarcasm.'

'I love sarcasm. It's like smacking people in the face but with words. You've taught me so well. I've nearly mastered its delivery as perfectly as you.'

He laughs. I laugh too, thankful for the humour he brings to days like today.

We stop at McDonald's for him to pick up a Big Mac and Fries. I opt for a Veggie Wrap, and we park up on a side street to eat. Chomping and chewing like this is his last day on earth, he demolishes his food before I'm even halfway through mine. 'I think I might dash to the loo before we go,' I say, opening the car door.

His mobile rings as I get out of the car, and he's still on the phone when I return. 'Catch you later,' he says and ends the call. 'That was my flatmate, Phil; the one who works for the British Transport Police. Looks like the reason for your holdup this morning was a jumper at Brixton Tube.' He pulls a pained grimace. 'It was a right mucky one by all accounts. Bloke all over the track.'

The spicy relish from the wrap repeats on me. Regardless of how many people there are in London, and, for that matter, middle-aged men, I can't help but dwell on the uneasy feeling that Marc could well be that person sprawled across the tracks. I throw the remainder of the wrap in with his rubbish and tell him to get a move on.

EIGHT

DAY 4

After dropping the kids at school, I pull on my running gear. I haven't managed to get out since Sunday, and I'm jittery. Withdrawal symptoms from the endorphin rush I get from pounding the streets. Running is my drug. It doses my body with freedom. My running repertoire is comprised of various routes. There's a six-miler up to and around Wandsworth Common, a shorter Tooting Common three-miler for when I only have a half-hour to spare, and street circuits of varying distances for when it's dark. It's another late shift today. I'm not due into work until two, so, after lacing my trainers, I quickly stretch before heading towards Wandsworth Common.

The sun is shining in a baby-blue sky, warming my skin as David Guetta pumps through my AirPods. They're new, the AirPods. Jim bought them for me last week. Not because it's my birthday or anything, but because that's the kind of thing he does. 'Not for nighttime runs, though,' he insisted.

Usually, when I find my rhythm, my worries and anxieties start to subside, and I can zone out, but Sasha and Marc invade my thoughts today. Despite my reassuring words to her, I've started to sprout a seed of worry. Has Marc been having an affair? Not with Pen. I don't think that's possible, but who else? I plan to have a dig around at work later. I know I will get to the root of his disappearance. My determination will succeed. It may take a few days, but it always wins.

My phone rings in the bedroom as I step my sweat-purged body into the shower. I step back out to check who's calling.

It's Sasha. 'How's it going?' I ask.

'I need you to see something.'

'What's happened?'

Noisy kids emerge in the background. Her voice becomes muffled. 'Sorry, I can't talk right now.'

'I'll try my best to stop by at some point. Call you later.'

I arrive at the station an hour before my shift starts. Not that Arthur acknowledges my efforts like he does my occasional lateness. I have a ton of paperwork to catch up on, so I grab a coffee and plough in. When Rob turns up, he briefs me on his findings from yesterday. Apparently, Jason Harper was suspected of taking a backhander in some client deal and "asked to leave" the software company he worked for. It was all kept very hush-hush because the client in question had associations with the company secretary. We view the Shane Baker interview from yesterday. He was let go due to insufficient evidence to charge him.

Despite our focused attempts, it's not until late afternoon that we get a tip-off from an old school friend of Baker's who we trace through social media. We head out to the given address west of Holborn. It feels like a treat, in a way, to escape the office and journey into the West End.

'My mum's got us tickets for my dad's sixtieth birthday up in that thing,' Rob says as we near the London Eye.

'That thing?' I say in a tone to suggest he needs to pay this London landmark a little more respect. As we wait in traffic, I stare at the ferris wheel revolving in London's sky. Jim and I have ridden the Eye twice, once in the day, once at night, way back before the kids, when life was so much simpler. I had loved the daytime ride so much, Jim surprised me one Saturday morning. 'I've got you a treat,' he said, opening the bedroom shutters to a glorious summer day. 'The weather has to be right. And tonight's the night.' He perched on the edge of the bed and handed me a printout of the tickets slotted amongst a bunch of red roses.

Such different experiences, but the night visit won the vote. He'd arranged a river sightseeing trip beforehand too. We drank bubbly and ate canapes as we cruised up the Thames capturing the best of London – St Paul's Cathedral, the Tower of London and the Houses of Parliament – before boarding the glass-encased pod. The thirty-minute ride turned out to be everything I had imagined. Some claim it's overrated and overpriced, but I don't agree. Seeing London twinkle a spectrum of colours, illuminating the night sky, is an experience you can only capture from views rising to one hundred and thirty-five metres high. We dined at the Oxo Tower afterwards and discussed our future – four kids and a holiday home in the South of France that were never to be.

We arrive at the given address in Holborn to find an overcrowded student flat. None of them have ever seen or heard of a Shane Baker.

'Bleeding waste of time,' Rob says as we leave.

'I need a favour.'

'What?'

'Before we go back to the station, would you drive me down to that house I went into the other night?'

'What's going on there?'

'Something to do with Jim.'

He looks at me quizzically. 'Whatever. You're lucky I like you a little bit.'

When I knock at Sasha's clinic door, she steps outside to tell me she's treating a patient but will be with me in ten. 'Make yourself at home,' she says, waving me over to the house to wait. 'The kids will let you in.'

George answers the door, scruffy after a day at school. He needs to visit the barbers, and ketchup stains his shirt. 'You need to be quiet,' he says, sniggering. 'Greta Thunberg's filming.'

I follow him into the kitchen. It's still a mess and smells of stale fish and chips. Hannah is sitting on a beanbag, and

Luke is kneeling, videoing her speaking about climate change. They both look quite the experts, concentrating intently on what they are doing. Across the room, Harry is lolling on another beanbag watching, amused. George whispers in my ear, sniggering, 'It's for her YouTube account.'

Hannah wears her hair in two plaits which rest on her chest. She looks so young, yet so mature, sitting crossed-legged, encouraging students to join the growing move-ment of global climate change strikes. 'One person can make such a huge difference. And that person is you,' she says, pointing a finger at the lens.

Luke stops the video. 'Let's rework that last bit. I'm going to zoom in, but you keep your finger still.'

'Rework that bit,' Harry laughs. 'She's not a fricking supermodel.'

'OK, Mr Videographer Extraordinaire,' Hannah says to Luke, blowing her fringe from her eyes.

'OK, Mr Videographer Extraordinaire,' George mimics.

Hannah turns to him. 'Get lost.'

Luke positions his phone like a professional. 'Ready?' He presses the start button. 'I'll edit it later and send it over. Let's add some music too. What do you fancy?'

'You're the expert, you choose.'

'You're the expert?' George is off again.

Hannah ignores her brother. 'Can you get some photos too for my Insta?'

Luke stands to catch her from different angles, taking several shots before crouching down to show her his endeavours.

'Can you get some more and more and more photos for my Insta?' George wiggles two-finger peace signs either side of his immature grin. 'My "we must all do our bit to save the planet," Insta.'

Harry reprimands his younger brother. 'Grow up, George.'

Sasha's entrance is well-timed. 'You lot aren't arguing again, are you?' She turns to me. 'Are they?'

I laugh. 'Just some healthy sibling rivalry, best ignored. Joe and Isabella are the same except they bicker over Lego bricks and colouring pencils.'

It comes out of I don't know where. Three days of pent-up stress and frustration, probably. It is as if her wrath has parachuted in and hijacked her placid nature. 'Grow up!' she screams at them. As silence fills the room, their four heads spin around simultaneously as if they have been choreographed.

Hannah runs over to her, concern flushing her cheeks. 'Mum, what's up?' She tugs Sasha's arm, but Sasha swings away from her.

'Your kids are young, Eva. You'd think mine would've grown up a bit by now.' She turns to her teens. 'Stop your stupid squabbling and get this place cleaned up.' She takes my hand, 'Come to the studio. I need to show you some-thing,' she says, dragging me away from an argument about whose turn it is to tackle the washing-up.

I have to increase my pace to keep up as she strides over to the studio. 'I found something you need to see. It's kept me awake all night.'

We pass Rob in the car. He winds down the window. 'Everything OK?'

I nod. 'I'll be with you soon.'

When we reach the clinic, she leads me over to the desk and opens her laptop. Her hands are shaking, and so is her voice. 'He's always taken care of the finances. It's not my thing.'

'It's not many people's thing.'

'He's much better at it than me. I should've taken more interest.'

'There's nothing to be ashamed of. You're a partnership.'

'*Were* a partnership.'

'Don't say that.' Something has flipped her. What has she found?

'When he was made redundant, he wrote himself a list of things to do. Jobs he's put off for ages – sorting the shed out, fixing the fence panel that blew down in those gales last October, that kind of thing.' She sweeps her hand around the room. 'He even added decorating in here. He was quite excited about it. His top priority, though, was sorting out our finances. I remember he said he was going to move our ISAs to earn more interest and look at switching energy providers. And look at remortgaging this place for a better deal. All that stuff you put off because it's too boring to contemplate.' She rummages around in her paperwork and hands me a piece of paper. 'Here it is, his master list. I found it in his filing cabinet.'

I glance down. It resembles what I struggled to create after Jim's accident – account names and numbers, passwords, contact details, policy particulars.

'So, I logged into our bank account again to see if he's used his debit card. He hasn't at all, but you see here.' She points to the heading, bank accounts. 'We've got our joint account, savings account, my business account – which he took care of too – and, look, there's another account in only his name I knew nothing about.' She clicks onto an HSBC site and references the sheet of paper to log on. 'So, this is what I found last night.'

I scan the transactions. The account balance stands at two hundred odd pounds.

'See.' She jabs a finger at the screen. 'Last week, a deposit of five thousand pounds.' She jabs faster. 'From Mr Peter Price.'

I look at her, confused. 'Who's he?'

'Pete the Prick, Pen's husband. Dog parlour pink Pen.'

I return my attention to the screen. 'The same amount was cashed at a bank on the fourth.' I look at her, questioningly. 'That was Tuesday, the day after he left.'

'That's right. And look where it was cashed from, Cambridge. And look.' Her finger slides down to the line below the five thousand pound withdrawal. 'Three hundred pounds was withdrawn from the cashpoint of the same bank the night before.'

I scan the transaction. 'What time?'

'Two minutes past six in the evening. So, now I know where he is. Cambridge.' She turns to me, her eyes glassy.

'Why Cambridge?'

She shrugs. 'He was born in Cambridge, and his family lived there for a while. But they moved to London when he was about ten or so. I don't think he knows anyone there now.'

He got up there pretty sharpish, I think to myself, but don't share that thought with her. There's no need to panic her at this point. I'll look at train times and work it out later. Perhaps he got a lift. But who with? 'How well does he know Pen's husband?'

She scoffs. 'Obviously better than I thought. As I mentioned the other day, they occasionally go jogging, and we get together with them and some of the other neighbours every few months.'

'Why would he have given Marc that kind of money?'

'I've no idea. I never even knew this account existed.'

'But he's never tried to hide it, otherwise he wouldn't have put it on this sheet,' I say, trying to calm her.

'I know this sounds irresponsible, but I take little interest in our finances. Marc takes care of that side of thing. That's bad, isn't it?'

I shake my head. 'In most relationships, one is usually better at looking after the finances. My mother-in-law was the same. Jim's father completely controlled everything. Sarah had her own bank account that he transferred a monthly allowance into, and she was content with that.'

'You are always so objective.'

'And so are you. This has shaken you.'

'And look at this. At the beginning of the year, there was a balance of seventeen hundred and twenty-seven pounds. Interest has been added on the first of each month, and nothing, until, look, last month, he made a cash withdrawal of fifteen hundred pounds from a bank at Cannon Street.

I've looked through my diary and in all the other accounts. I've no idea what that was used for.'

'I don't suppose you can remember what he was doing on that day. Why was he uptown?'

She shakes her head.

'We need to see his diary.' My phone beeps. I take it out of my pocket. It's Rob.

Will you be long? Thought I might go and find something to eat.

'I have to go. I'm sorry, I can't keep Rob waiting any longer. We need to get back to work.'

Angst knots her face, but my hands are tied. I can't pull any strings for her at the moment. 'I've got three days off after today. I'll give this some thought and pop over tomorrow. Call me if you find anything else out.'

Sighing heavily, she clicks the laptop shut. 'Cambridge? Why Cambridge? And what did Pete give him five grand for?'

'Can't you go and ask him?'

'I need to get him on his own. What if Pen knows nothing about it, and there was a reason Pete never told her.'

'Quick question before I go,' I say before she opens the door. 'Did Marc have a life insurance policy?'

She nods at the sheet of paper still in her hand. 'We both did. We took them out when the kids were born.'

'Have there been any changes to the policy that you're aware of?'

'All the details are on here. I checked everything this morning. There've been no changes.'

'Can I get a copy of that?'

She goes back to her printer to photocopy the sheet of paper. A lonely tear drops down her face. 'I'm not like you, Eva. I can't cope with all this.'

'You can, and you will. You have to keep strong.'

'But it's been more than forty-eight hours now. And there's still no word from him.'

NINE

Back at the station, I call the kids to say goodnight. Isabella spills a mouthful of mother guilt. 'I miss you tonight, Mummy,' she says in the cute voice that she seems to save for moments like these. 'Daddy's grumpy. He's hidden our iPads. I wish you were here.'

'Where's Mel?'

'Sick. She had to go home.'

Oh, no. This is all I need. Although it rarely does, I hate it when this happens. I always try and arrange cover, but not even a tried-and-tested childcare plan is foolproof. Even Mary Poppins sometimes needs a spoonful of medicine. 'If you are the best-behaved children in the world for Daddy tonight, I'll take you to school in the morning and pick you up.'

'Do you promise, Mummy?'

'I promise. Now go and kiss Daddy and tell him you love him.'

'Can we go for special ice creams after school tomorrow, then?'

'Yes, we can, sweetheart.'

'Promise?'

'I promise.'

I call Jim to tell him to call Mick – a friend of ours who lives alone in a two-bedroomed flat in the adjacent road. A retired actor, he drives a cab at the weekends for beer money and will always help us out with lifts when he is available. We met him when we first moved into our house, and Jim needed a ride to a hospital appointment. When I'm working lates, he often comes over to play poker with Jim and a couple of their mates, and he'll always help out when he can.

'Stop panicking,' Jim says. 'I've already called him. He's stopping by soon.'

I catch up on paperwork, then try and focus on the Jason Harper case, but knowing Jim is on his own with the kids does nothing for my concentration.

Neither does Rob's hunger. 'I'm popping out for food. Want anything?'

I shake my head. 'Your appetite is the size of an industrial hoover.'

I wander over to the kitchen area and make myself a strong black coffee, my mind drifting to Marc. Did he borrow that five grand from Pete on the pretence of a short-term borrowing arrangement, only to use it to run off with another woman? And what about that fifteen hundred pounds?

I search National Rail Enquiries for trains to Cambridge. The Tube Marc took on Monday must have departed around four o'clock. The quickest route would have been the Underground up to King's Cross, then a dash for a British Rail train to Cambridge. Assuming no delays, and he legged it from the station or took a cab, it would have taken about an hour and a half in total. Yes, it is possible he made it to Cambridge Market Square by 6pm to withdraw that money. But why?

After some hesitation, I pull up the Police National Computer. I pause and glance over my shoulder, knocking my knuckles together. It's pretty busy in here tonight. A cluster of detectives are huddled at a workstation, others are busy on the phone. Gossiping Gloria – one of the admin team – nods over at me and adjusts her tortoiseshell glasses. Turning back to the screen, I bite down on the knuckles of my index fingers and think for a while. Another glance over my shoulder, and I see Gloria has joined the gathering at the workstation. I take a deep breath and type Marc's details into the PNC. I don't know what I'm looking for, but that twisty feeling in my gut, that usually means I'm right, tells me I'll find something. It doesn't take long. It pops up like a Freddie Krueger jack-in-the-box. I scan the details and gasp. Last month, Marc received an eighteen-month driving ban and a fifteen hundred pound fine for being under the influence of alcohol while driving a motor vehicle. I reread the entry several times. Sasha told me she always drives everywhere these days, but she never mentioned anything about this. Maybe she's too embarrassed. Maybe she doesn't know.

I search some more, but there's nothing.

I trawl through his social media accounts. He's on

LinkedIn, "Seeking a new opportunity in the IT Security Industry", but there's nothing more that provokes me to investigate further. With a few exceptions – which arouse nothing of interest – all his connections appear to be people in similar roles. I can't find him on Twitter or Instagram. He has a Facebook page, but hasn't posted since New Year when he put up a picture of Sasha, Ralph and the kids, wishing all his friends and family, "All the best for the year ahead". I flick through other posts, scrolling back a few years, but they only show the typical traits of a family man: pictures of him cheering on Harry in a rugby match, sailing with Hannah and George on Lake Windermere, date night with Sasha.

So why the hell has he walked out?

Later in the evening, a call comes through on the arrest of a drug dealer we've had on surveillance, and he's on his way to the station. I prepare for the interview, and this takes up the rest of the shift. It's gone midnight before I leave, and I sigh with relief when I get in the car. I'll still be working, but at least I have three days away from the station, although a job like this never gives you real time off.

As I put my key in the ignition, my phone beeps. It's Sasha asking me to call her when I can. I find her number and tap it.

She answers straight away, sniffling. 'I know it's late, but I've tried so hard to do it myself. I need your help. I'm so useless. No wonder he left me.' Her voice is desperate, in stark contrast to the strong bold Sasha, I know.

'What's happened?'

'I want to go to Cambridge to try and find him,' she manages to say between suppressed sobs. 'I've tried to design this missing person leaflet like one I found online, but I can't get the text to line up, and it looks crap. Usually, I'd ask the kids, but...' Tears rob the rest of her words.

My offer of help beats my rationality. It's late, and I should go home. 'Calm down. I'm in your area. I'll be with you soon. But I can't stay long.'

What am I thinking?

There's no traffic, so it's a clear ride to her house. She's waiting at the studio door when I pull up, her face pale and tear-stained. 'I'm sorry to mix you up in all of this, but if the police won't do anything, I need to take control of things myself,' she says, shoving the leaflet under my nose.

'What's your plan?' I ask as I correct spelling mistakes and fiddle with fonts.

'I'm driving up to Cambridge on Sunday. I've found a map of the town. The bank where he cashed that five grand from is next to the Market Square. I'm going to hand it around the stallholders and the shops in the near vicinity. You never know,' she says with a smidgen of hope that's gut-wrenching to hear. 'I can't just sit around. I have to do something.'

She's wasting her energy, but I've seen this so many times before. People taking the law into their own hands when they think the police are failing. What they don't realise is that we sacrifice sleep and skip meals in our inordinate desire to expose the truth. They can't see behind the scenes. Often things are so tangled up that we have to separate the threads slowly, with patience, so when everything finally gets unravelled, the strands of evidence don't fray and snap or come back to strangle us. So, often, this takes far longer than people's forbearance can cope with.

'Will the same stallholders be there on a Sunday?' I ask.

'I can't go during the week. I've got clients.'

I try to reason with her. Is this a good use of her time? But she's adamant. After proofing our efforts and sending the file to print two hundred copies, she offers me a drink.

I shake my head. I need to get home. I'm wondering if I should tell her about my findings today. Too late. I blurt it out. 'Do you know if Marc has a criminal record of any kind?'

She turns to me aghast. 'No, why?'

Every sinew in my body is screaming at me to stop.

'What are you trying to say?'

'I need to talk to you about something.'

Sasha gives me a look which suggests she already knows she's not going to like what I'm going to tell her. 'Go for it.' She stands to take the first batch of leaflets from the printer.

I pause.

Her eyes widen. 'You're worrying me now. Spill.'

My anxiety spares her a further few seconds from the torture my words are going to inflict. I hate these moments; relaying information that will crush people. But there's been worse. I'm not exactly going to tell her that her husband is a paedophile or a murderer, but still, this is going to hurt.

Unless she already knows.

'Marc does have a criminal record.'

Her hand flies to her heart. 'Oh, God. What's he done?'

'Drink-driving. He received an eighteen month ban and a fifteen hundred pound fine.'

'How do you know?'

'It doesn't matter, but you absolutely can't repeat to a living soul you heard this from me.'

'You sure you've got the right person?'

I nod. No words are going to lighten the load.

Her face pales. She shrinks into the chair and stares at her husband's face smiling up from the leaflets in her hand. 'That makes sense.' She slams the leaflets on the desk. 'Do you remember me telling you about that sickening pile-up on the M3 we narrowly escaped last Christmas?'

'I do. You were stuck for four hours watching the emergency services clear it up.'

'That's right. Marc was so badly shaken up, I ended up driving us home.' She pauses, as if she is trying to get the timeline right in her head. 'Then there was the collision with that car with the toddler. Both incidences terrified him.'

'Jim's the same. He's never got behind the wheel again.'

She gasps. 'That's why he sold his car. Oh, God, this is getting worse. He said we didn't need two cars while he was out of work and, as he was anxious driving anyway, we might as well save the costs of being a two-car family.' Sasha looks at the leaflet again. 'You lying bastard!' she yells at the picture of her husband's face.

The printer beeps. She reloads it with paper. 'Now I think about it, I know the day it happened.' Sasha pauses while her brain recalls the details. 'He drove down to

Croydon for a job interview in the morning. It was around the middle of January. I remember because there was a forecast of snow, and he was debating whether to take the train.' She snorts. 'He didn't even want the job but said the experience would look good on his CV, so he could hack it until something more suitable came up. On the way back, he stopped off in Thornton Heath for lunch with an old friend of his, Oli, from uni. I never thought anything of it. He must have drunk at that lunch and got caught afterwards because he didn't come home that night. He told me the interviewer got held up, and the lunch with Oli turned into dinner, so he was staying there. I wonder who bailed him out? It must have been Oli. He must have driven his car home the next evening too. That's why he withdrew that fifteen hundred pounds from his bank account. He needed to settle the fine and didn't want to pay it out of our joint account. And that's why he made me sell the car and always makes me drive now.' She slaps her hands on top of her head in anguish. 'Why didn't he share all this with me? Isn't that what marriage is all about? Sharing good times with the bad.'

She looks at me with such sadness, a lump appears in the back of my throat. A tumour of pity I swallow before it grows any bigger. Arthur's voice rings in my head. "Don't get involved in their story". 'Only he can tell you that.'

'God, it's like I never knew him.'

Her tears recommence, but this time they are not of distress and sorrow. They are of justifiable resentment. I've seen it so many times. Another couple playing the marriage game – but not by the same rules.

TEN

DAY 5

When I drop the kids at school, a yummy mummy accosts me at the gates. The designer-clothes-and-fancy-handbag type, privileged enough to employ a full-time nanny even though they don't have a job. Claudia Walters-Stewart represents the kind of woman I haven't got the time for but need to be polite to for the sake of my daughter. Isabella and her daughter Amelia are bffs.

'Eva,' she calls out, waving her manicured nails in time to her voice which sounds as if tiny unicorns are going to dance out of her rear end. Rob's sarcasm has undoubtedly rubbed off on me lately. 'We need to discuss Isabella.'

Oh, do we now?

I grit my teeth. I slept badly last night. After calling in on Sasha, I stopped at the twenty-four-hour supermarket to pick up ingredients for this cake I foolishly agreed to take responsibility for. Why, oh why? Then the kids delighted me with prods and pokes at six.

Isabella cowers behind me. 'Sure, let me see my children off, and I'll be happy to chat.' When did I get so good at lying? I kiss Joe and Isabella goodbye while trying to find the pseudo-smile I save for situations like this. I turn to face Claudia. 'How're things?'

She pounces straight in like a jaguar on its prey. 'Amelia told me Isabella said her mummy carries a gun for her job, and she will bring it into school and shoot her if she won't be her friend. And, as you can imagine, Amelia is dreadfully upset about this.'

Her allegation tips me off balance; I grab the railing. 'I thought they were friends?' I say to give myself time to think of a suitable answer.

'It appears not. Hasn't Isabella told you?'

'Told me what?'

'That she threatened my Amelia.'

'I can assure you, Claudia. I do not carry a gun. I will have a chat with Isabella at the weekend to hear her side of the story.'

'I want to go and discuss it with the head. Now.'

'As I said, please let me talk to my daughter first.' I walk away, hearing her tut as she stomps off towards her clique of cronies, all staring at me, crowded around her Range Rover.

There's no denying it, Claudia Walters-Stewart has wound me up. I drive home faster than I should. Isabella wouldn't say such a thing, would she?

I wasn't going to run today, but that woman has worked

me up so much, I know it's the only thing that's going to get me through the day. Damn her. I quickly catch up on emails regarding a couple of cases currently awaiting trial, before changing into some shorts and a T-shirt. I tie my hair into a ponytail and head out towards Tooting Common. I need to make that cake, so there's only time for a three-miler. But it's half-hour well spent sweating Claudia Whatever out of my system.

'So, I guess lunch is delayed?' Jim says when he gets in from his Friday morning session at a local charity for the homeless. He started volunteering there way before we got together. It's coming up for his twelfth year now, and he still looks forward to it every week. He teaches people who have never even peeled an onion to cook homemade meals. Unlike me, he is a dab hand in the culinary skills department. I used to join him weekly before Joe was born and occasionally still go along to help – in the office rather than the kitchen, though.

He grins at the cake mixture daubed across the backsplash, and the entire contents of our baking collection mounting in the sink. I didn't even know we owned this much equipment: whisks and spoons and spatulas, tins and bowls and measuring jugs. Mel must have acquired it over the years. She often leaves a receipt with a note to say what she has bought, but I never pay much attention. I trust her enough to periodically throw a couple of twenties in the money box she uses for ad hoc purchases.

'Nice effort.' Jim nods approval at my baking attempt, which doesn't deserve such a liberal compliment.

'You should have made it.'

'You know I don't like making cakes,' he says.

I snort, glancing at my watch. I want to speak to him about the yummy mummy's accusation, but it's only two hours until school pickup, and I promised Sasha I'd pop in. 'Can we do dinner, instead of lunch? I've got a few jobs to do before I need to get the kids from school.'

'Can't even spare ten minutes with your husband?'

I try the wide eyes, pouting look. It usually works. 'I'll sort a takeaway tonight.'

He rolls his eyes and says he'll put some wine in the fridge.

After clearing up, I find a tin for the cake and search for the candles and personalised name cake topper I ordered online. If it tastes bad, at least it might look good.

When I arrive at Napier Close, Sasha opens the studio door and shouts out, 'Be with you in a minute!'

I check my phone for updates when a car pulling up outside Pen's Parlour catches my attention. I watch a small woman get out with a cockerpoo as, concurrently, the door to Pen's Parlour opens, and ginger-haired Tom slips out to the side – dogless, again. I watch him walk to his house opposite, tucking his shirt into his jeans, and shake my head.

Sasha waves off her client and beckons me towards the house. I take my bag and the cake and follow her in. Stormzy is blaring out from the kitchen.

'The cake?' she says, managing a smile.

'Don't hold out for any masterpiece.' I lift the lid and give her a peek.

'You made it yourself,' she gasps.

'Don't look so surprised,' I say, faking a hurtful face. 'Nightmare! I left it a bit late and couldn't find anyone to make it. I've got some decorations and candles to go on the top.'

She kisses my cheek, thanks me profusely for saving her the trouble and nods towards the stairs. 'Sounds like the boys are in the kitchen, so pop it in my bedroom. It's the coolest room in the house. I'll make room in the fridge later. I had a Tesco delivery this morning, and it's full of party food.'

I climb the stairs to her room, a large double at the front of the house. As I enter, I nearly drop the cake in fright. Harry's walking out of the en suite.

'Sorry, I didn't mean to alarm you. I was using the toilet.'

Strange, I think, he didn't pull the chain. And why did he come in here to use the toilet?

'Let me take that for you.' Smiling broadly, he reaches out to empty my arms.

I pull the cake out of his reach. 'No problem. This is something for your mum.'

He glances around the room, and his eyes stop at a chest of drawers. On top of it lies some bottles of aftershave and a silver dish containing a few odd coins. He shifts them both aside. 'Here, put it on there,' he says and politely excuses himself and darts off downstairs.

I poke around the bedroom. I don't know what I'm snooping for, and nothing strikes me as out of the ordinary. It's your average couple's personal space painted plain white. Towelling dressing gowns hang from hooks on the back of the door. A peace lily plant grows in the corner next to the window. I walk over to Marc's bedside cabinet. Books scatter the surface, along with a photo frame turned face down. I lift it up. It's of Sasha and Marc on their wedding day, laughing in love as the light from the day's brilliant sun creates a halo above his head. I can see why she can't bear to look at it at the moment. There's one of those placemats with his name on it. The last resort type of gift you buy for the kids to give to their dad on his birthday when they are still too young to choose a present themselves, and you've run out of ideas. It has a picture of a young Harry, Hannah and George in the background, overwritten with:

Marc
A born warrior, you are sincere
People appreciate your honesty and straightforwardness

Ouch! It must hurt her looking at that too. I open the drawers but find nothing out of the ordinary – a couple more books, a packet of tissues, a phone charger.

What is the story here? There is one; I know. And I will find it. But something tells me it's not going to make good reading.

Wardrobes with sliding doors line the walls leading to the en suite. The ones on the left are open. Shirts, jackets and trousers hang neatly below a shelf of jumpers and tops. Marc's side, I guess. I check inside the jacket pockets but find nothing. Ties and belts dangle from hooks on the inside wall.

There must be something.

Below the clothes sits a rack of shoes and trainers, and a row of boxes covers the carpeted floor. I bend down and open them in turn, only to find folded scarfs, hats and gloves. The box at the bottom is pine green with a gold logo. I remove the lid to find a black pair of polished brogues and a mini shoe cleaning kit. I lift the shoes out and shake one in each hand. Worth a try? Jim's voice disturbs my thoughts. "You need to keep out of their business", but it's overridden by Arthur's "No stone can be left unturned in this game". Out falls a small plastic pouch containing at a guess, a couple of grams of coke.

Marc? Coke? Or is this what Harry was really doing in here?

Sasha's voice crescendos up the stairs. 'Eva! Are you OK up there?'

I stuff everything back where I found it and dash into the en suite.

She enters the bedroom as I flush the loo. 'You in here?'

'Just using the toilet,' I say, walking out past the wardrobes. 'I think Harry sussed me. He was in here when I got up here. I should have left the cake downstairs.'

'What was he doing in here?'

'Using the toilet.'

'Oh, no. Don't say the kids' loo's blocked again.' She rolls her eyes. 'Another thing Marc was meant to be fixing. We've got a problem with all the blasted loos in this house. They're forever getting blocked. Actually, it's a problem with the whole estate. Marc reckons it's the cheap sanitary-ware the builders sourced when these houses were built.'

She sits on a patchwork throw at the end of the bed, huffing and puffing. The throw is quilted and beautifully crafted in patterns of blue. Squares of stripes and spots, checks and stars are stitched together and bordered by cobalt blue piping. She stretches back on it with her hands facing the tufted headboard. 'I called Marc's friend, Oli, in Thornton Heath. The one he met up with on his way back from that interview. He was reluctant to split on Marc, but I got it out of him in the end. He knew about the drink-driving ban.' She snorts. 'Why didn't he tell me?'

'Perhaps he was too ashamed?'

'Before we go downstairs, I need to tell you something.' Her tone suggests more bad news coming my way. 'When you left last night, I did a closer search of our joint bank account. Something's not quite right. Over the last few months, he's been withdrawing one hundred and fifty pounds from the cashpoint every Friday morning.'

'And that's unusual?'

She nods. 'He usually withdraws five hundred on the first of each month, and that generally lasts us the whole month for bits and bobs, money for the kids, odd bits of shopping, that type of thing. He's been withdrawing this extra one-fifty weekly on top of that.'

'And you have no idea what he's been using it for?'

'No clue at all. We've cut back our spending since he was made redundant. Most Fridays, when the twins go to their youth club, he used to take me out. I'm sure I've told you before. Only to a local restaurant, but it was our night. He and I; the kids never came. But since he lost his job, he's been cooking and, on a Friday, he's made a point of making something special for the two of us and getting a decent bottle of wine in. Every Friday, without fail. But not one hundred and fifty pounds worth of niceness.' She curls her arms over her head, grimacing at me. 'It's all leading to the same conclusion, isn't it?' Her nose briefly turns up as if she can't stand the smell of her words. 'He was spending it on another woman. There's no other explanation. While I was working, he must've been seeing someone else.'

I sit down beside her and slide my arm across her back. 'I've already told you.' I squeeze her towards me. 'You mustn't make hasty assumptions. It's not helpful.'

'Then what has he been spending that much money on?'

I wish I could give her an explanation. 'We'll work it out.' I contemplate telling her about my discovery in her husband's shoes, but I need to give it more thought. What was Harry really doing in this room? Has he got something to do with the drugs I found? 'Did you get any further on the five grand?'

'I don't know how to approach Pete. Should I involve Pen?'

'Might get awkward if you don't. But then again, if he's kept it from her for a reason, it might cause more trouble than it's worth. He might have a rational explanation.'

She sighs. 'Come on, let's go back downstairs.'

In the kitchen, Harry and Luke are tucking into cheesy-smelling food from cardboard boxes and laughing at something they are watching on Luke's laptop. Sasha snatches the remote and turns the music down. 'You boys should be eating brain food, not all that rubbish.'

'We were starving after the exam,' Luke says, apologetically.

'I'm gasping. Cuppa?' Sasha asks the room in general; and questions the boys on how their exam went this morning.

Luke gives the thumbs-up sign, as Harry swears he has messed it up like all the rest.

'It wasn't that bad,' Luke says.

'Not if you've got a fricking calculator for a brain.'

Sasha waves a knife at her son. 'Stop with the effing and blinding, Harry O'Sullivan. It doesn't suit you.'

'I'll be lucky to get to uni at this rate.' Harry pauses to stuff a handful of nachos in his mouth. 'I got a text from Dad this morning,' he says, crunching his food.

'Me too,' Sasha says, quickly buttering slices of bread. 'What did yours say?'

A shiver of disapproval flutters through me. I look at the floor. Harry needs the truth.

'He wished me good luck with the exam and said he couldn't make it back for the party.' He shrugs his ambivalence. 'I guess he's busy, and it's a long way to come, but it is my eighteenth. He said he'd take me down the pub for my first legal pint next weekend to make up for it.'

'It's only a week away. It'll go in no time, and he'll be back.'

I throw Sasha a look, but her guilt doesn't allow her to cast one back. She arranges some ham and salad on two slices of bread and dollops mayonnaise on the others. 'It will go in a flash, don't you worry,' she says as the doorbell rings.

Talk about saved by the bell.

ELEVEN

'Who could that be?' Sasha asks, her dejected eyes shining a sliver of hope. She throws the sandwiches onto two plates and hands me one before going to answer the door.

I bite into the sandwich and watch the boys glued to the laptop. Two ordinary teenagers belly laughing at some videos. Seconds later, an attractive-looking woman strides in, smartly turned out in an animal-print shirt dress and brutal heels. 'I thought I might find you here,' she says to Harry and Luke. She unloads a stack of plastic containers on the worktop. 'Sixty homemade sausage rolls and my most-talked-about pasta salad,' she says, swinging her sleek, shoulder-length hair from her face.

The boys steal themselves from the screen. Luke nods at her and nudges Harry. 'Come on, let's go up to your room.'

'Teenagers,' the woman sighs as they saunter out. 'I live in the hope that one day, he might, just might, appreciate me.' She slips her bag off her shoulder, places it on a stool, and flicks the kettle switch.

Sasha lays a hand on the woman's shoulder. 'He loves you really.' She introduces us. 'Annie, this is my friend, Eva. Eva, meet my neighbour, Annie. Art's wife – Luke's Mum. The friend who always makes me feel under dressed.' Sasha pulls a face as she points at her Lycra leggings and work T-shirt, then at Annie. She's wrong, though. When not in her physio attire, Sasha can always be seen in feminine dresses: floral ones with delicate pleats and girly bows.

Annie laughs. She is subtly made up, her lips are pale pink, and there's no mistaking that she takes maximum advantage of her husband's professional knowledge. Working out is a priority in her life.

'Luke's always lovely when he's here, if that's any consolation. Let him get over these exams, and you'll have your boy back. Harry has been dreadfully moody all year.'

'One can only dream. Luke's been moody for months, too.' She throws her hands in the air in theatrical frustration. 'Roll on a week today, and it'll all be over.'

Sasha opens the dishwasher and removes three unwashed cups, squirting them with washing-up liquid. 'Harry's worse than Luke, I can tell you. From what I can gather, anyway. He's probably more polite for me than you, though.' She sighs. 'It won't be long before I have George to contend with too. I don't know, all this male testosterone.'

'The weather's holding up for tomorrow. What're your plans? You still going to open up the house?' Annie asks as she perches herself on a kitchen stool.

'I don't think I need to, do you?'

Annie shakes her head, unclipping the lid of one of her containers. 'I checked the forecast; it's going to be warm all day tomorrow. Save yourself the trouble, shut the house and keep everyone outside. They can use the loo in your studio.' She offers me one of her golden sausage rolls. Their fresh-from-the-oven smell prevents me from refusing. 'What else do you need me to do?'

'Nothing, thanks. I've no more clients today, and I'm pretty organised. I could do with some help tomorrow setting up.'

'I'll pitch in as soon as I get back from the shop.' She reaches towards the container, patting her firm tummy as if she needs the approval to help herself to a sausage roll. 'Art told me Marc has gone away to Scotland. That was a bit sudden, wasn't it?'

Sasha shoots me a warning look as I bite into a mouthful of sausage roll. Flakes of pastry shower onto my lap. 'A great opportunity came up we just couldn't turn down,' Sasha replies. 'The money was too good. Bit of an inopportune time, what with Harry's exams and his eighteenth tomorrow, but beggars can't be choosers.'

'How long for?'

'Two weeks,' says Sasha, making the tea.

'Two weeks! Not good timing with the boys' A levels.' Annie looks at me and says, 'Luke's been joining the revision sessions that Marc's been giving Harry. Neither Art nor I are the academic type.'

'I'm not sure Marc can teach Luke much more. He's such a bright boy,' says Sasha. She prods my arm. 'Did I tell you Annie owns a boutique up on the High Road?'

'Square One Womenswear, thirty per cent discount for new clients,' Annie says, looking me up and down as if it's a deal I shouldn't decline. She's probably right. I feel under-dressed in my jeans and favourite trainers that I should have thrown out yonks ago. At least I've got a decent shirt on. She gives me the low-down on the latest trends she has in stock. I try to look interested, honestly, I do, but fashion has never been my thing. Not that I don't take pride in what I wear, it just doesn't have to be the latest craze.

That twisty feeling is back, knotting my stomach. I'd quite like to have a conversation with this woman. But not in the presence of Sasha. 'In fact, I could do with something new for the party tomorrow night,' I say.

'I'm going there now to relieve my Friday girl, so if you want to come on down, I have a number of items I can see someone as slim as you in,' she says in that fake confident tone of a saleswoman who has a ton of stock to shift.

Shopping has never been a pastime I enjoy, especially now with post-pregnancy lumps and bumps to my armour. All that traipsing around rails packed with over-whelming choice and trying to look good in current trends under unflattering lighting and distorted mirrors that allow zero forgiveness for having contributed to evolution. I've even given up ordering online for myself because I end up with stuff I don't particularly like and don't get around to returning, so it ends up in the local charity shop. I tend to brave it and have an extravagant spree once a year, praying for the day I'll find that magical shop where I'll spend an hour and leave with enough clothes to stock my wardrobe for the rest of my life.

I gulp down my tea. 'I have to go and pick up my kids

now. Are you there tomorrow morning? I'll have them with me, but I'll bring their iPads.'

'I have bits and pieces to entertain children, so you'll be safe for a good hour. Saturdays are usually busy, but if you can come before ten, it's not too bad. To save time, I'll pick out some items I know you'll look great in and have them ready for you.' She turns to Sasha. 'Fancy coming too? I had a delivery this week. There's a great maxi that has your name written all over it from the halter neckline to the floor-length hemline. Oh, God, what's wrong?'

Neither of us has noticed Sasha silently sobbing. Annie rushes to her, looking at me questioningly. She puts her arms around her.

'Marc's not really in Scotland,' Sasha snivels, her shoulders shaking.

Annie looks over at me again, but I look away. This is Sasha's story to tell. 'What do you mean?' Annie asks.

'He's left us. And I have no idea where he's gone.'

Annie can't find any words, but who can blame her? It's not every day a friend tells you their husband has disappeared. Annie gawps as she listens to Sasha's update. 'Art never mentioned anything to me,' Annie says. I can't work out if this bothers her or not. It would if I were her. Jim doesn't keep anything from me.

Sasha says, 'Not many people know. I don't want the kids to find out until Harry has finished his exams.'

Annie, unintentionally I believe, raises her voice. 'You've kept this from the kids?'

Sasha holds up her hand. 'I know. I know. Don't go there.'

Annie's cheeks pale beneath her carefully applied blusher. She goes to speak but stops herself.

'What is it?' Sasha asks.

'I don't know if I should say.'

'Say what?'

Annie looks from me to Sasha and then to the floor.

'Come on, tell me,' Sasha says.

'I don't know if it's of any significance, or if I should even mention it, but I saw Marc one morning last week, in that coffee shop, near the boutique. What's it called?' She clicks her fingers in the air several times. 'The Wild Café.'

'I know the one. I didn't know he went in there. Was he alone?'

Annie shakes her head.

'Was he with a woman?'

Annie nods.

'Who? Who? You have to tell me.'

'Well, I thought it strange they hadn't met here or at her house.'

Sasha frowns. 'Who?'

'Alisha.'

'As in Alisha and Tom?'

Annie nods.

'Neighbours Alisha and Tom?' Sasha asks, her forehead furrowed.

'That's right. It surprised me too. I didn't know they knew each other that well.'

'Nor did I. How well?'

'I went in there to buy a quick coffee. And there they were engrossed in some pretty heavy conversation.'

TWELVE

Sasha stares incredulously at Annie, her voice barely a whisper. 'Did you hear what they were talking about?'

Annie shakes her head. 'I was only in there briefly, and I didn't notice them until I was paying.'

'Did they see you?'

'I don't think so. They were too absorbed in whatever they were discussing.' Annie glances up at the clock and grabs her handbag. 'I'm sorry if this is news you didn't want to hear, but I felt I should share it with you in the circumstances.'

'Of course, of course.'

'Must dash. I'll see myself out.'

She's in such a hurry to leave, we hear her bump into the table along the hallway.

Sasha glares at me. Her mouth is open so wide you could fit a golf ball in there without it touching her teeth. She waits for the thud of the front door. 'What was that all about?'

'Who is this Alisha?' I ask.

'I told you about her the other day. She's married to Tom, the graphic designer. The guy we met coming out of Pen's Parlour on Tuesday.'

Yep, I know who Tom is. The man without a dog.

'She's a lawyer. Works up in the City. She's also a client of mine who I see on an ad hoc basis. She suffers from recurring back pain. Workaholic. It's the way she sits at her desk for too many hours. She's quite a nice lady and very attractive. She's got these amazing blue eyes.' She pauses, wincing, then adds. 'Do you think she and Marc are having an affair?'

I take her hand, squeezing it tightly. 'I keep telling you – stop jumping to conclusions.'

'Then what were they doing together?'

'I could give you many reasons, but I have to go. I can't be late picking up the kids.'

'Will you come over there with me later?'

'Where?'

'Alisha's. She's working from home today. She called me this morning to ask if I could fit her in for an appointment today, but I was fully booked. '

How am I going to fit that in?

'Please? Eva, please.'

'What're you going to say to her?'

'I'm going to ask her what she was doing with Marc in that café last week. My head's all over the place. I know I'm not thinking straight. I need you with me to gauge her reaction.'

'I promised the kids the park and ice creams after school. I can't let them down.'

'That'll work. Hannah will be home by then. You know how much she loves them. They'll be fine with her while we chat to Alisha.'

The kids are hanging off the headteacher's arm when I arrive out of breath to an empty playground. 'You're never on time, Mummy,' Joe says, which is a tad unfair. I've only been late picking them up on a couple of occasions. Isabella's downturned mouth boosts the guilt her brother hurls my way. 'You're always late.'

'Pickup is three-twenty, Mrs Barnes. We try to teach the children good timekeeping here,' Mrs Miller says with the air of superiority only a headteacher can get away with.

'Sorry, you two. I couldn't find a parking space, so I had to leave the car a few streets away.'

'I've sent you an email, Mrs Barnes. Perhaps you could send me a reply when you get home?'

'Sure. Anything we need to discuss now?' I ask.

'No, no. Have a wonderful weekend.'

I grab the kids' hands. 'Come on. It's ice cream time.' I wish Mrs Miller a happy weekend before she has the chance to lecture me any more.

I take them to the common and watch them run to the café. It's their favourite place. A large wooden cabin, surrounded by trees, famous for its homemade ice cream served in fancy waffle cones half coated with rich Belgian chocolate. Joe sprinkles on the guilt. 'Can we have extra toppings today?'

I can't endure an argument. 'Go on. Just this once.' He smiles for the first time since pickup.

After our sugar overload, we wander over to the adjacent playground, the kids chatting without pause. I park myself at the end of a bench, relishing the smiles now gracing their innocent faces. They scamper off to play, holding hands and squealing. They have taught me that, for them, happiness is simple. I savour the time watching them climb and swing, see-saw and slide their way around the equipment.

Why can't life always be this simple?

I'm replying to Mrs Miller's email on my phone, agreeing to go and see her first thing on Monday morning, when Isabella comes running towards me, her arms held wide. I spring up and catch her, holding her close against me. 'I love you so much, Mummy,' she says, and I tell her not as much as I love her.

I lead her away from the bench and the ears of other mothers, scanning the playground for Joe. There he is, safely occupied with other similar-aged children on a wooden pirate ship. I tidy loose strands of Isabella's dark hair back into the bunches I tied for her this morning. 'Can I ask you something?'

Her smile vanishes with my contentment. 'Am I in trouble?' She stiffens in my arms and looks to the ground.

I find a quiet grassy area and sit crossed legged, with her in the same position opposite me. 'Not at all.' I place my fingers below her chin and gently lift her eyes to meet mine. 'I mean that. And I won't be cross. As long as... what?' I hold her beautiful face, overcome with love for my fragile daughter who, eight years ago, due to family fabrication and deceit, nearly didn't make it into this world.

'As long as I don't lie.'

'That's right.' I pause for a moment wondering how best to approach this tricky subject without ruining our precious time together. 'Amelia's mummy asked to talk to me this morning.'

Her chin presses down, but I won't allow my fingers to give. I raise her chin, so her eyes meet mine, and I ask her to explain her troubles.

She doesn't deny it, but her confirmation accompanies the painful truth no mother ever wants to hear. Angry tears burst out of her eyes like the words from her mouth. 'Amelia calls me horrible names. She's so mean. She says I'm ugly, and you don't love us, because you make Mel pick us up from school. And she pulls my hair.' More words spill, tripping over each other until so merged with snot and tears, they are no longer understandable.

Her eruption floods me with a torrent of rage that I fight to contain for another time and another place. 'How long has this been going on?'

'F... fo... forever,' she stutters through her tears. 'I thought if I told her you were a policewoman, and you had a gun, she would stop. Please don't be angry with me.'

I cup her innocent face in my hands. Not so innocent, it seems. 'My darling girl. I want you to listen to me and believe what I say. Firstly, I'm not at all angry with you. Secondly, none of this is your fault and, thirdly, I do not carry a gun. On Monday, we'll go and speak to Mrs Miller and sort all this out.'

My heart beats out of time for my daughter's saddened eyes weeping in her pink face, and I have to fight the mental image of meeting up with Claudia Walters-Stewart, pulling her hair and kicking her right where her unicorns sleep at night. I take a deep breath as I wipe her eyes, unsticking her eyelashes glued together from her tears. 'Come on. Go get your brother. I'm taking you somewhere.'

'Where? Where?'

'It's a surprise,' I say, looking to the heavens. Please, Hannah, be home when we arrive. I watch as Isabella skitters over to Joe as if our chat has lightened her step, and I can't help wondering if I were a yummy mummy and around for my kids more, would we have needed this conversation?

'Hide-and-seek or Pictionary?' Hannah asks as she scoops the kids into her skinny arms.

Sasha and I leave them debating which of their favourite games will win the vote, and we head to Alisha and Tom's place. Of all the houses in the close, theirs is the most well-kept. The weatherboarding is painted a French grey, and the woodwork white. A mass of flowering shrubs packs the borders, and on either side of the doorstep sit two lollipop bay trees in pots which match the paintwork of the navy blue door. 'I called her earlier to say I needed a quick word,' Sasha says, ringing the doorbell.

Alisha appears straight away. Tall and graceful with a

long face like a greyhound, she's the type of woman who makes you stop and stare. Her sleek, bobbed hair shines like glass. 'Sorry, I'm still a little busy with work. I'll be ten minutes.' She has a plummy voice which reminds me of Jim's father. She opens the door wider. 'You're welcome to come in and wait.'

Sasha throws me a look to ask me if that's OK. I smile and nod, and Sasha introduces us as we walk in. The inside of the house reflects the perfection of the outside and is the same layout to Sasha's. The hall is beautifully decorated with large abstract paintings. A porcelain vase of fresh flowers swamps a glass console, their velvety fragrance scenting the air. 'I'm having an introduction video made for my website,' she tells us as she delicately rearranges a gerbera with her long, thin fingers. There's a framed photograph of her in a black gown on her graduation day, which she rotates five degrees to the left before returning it to its original position.

'I thought you worked for some firm in the City,' Sasha says as Alisha leads us along the hall.

'I do, but I also run a small private practice. Well, I say small. It's grown more than I anticipated in the last year. Business is booming, so I'm updating my website.'

'What do you do?' I ask as she leads us along the hallway.

'I'm an intellectual property lawyer. Well, that's what I specialise in, but I take on various cases in my private work.'

Her kitchen is as pristine as a show home. She obviously doesn't have kids. Classical music softly plays from a

Bose system positioned on a unit at the end of the light and airy room. 'Hi Sasha, Eva,' a voice sounds as we enter, and I'm surprised to see Luke standing in the breakfast room area, where a glazed boxed canvas, depicting an uninhibited soirée of flowers, practically covers the entire far wall. He has one hand on his hip and holds a high-tech camera in the other. 'My first official paid job,' he says, with a proud smile.

'We need to finish filming one final piece, and I'll be with you,' Alisha says, gesturing for us to take a seat at the breakfast bar. She claps her hands and folds them together in front of her chest. 'Can I get you both a drink?'

'Water, please,' Sasha says, and I ask for the same.

'Still or sparkling?' she asks, opening the fridge door.

We both opt for sparkling, and she pulls out two bottles of San Pellegrino I've only ever seen in restaurants. She fills two glasses with ice and lemon and brings them over to us on a mirrored tray with gold handles. 'I won't be long.'

We watch them finish. I'm reminded how mature Luke is for an eighteen-year-old. He's quite a natural at this videoing business. He fixes his camera to a tripod and tells Alisha to switch position. 'Turn slightly to face me,' he says, with the confidence of a professional. He strides over to her and gently guides her shoulder to the right, then steps back behind the lens. 'Now, I want you to move to the left.' He bends to look through the viewfinder. 'Let's capture more of the colours in that striking canvas behind you.' The evening sun shines on her face, accenting her high cheekbones. He walks over to the plantation shutters and adjusts the panels, then returns to fine-tune the microphone.

'You're quite a pro, Luke,' Alisha says, shuffling along the sofa. 'You should be studying media or photography at uni.'

'My parents insisted I'd be better off with a computing degree. They see videography as more of a hobby. I get their point. So, I'm going to pursue my computing and take some side courses to improve my media skills. In the meantime, when my A levels are over, plans are afoot to go full steam ahead with a techie vlog I've been working on.'

'Where are you going to uni?' I ask.

'Imperial College.' He turns back to Alisha.

It takes longer than the estimated ten minutes. I get my phone out of my back pocket and text Jim to say I'll bring a takeaway home with me. He texts straight back.

No, let's get the kids to bed first and get a delivery later X

Two other texts arrive in quick succession.

It's Friday night, after all X

And you're not working for once X

Once Luke has finished, he packs up his bag. 'Is it OK to pop to your study and upload this final piece on your computer?'

'Sure,' says Alisha, and she disappears into the hallway after him, telling us she'll be with us in a minute.

'Do you think she and Marc could be having an affair?' Sasha whispers.

'Sasha!' I cast her a look. Really?

'I know, I know. I can't, for the life of me, think what he was doing with her.'

Alisha returns and seats herself opposite us. 'Now what can I do for you?' she says as if we are clients.

Sasha sits up straight. 'I'll cut to the chase, Alisha,' she says, a little too confrontational. 'I need to know why you and Marc met last week in the Wild Café.'

Alisha sits up straighter and steeples her fingers. She sucks her lips in, looking from Sasha to me and back again. She takes a deep breath. 'I can't tell you that.'

THIRTEEN

'Why not?' Sasha bangs her bottle of water on the table.

'I'm sorry, but client confidentiality does not allow me to discuss the private affairs of my clients. You'll have to ask his permission for me to discuss his business.'

'I can't.'

Alisha takes a sip of water.

What does she know?

Sasha drops her head and rests her chin in her hand, massaging her cheeks with long hard strokes. She pauses and looks up, and her story propels out of her mouth like projectile vomit, covering the room with a nasty sense of unease.

Alisha reaches forward and slides her slender hand along the table towards Sasha. Her voice softens as if to cushion her words. 'I'm so sorry for your situation, but I can't discuss client details with anyone. No one at all. Unless I thought he was committing a crime. He could come back tomorrow, and I would be in dreadful trouble if he found out I betrayed his trust. Especially since he went to the police with a request not to be found.'

Sasha tries to reason with her, but there's no breaking down Alisha's barrier of professionalism.

There's an awkward silence. 'Look,' Alisha says. 'I don't want to add fuel to an already burning fire, but can I suggest you talk to Annie?'

'Annie,' Sasha repeats, with a frown.

'Monday, that was the day he disappeared, right?'

Sasha nods.

'I was leaving for work, and I saw her arguing with Marc outside Art's gym. It was early.' She pauses for a moment. 'I usually leave around six, but I was late on Monday because I was going straight to a breakfast meeting with a client, so I reckon it was more like six-fifteen.'

'What were they arguing about?'

'I don't know, I couldn't make it out, but it was pretty heated. I'm surprised no one else heard.'

'Annie never mentioned anything.'

'Please could I ask you to keep my name out of this?'

Sasha smashes her clenched fist on the table, anguish paining her face. 'What is happening?'

'Where've you been?' Jim asks when I finally get home with the kids. 'You haven't answered my texts.'

I bend down to kiss away his annoyance, ignoring his rolling eyes. 'I took the kids to the park for ice cream and popped to Sasha's. Hannah gave them dinner. I've sent them to run a bath. I'll get them to bed; they're whacked. You order the takeaway. I'm starving.'

'You need to go through this playlist for the party,' he calls after me.

By the time I've bathed the kids, read them two stories apiece and got them off to sleep, an hour has passed before I get back downstairs to the smell of onion bhaji and chicken tikka masala. Jim's iPhone is belting out a Michael Jackson tune. I throw him a questioning look. 'Enough of the face, it's from the party playlist,' he says with a grin. 'I've done my homework. It's up there as a tune to include.'

Two generous glasses of wine sit on the table and a box in a brown paper bag rests on my dinner plate. 'What's this?'

'Look and see.'

I open the box to a treasure chest of chocolate heaven. 'My favourite. You're the best.'

'I try to be.'

'I'll save them for dessert.'

'At last, sitting down for a meal with my wife.' He raises his glass. 'Cheers.' He takes a sip of wine. 'The kids really miss you when you're not here, you know.'

'Let's not go there.' He has a habit of bringing this subject up when I haven't got the bandwidth to answer.

'We need to discuss it. Anyway, it's not only them. I do too.'

'We've been here before, and nothing's changed. They need to understand I have to earn a living. You do tell them that, don't you?'

He nods. 'Come on. I've hardly seen you all week. What's been going on?'

I drain half my glass of wine. 'Where do I start?' I bite into a samosa and tell him about the unpleasant encounter with Claudia Walters-Stewart and the outburst from Isabella in the park.

After threatening to give Claudia Walters-Stewart what for first thing on Monday morning, he says, 'We need to get out of London. For the kids' sake.'

I sit back in my chair. 'Where did that come from?'

He shrugs. 'I guess I'm getting old.'

'You're only forty.' I change the subject and we discuss his work before he asks, 'Any news on Marc?'

'Lots.'

'And?'

Knowing he won't be happy about the amount of time I've dedicated to poking my nose in where I shouldn't, especially at the expense of everything else going on in our lives, I hesitate.

'And?'

'It's all a bit baffling. I'll tell you, but you can't be angry with me.'

I get up to fetch some serving spoons, while he refills our glasses. 'It's messy, and the more I delve into it, the more mysterious it gets.'

'Sum it up.'

I think for a while. 'What's that saying? Don't judge a book by its cover? Well, each day since his disappearance, it has become increasingly apparent that there is more to

Marc than the happy family man he presented to the world.'

'What's happened now?'

'Marc's computer has been completely wiped. His laptop has gone, but I'm ninety-nine per cent sure that he didn't have it with him on Monday when he left. Sasha thinks it was in his office, but she's not definite on that. Then there's the bit about Art driving him to the doctors last Friday. He was prescribed anti-depressants, but no one knew he was depressed. Sasha found the pills, so he didn't take them with him. The couple who live diagonally opposite them are a bit weird. Pete and Penelope – Pen, she calls herself – have you ever met them?'

Jim shakes his head as he piles his plate with pilau rice.

'She's a dog groomer and I'm pretty sure that she's having an affair with the guy opposite, Tom. You met him?'

Jim shakes his head again.

'No proof, but I've seen him coming out of the parlour twice without a dog.'

'There could be other reasons.'

'Fair point, but Pen didn't hold back on how she felt about her husband. Pete's a city dealer. She refers to him as Pete the Prick. Sasha found a deposit in Marc's bank account last week for five thousand pounds – guess who from?'

He passes me a spoon as he shrugs.

'Pete. Furthermore, five grand was withdrawn from Marc's account from a bank in Cambridge on Tuesday. And he withdrew three hundred pounds from the cashpoint of the same bank at six o'clock Monday evening.'

'Cambridge? On Monday when he disappeared? I thought you saw him in the afternoon. He couldn't have got to Cambridge that quickly, surely.'

'I worked it out. He could have, but who knows if it was even him who withdrew the money? Now, here's the bit you're not going to believe. I found out that, last month, Marc was done for drink-driving.'

'What?'

'Sasha didn't know either.'

He goes to put a mouthful of food in his mouth but stops and frowns. 'So, how do you?'

'You said you wouldn't get angry with me.'

'Eva?'

I grit my teeth, waiting for the fallout.

He gawps. 'You didn't look on the PNC?'

I nod.

'Eva! You'll get the boot. Not to mention a criminal record.'

'They only do spot checks. The chances of one being done on me for this are minimal.'

'But not impossible.'

I can't argue with that. I know the risks – policing the police. Now and again – rarely in fact, but it does happen – I've heard of officers of all ranks receive a request for information asking what led them to query the police national computer. In the past, police personnel have been caught selling information for various nefarious reasons such as organised-crime syndicates seeking particular details. There have also been cases of officers suspecting their partners of having extramarital affairs and so have checked on their movements. And person checks, where someone would approach a "friendly" officer because they believed their daughter's new boyfriend was a bit "shady". Misuse is quite rare these days, but some cops still think they are smart enough to beat the system.

'Don't make me feel even more guilty than I already do.'

'Did you tell Sasha?' he asks.

I nod, and he shakes his head at me like he does when Isabella has been a naughty girl.

I eat a few mouthfuls of food. 'That's not all.' In for a penny... I tell him about the coke I found in Marc's wardrobe. 'And while I was up there, something else happened. What do you think of this? Harry was up in their bedroom, acting all suspicious. He said he was using the loo.'

'So, what's odd about that?'

'He didn't flush, and there was no sign the toilet had been used when I went in there, nor the sink.' I spoon a second helping of chicken onto our plates. 'I can't say for sure, but I think he may have been doing something in Marc's wardrobe. Putting the coke in there? Or getting some out.' I share out the remaining chana masala and sag aloo.

'Was it definitely coke?'

I nod.

'How much are we talking about?'

'A couple of grams.'

Absorbed in thought, I swirl curry around my plate.

'Marc spoke to me about Harry recently. He was

worried about him because he'd become moody and withdrawn,' Jim said.

'And? What was the outcome?'

'Harry is stressed about the exams. He's worried he won't get the grades for the uni course he wants to do.'

'Do you think the coke was Harry's?' I say.

'He seems too sensible to be dabbling in that kind of thing. Plus, why would he hide it in Marc's wardrobe?'

I continue the saga with the weekly one hundred and fifty cash withdrawal and Marc's meeting with Alisha.

Jim listens as if he can't believe I'm talking about Marc, our friend.

'Have you ever seen Marc do coke?' I ask.

He scrunches up his nose. 'That's as bizarre as the idea of him having an affair.'

'See what I mean? There's more to this than meets the eye. Sasha knows it too. Maybe he has no intention of returning.'

'Can't you go to Arthur with what you've found?'

I sigh heavily and push my empty glass towards him. 'If Arthur even suspects what I've done, as you say, it'll be curtains for me.' I take another large sip of wine, debating whether to carry on. 'There's something else too.' He looks up from his food, arching an eyebrow, and I tell him about our chat with Alisha, and that she saw Annie and Marc arguing on the morning of his disappearance.

'Why doesn't Sasha go to the police again? That's the logical thing here, isn't it?'

'I don't want her to.'

'Why?'

'Because however much she tries to keep me out of it, she'll let slip I'm a friend and I've found out stuff for her I shouldn't have.'

'See, what did I tell you? You should've left well alone in the first place. All this would've come out eventually. You're risking your career, for what? Come on, darling. Think about it.'

I don't tell him the real reason for my trip to Annie's in the morning. Sometimes, there's only so far you can push people.

FOURTEEN

DAY 6

'You! Going shopping?' Jim exclaims as if I've announced an impromptu trip to Mars. He's manoeuvring himself around the table, cutlery perched on his lap while I fry eggs and bacon for breakfast, as I typically do on my weekends off. The weather is so good, I've opened the patio doors to clear the lingering smell of last night's takeaway. The morning rays beam particle-scattered sunlight across the room.

'I've got nothing to wear tonight,' I say, humming along to Handel treating us to his *Water Music* via our Echo Dot speaker. Another present Jim surprised me with a few months ago that I haven't stopped using. The ability to have our favourite melody at our immediate disposal has made me fall in love with Alexa. I turn the volume up to drown out the sound of Saturday morning CBBC. 'You want a hand?' I ask. He looks tired, his complexion grey, and every movement appears to be an effort for him.

'I'm fine. Leave the kids here with me.'

'They won't be a problem. I've loaded a new game on their iPads that they can play together, and I'll bribe them with some sweets.' I drop slices of bread in the toaster. 'It's a lovely day. I think I'll take them to the park again after shopping or maybe swimming.' I pour four glasses of orange juice. 'I must make time to do some clearing up out the front. Those weeds are driving me crazy. And we need to get some oil on your wheel bearings. Get the kids, can you? They're watching TV. I've called them once already. God, I wish they would come the first time they're called.'

'Where're you planning on going?'

'Sasha's neighbour Annie owns a clothes shop up on Streatham High Road. When I met her yesterday, she offered me a discount.' I reach for the toast as it pops out of the toaster.

'I thought we agreed you weren't going to get involved?'

'Remind me to put some sunscreen on the kids before we go. It's hot out there today,' I say, taking the butter out of the fridge. 'Shall we eat out on the decking? I'll put the umbrella up if the sun's too much for you. Oh, by the way, we're out of coffee, I'll pick some up later. Shall I make a pot of tea?'

He shakes his head. He knows me so well.

Annie's shop is more exclusive than I expected. The lighting is subtle, and gentle background music thrums throughout like an exclusive West End boutique. She greets us with eager enthusiasm as if she can see the pound signs of a potential sale. 'What beautiful children,' she says, patting Joe and Isabella on their heads. 'You take after your mummy.'

I can't help but stare at her in bewilderment. They may be my kids, but with their abundance of black hair, dark eyes and lush lashes as long and as thick as mine *after* I've applied three coats of mascara, they are the image of their dad through and through.

'Come with me and give your mummy some time to herself.' She guides them behind the counter to a mini children's entertainment centre. A small-scale table and chairs, toys and colouring books and pens are cunningly arranged to allow for the perfect in-store retail experience for the eager shopper. 'Browse away,' she sort of orders me. 'I'll keep an eye on these two for you.'

'What is that lovely smell?' I ask, peering around the colourful explosion of summery clothes. Where to begin? There are so many styles and so much choice – an Aladdin's cave for the serious shopper.

'My signature aroma – lime, basil and mandarin – I have a diffuser out the back. Everyone comments on it. I shouldn't say this, but I've got a sale starting on Monday. If you promise not to say a dicky to anyone, I'll sell to you at the discounted price. What exactly are you looking for?'

'Something for Harry's eighteenth tonight.'

'Something eye-catching. What size are you, eight, ten?'

'All depends on the style.' I suck in my post-pregnancy

pouch, which Jim tells me is in my imagination, but I beg to differ.

'I have just the thing for a black tie do.' She walks over to the side wall and pulls out a black dress. 'You can never go wrong with an LBD, and this design flatters any figure,' she says, which I take to mean that its ruffled middle will hide the fact that I've delivered two kids.

She whips out a baby-pink jacket with black buttons and trim to the pockets – if that's the way to describe it. This is not my area of expertise. 'This jacket complements it perfectly. Or maybe you'd prefer something more formal which you could get away with for any occasion.' She reaches for a light tan suede jacket and slips the dress inside its sleeves.

I don't think she has quite sussed my budget.

'I'll tell you what. Why don't we pick a few things out for you, and you can try them all on? That way, you don't have to keep dressing and undressing. How about these to go with the pink jacket?' She grabs a pair of pink and black leopard print skinny jeans.

I stifle a giggle. She hasn't sussed my taste either.

'Try them. You never know. And what about this? It's a little less formal.' She swings a skirt and matching top off the rails. 'You can always dress down items with a scarf, you know.' She opens the lid of a large wicker basket and rummages around to find the colour she's looking for. 'These are just to try. If you like any of them, I can get you a packaged one from my storeroom. When you've chosen what you like, I can accessorize too. Any item can be jazzed up.' She points to a shabby chic cabinet below an ornate mirror, arranged with earrings and brooches, necklaces and bags. 'Sasha was out the front when I left this morning, busy with some decorations. Pity Marc won't be at the party tonight.' Flitting around the store, she gathers items like a bird trying to assemble a nest. 'This is a good one, such a sleek style. A real showstopper. You can match it with different coloured camisoles.' She reaches for a short dress with a plunging neckline.

What was I thinking, coming here?

'Or this sexy number is great because you can wear suspenders underneath and they won't show through. A dress to impress, designed to trim the waistline and flatter from every angle. Not that you have a waistline needing attention.' She holds the dress towards the ceiling and waggles it. 'Don't you just love the way all these sequins shimmer in the light?'

No, I don't want to look like a disco ball. I smile and nod in agreement.

A few customers trickle in. 'I'll be with you in a minute,' Annie calls out to them. 'Please feel free to look around. There's no rush.' With her arms loaded, she motions me into the changing room and hooks her questionable attempts to restyle me onto the back of the door. 'Very strange about Marc, don't you think? I spoke to Art about it last night. Art knows him much better than I do. They sometimes go jogging together. We've gone through all the scenarios, but none of them make any sense.' She glances down at my feet. 'You need some shoes to try on all these with. Give me a sec.' I watch her fade amongst the rails and reappear with a pair of ankle-breaking stilettos.

This is getting worse.

'This classic style will go with most of what I've picked out. Once you've chosen what you like, you can try on some different styles to complete your outfit. Call me if you need a different size or help zipping up.'

She leaves me staring at my reflection, exhausted before I've even started.

As I kick off my trainers and tug off my jeans to begin the painful process of elimination, I hear her repeat her sales technique with her other victims. She tries her hardest but doesn't succeed in getting them into a changing room. When the doorbell chimes, I hear her tut and mumble something about time-wasters as she rushes back to ask me how I'm doing. When I confirm I'm still trying items on, I hear her talking to Isabella. 'Did your mummy plait your hair?'

'Yes,' Isabella replies.

'It's so long.'

'I'll be able to sit on it soon.'

'You're a very pretty girl. Like your mummy. And what about you? Are you as handsome as your daddy?'

There's no reply, but I can imagine Joe nodding. I wrangle with one of the dresses, trying to decipher how I'm meant to wear it.

'I thought so. What's your daddy up to today then, having a rest?'

'No, he's working,' I hear Joe say.

'What does he do?'

'He's an author.'

In the changing room, I gape at my image – nose

screwed up – in the three-way mirror wearing a yellow linen one-shoulder dress, feeling like a right lemon. It clashes dreadfully with my blonde hair.

She raps on the door. 'Which one are you leaning towards?'

I step outside, gritting my teeth to stop myself swearing.

'Very nice, you like it?' she asks.

Nice? It's the most unflattering thing I've ever tried on. Besides, won't the other shoulder get cold? 'I'd prefer something more… symmetrical.'

'The trouble with this fabric is it wrinkles too easily. Try some of the others.' She stands watching me. I wish she wouldn't. 'I always thought Marc was the ultimate family man. He's always doing something with his kids. Don't tell her I said this – it could come across wrong – but I've always been a little jealous of Sasha. She's got it all, hasn't she? The pretty face, the great figure, her own successful business, the committed husband and father? I still can't believe he's gone, you know.' She carries on like the village gossip. I'm itching to ask her what she was arguing with Marc about on the day he left, but I know it will be safer coming from Sasha.

She closes the door and leaves me to it. My patience dwindles as I rush through trying on the other outfits. This was a mistake. I should've caught the Tube into town. They are all too uncomfortable – both in size and style. I look at the price tag of a maxi dress and don't even bother to take it off the hanger. Annie knocks on the door again; a buzzing fly that refuses to leave you in peace.

'How about this one?' she suggests, handing me a midi

dress with lace cap sleeves. 'This is the black. It comes in red too – a lovely ruby red. I'll get it for you. The tie belt cinches around the waist – a definite flattering number. And I've got a classy metallic bag which will suit either colour. Let me take away what you're not interested in.' She runs off to fetch the red dress, then grabs the unwanted clothes and leaves me to it.

Her latest offering is the only one that achieves a smile as I twirl and turn to look at myself from all angles in the mirror. The stilettos have to go, though. I've got a pair of black kitten heels somewhere at home that will polish up well enough. Slipping back into my jeans and T-shirt, I take the dress to the till where she is prinking her hair in a compact mirror. She stops to whip the dress from my hands. 'You've gone for the ruby red. I thought you might.'

The kids are sitting like little stars, colouring in pictures of the sky. I stand, staring at them for a few minutes while Annie finishes replacing all the items I found unsuitable.

'What about shoes and bag?'

I tell her my plans, and she asks me about jewellery, but I tell her it's not my thing.

'Aren't they little angels?' she says, nodding over to the kids while she parcels the dress in tissue. 'Such a credit to you.'

The kids wander over, and I slip a packet of jelly babies out of my bag and hand it to Isabella. 'Make sure you share.'

'I like it when you don't work on Saturdays, Mummy,' Isabella says, 'it's so much more fun.' She offers Annie one of her sweets. 'My mummy's a policewoman, but don't worry, she doesn't carry a gun.' She returns to her colouring.

Annie shuffles back a step. 'Are you really? A policewoman?'

'I am indeed, but don't worry, she's telling the truth. I honestly don't carry a weapon of any description.' I laugh, but she doesn't.

Flustered, she applies her promised discounts and processes my payment. 'So, what made you want to become a policewoman?' she asks while she is waiting for the transaction to process.

I tell her the truth. That my childhood was riddled with deceitful bastards and ever since, I've wanted to contribute towards ridding the world of them, which clearly flusters her some more. Her cheeks redden, and she removes the silk scarf she wears around her neck like an air hostess. She quickly slips my purchase into an Annie's-embossed glossy bag, and tells the kids it's time to go. Isabella protests that she wants to stay and finish her picture. Annie whips the book from under Isabella's crayon. 'Take it with you – a present from me. Be sure to finish colouring all the pictures and bring it to show me next time.'

Her voice rises in vocal pitch as she swings the bag's ribbon handles towards the door. 'Have a good day.'

'I don't like that lady, Mummy,' Joe says as we walk to the car. 'She talks too much.'

Cutely intuitive, it's not only in his physical appearance that my son takes after his father. This Annie warrants further investigation.

FIFTEEN

Harry's looking suave in black tie when he greets us. He is standing with a broad-shouldered man with a close-cropped, grey beard who is dressed in a tuxedo too. 'You must be Jim and Eva. Sasha has told me all about you.' He holds out a large hand. 'I'm Art,' he says, 'the designated security officer for the night.' His tone suggests he's happy with this arrangement. 'I'll be on guard to prevent any crashers who might decide to rock up.' Two cars are parked in the entrance of the close to stop any unwanted visitors.

More guests arrive, half our age it seems, and Harry high-fives them. Jim discusses his upcoming appointment on Monday with Art, while I glance around the horseshoe crescent decorated party-style with black, white and silver balloons – fitting for a boy becoming a man. The party is already in full swing. There are more people here than I imagined. A vast banner marking Harry's coming of age is hooked to the brickwork of Sasha's studio. This is typical Sasha, digging deep to ensure perfection.

She appears with a tray of fizz-filled flutes each topped with a cherry on a cocktail stick. Harry scoops up four. 'Steady on, you've already had a few.' Sasha says. She's dressed in a brightly coloured maxi dress which I saw in Annie's boutique this morning. 'Welcome, have a glass of this,' she says, offering me a drink. 'You look fantastic. I'm glad Annie found you something.'

A mask of party makeup – red-glossed lips, heavy eyeshadow and glittered cheeks – and a conscious effort to smile for her son's important night, attempt to disguise the pain in her face, but she doesn't fool me. 'At last, the official DJ has arrived!' she says. 'I'm glad you're finally here. George keeps putting on his dreadful rap music.'

'Sorry, I had trouble getting the kids settled. They wanted to come too. The cab I'd ordered drove off, and we had to wait for another.'

'You could've brought them along. We wouldn't have minded. But I'm sure it's good for you and Jim to have a night out together, just the two of you. At least you can have a couple of drinks.'

I finger a sparkling line of eighteenth bunting gently flapping in between the eucalyptus trees. 'You've decorated the place beautifully.'

'Pen, Art and the kids pitched in this morning, and family have brought food which has helped. More teenagers have turned up than Harry told me about, though, which is slightly worrying. I thought he was only inviting a couple of his closest friends, but it's turned out to be a lot more than that. I'm thankful the weather has been kind to us. It's all going to plan. Well, nearly.' She leans over and whispers regretfully in my ear. 'If only Marc were here.'

A group of guests gather by the food, nibbling cocktail sausages and sandwiches, mini pizzas and Annie's sausage rolls. Harry's friends and a few older couples surround a makeshift bar: a sheet-covered table with a garland of balloons, threaded with tiny lights, draped across the front. On top sits a selection of spirits and behind is an old book-shelf stocked with different sized glasses. Pen is jiggling a cocktail shaker beside a tall, middle-aged man with dark, gelled hair who I'm guessing must be Pete. His shirt is half unbuttoned, displaying a chest of grey fur.

'I'll show you to the speakers and you can start your music, Jim.' Sasha leads us off towards the action, leaving Art to guard the entrance.

'Eva! Eva!' Hannah calls out, waving me over. 'Come and try this, it's delicious.' Standing behind the pearly gates for sugar cravers, Hannah is waving a bamboo skewer stabbed into what looks like a chunk of peanut brittle. There's a chocolate fountain on the table and trays of marshmallows, chopped fruit, and mini donuts iced with different coloured toppings. Another girl is standing with her, spinning sugar in a candyfloss maker. She's wearing a blue gingham pinafore and has her hair in plaits like Dorothy from *The Wizard of Oz*.

Annie is there too, impeccably turned out, holding a glass of fizz. 'Look at you – what a fabulous dress. You must have got that from somewhere special!' She gives a wink and a cocky smile.

'I'm pleased with it, thanks.' And I mean it. Jim had

commented on it too, saying how nice it is to see me out of my uniform jeans and shirt.

'The shoes look OK too,' she says.

I silently will her not to ask about a bag. I couldn't find one earlier, so I chucked everything I need into the back of Jim's wheelchair rucksack.

'This is Grace, my bestie,' Hannah says, introducing me to her friend. She twizzles the peanut brittle under the liquid chocolate before passing it to me. I don't fancy her offering, it's an unsuitable complement for the fizz, but I don't want to offend her.

'The marshmallows are my favourite,' she declares, loading another skewer with pink and white sugary fluff. 'Want to try one, Annie?'

'Maybe later,' Annie says, running a hand over her flat tummy.

I take a bite of the sugar overdose as Luke springs up with a camera and insists we hold still for a second or two. Hannah stiffens. She pulls her shoulders back and sticks her chest out as he shoots away. 'Would you mind moving behind the table please, Eva?' he asks me. 'I want one of the four of you together.' I oblige, gritting my teeth. Posing for photos is not my favourite thing. Luke works the lens. He lunges forward and nudges me on the shoulder. 'Move in, closer, closer,' he says, 'that's it, just right, stay there.' Hannah stifles her giggles as he crouches down and snaps away. 'Thanks,' he says, springing up and giving us a wave of gratitude before gliding along to his next target.

Grace nudges Hannah as she joins the tips of her thumbs and forefingers into the shape of a heart and pumps it in Luke's direction. Hannah slaps her friend's hands.

'He's very enthusiastic, isn't he?' I say to Annie.

'He's always been into photography. Since he was this high.' She drops her palm towards the ground. 'My brother bought him a cheap camera for Christmas one year. He wouldn't put it down – even took it to bed with him.' She laughs with fondness at the memory. 'The amount we spent on paper and ink getting all his photos printed cost us more than the bloody thing itself.' She takes a sip of her drink. 'He wanted to study photography at university.'

'Media,' says Hannah, blushing. 'He wants to study media.'

'Yes, yes, that's the word,' Annie says, nodding. 'But Art and I,' she pats Hannah's shoulder, 'and your dad too, managed to persuade him that computers are the way forward. I have to say, they've been his thing since he was little too. We said to him, there's more money in computers than cameras. We're right, aren't we?' She doesn't sound too sure. 'He can come back to his photography any time.'

'Who does he get his talent from?' I ask.

'Who knows!' she says, waving to someone. 'My husband wants me.' Off she totters in her shiny heels that I would refuse to own, even if she'd thrown them in with my dress for free.

A group of teenagers approach the table, and I leave them to Hannah and her sweet delights to go in search of Jim. A shrill voice calls out my name. I turn to see Pen beckoning me over towards the bar. 'We're swamped here.

Couldn't help for a while, could you? Until the rush dies down. I agreed to hand around these glasses of Prosecco.'

Swiping an apron hooked around the frame of the bookshelf behind her, she presses it into my chest. 'Have you met Pete, my husband?' She prods his arm. 'Pete, this is Sasha's friend, the copper. You remember me telling you about her?'

He pauses pouring vodka and looks me up and down as if to determine my suitability for the role his wife has bullied me into. That one look tells me that, yep, Pen is right. Her husband is a prick. He holds out a hand which I pretend I haven't seen as I start to cough uncontrollably on the choking smell of expensive aftershave.

'See, I told you to stop putting so much of that over-priced crap on,' Pen says, jutting her scowling head out towards him. He laughs and waves her off, continuing with his assigned duties for the night. She points to a wheel-barrow filled with ice, cans and bottles. 'Beers and soft drinks in there.' Tapping her fingers along the top of the bottles on the table, she names each of the spirits on offer. 'Oh, and in this jug here, is my special Pimm's recipe. Watch what the youngsters are drinking. I don't fancy cleaning up the after-effects of teenage alcoholic gluttony. Oh, and that there,' she points to a highball tumbler, 'is my attempt at a Long Island iced tea.' I thought Harry's friend asked for three, but he only wanted two, so have it if you want. I'm more of a Pimm's girl myself.'

Thanking her, I take a sip of her potent creation which makes me cough nearly as much as her husband's after-shave. She's been far too liberal with the tequila, or maybe

143

the rum? It's been ten years since I played bartender. Way back during the early days of Jim and me when I was a student, and he worked in the City. The days when he tried to woo me with his lavish lifestyle and generous bank account but, much to his annoyance, I insisted on working part-time in a local bar to pay my way.

After a while, a young couple – early twenties – approach us. Hands clasped, shoulders touching, they ask what cocktails are on offer. I scan the spirits and reply, 'I could make a Mojito or a Cosmopolitan.' There are several others I could add to my offering, but best to keep things simple.

They glance at each other and chorus, 'Mojito,' laughing together with a chemical blend of affection which makes me stop and stare. The woman relaxes her head on the man's shoulder. He glides her in front of him and enfolds her in his arms. She giggles with the thrill. He lifts her off her feet as Bruno Mars's "Just the Way you Are" blares from the speakers. I look away, her squeals of laughter evoking painful nostalgia for the couple Jim and I once were. That song came out in 2010. It was our song. It was played at our wedding. My stomach flips, the memories of his accident torturing me. All the long hours I sat at his bedside clinging to his hand, humming this tune, singing the lyrics, desperately trying to provoke a reaction in him. A twitch of his lips, a blink of his eye, anything to let me know he was still with me. I sidestep to look around the people queuing for drinks to find him. Jim is talking to Sasha but leans aside in his chair to mouth he loves me.

Pete interrupts. 'You've done this before,' he says with

a creepy smile which, I've noticed, he saves for the females. A smile sure to offend the wrong woman. I've also clocked the way he stares at them that little bit too long.

Time to find out a little more about this man.

'Not for many years, but you don't forget.' We exchange friendly banter, and I ask him where he works.

'I'm a commodities trader,' he replies in a manner that suggests I should be impressed. 'For a firm in the West End.'

Walking over to the wheelbarrow, I ask about his job, acting like I give a damn. I pick up a beer and offer him one.

'Not for me. I'm racing tomorrow.'

'Racing?'

'Yes. I'm running a ten kilometre up in Hyde Park tomorrow.'

'For charity?'

'Usually for the kids' cancer unit at Great Ormond Street, but it's for Pride tomorrow.'

He's not all bad.

We serve several guests and Harry appears. He slurs his words, looking at me. 'Double vodka and tonic and a can of Coke.'

Pete butts in as if Harry had requested him. 'Coke,' he exclaims, 'on your eighteenth? What's wrong with you?'

'It's for Luke. He's on video duty. Can't have distorted memories of tonight.'

'I thought the only coke your age group participated in was of the powdered variety,' Pete guffaws.

'What about all your other friends?' I ask. 'Anything for them?'

'I'll let them get their own,' Harry says.

'Are they friends from school?'

Harry nods. 'Mostly.'

I serve his drinks, and when there's no one left waiting, I remove my apron. I need to find Jim. He'll be wondering where I am. Plus I need the toilet. 'I'm sure you can cope without me now.'

'No, please stay,' Pete says. 'It's always good to get to know the neighbours' friends a little better.'

'Maybe later if it gets busy again,' I say, looping the apron back around the bookcase.

'Let me at least make you a drink,' he says, picking up the vodka.

I tell him not to worry. After Pen's heady creation, I'll stick to the beer. Delving into the wheelbarrow, I root through the ice and pick out a bottle of Bud. Once I've left him, I turn to confirm my suspicions. Yep, he's still perving after me like a lecherous old git.

The queue for the toilet snakes out of Sasha's studio. I search for her to ask if I can go into the house, stopping to watch Luke, now meandering around with his video recorder. The way he manoeuvres himself fascinates me – such a skilful manipulator of the lens. He stops here, pauses there, zooming in and out like a seasoned pro. Harry staggers towards him, his bow tie unravelled and hanging around his neck. He slaps a hand on Luke's shoulder and says something, and they both burst into laughter.

As I peer around for Sasha, I see her slip into the house

with Annie. Great, I'll be able to use the loo inside. They've left the door ajar. Raised voices come from the kitchen. I sneak along the hallway and peer through the crack in the door, curious to hear what they are arguing about. They are standing sideways on to me, by the centre island.

'We had words that got a little heated, that's all,' Annie says.

Sasha's inquisitive tone craves the truth. 'What about?'

Annie pauses, crossing her arms across her chest.

'You have to tell me.'

'Look, it's not important. Totally irrelevant.'

Sasha shakes Annie's arms. 'Everything is relevant. Every single thing.'

Annie sighs. 'He owes me and Art money, and we need it back.'

SIXTEEN

'Money for what?' Sasha asks. Annie turns towards the door as Sasha roughly grabs the sleeve of her dress. The fabric rips. 'Oh, my God, I'm so sorry,' Sasha says, obviously appalled at her uncharacteristic display of aggression.

Annie, her mouth agape, strokes the ripped material in horror. I'm watching from a distance but can feel the tension. One of them was bound to snap.

'What did he owe you money for?' Sasha repeats. 'Tell me.'

'It's not my story to tell. It's between Marc and Art.' Annie turns to walk out. This time Sasha doesn't try and stop her. 'It's nothing sinister if that's what you think,' Annie turns and adds.

'Annie, please.'

Annie pauses in the doorway. She stands still for a few seconds and tilts her head to the side. 'He said he was short for the month. You had some bonds coming up for maturity, and he wanted a short-term loan, that's all. I told you it was inconsequential.'

I press myself up against the hall wall, praying she won't glance back when she walks to the front door. When the door slams, echoing along the hallway, I rush into the kitchen.

'Did you hear that?' Sasha asks. Her shining eyes mirror her glossy lips.

I nod as I place my empty beer bottle on the worktop.

'We've never had any bonds. Not that I know of, anyway.' She sucks in air and looks to the ceiling, her lower lip trembling as much as her hands. 'I mustn't cry. Not tonight. It's not fair on Harry.' She takes several deep breaths and drives her fisted hand down hard on the chopping board. 'God, I miss him.'

I hug her because that's all I can do. Words can't counteract her suffering.

'I will get to the bottom of this. I will,' she says with dogged determination. She dabs her eyes and takes another deep breath, smashing her hand down again. 'I need to get back out there.'

After I've used the loo, I wander outside, where the party atmosphere has changed. Alcohol has soaked into bloodstreams. Chat is faster and laughter louder. The summer sun is dipping beneath the horizon, but its golden rays are still illuminating London's sky. Upbeat music thumps through the celebrations, injecting rhythm into a group of teenagers dancing on an improvised dance floor in the parking area between Sasha and Marc's and Art and Annie's houses. Harry is in the mix, joking with his mates, much more confident than I've ever seen him. He surprises me. I've always had him down as an adolescent wallflower.

I look around and spot Annie by the entrance to the close in an intense discussion with Art. It's time to find out what is going on around here. I sneak along the side of the house with the SOLD sign standing proud in the garden and slide behind a car parked in front of Pen's Parlour.

Annie is revealing the mess of her sleeve to Art.

'Why did you have to argue with Marc in the first place?' Art grabs his wife's hand, examining the tear before releasing her arm with contentious force.

'Careful.' She shakes her arm.

Art folds his arms across his jacket.

A voice disturbs their squabble. 'Hi, is this Hazza's eighteenth?'

Art smiles at the new arrivals and asks their names. Cross-referencing his list attached to a clipboard, he lets them in as Annie flounces off back towards the party.

The wind is picking up. A chill sweeps through me. Shivering, I look around for Jim. I left my cardigan on the back of his chair. There he is, by the bar, thumbing his iPhone with Harry looking over his shoulder. Making a beeline for him, I pass Hannah, still manning dessert of the day with Grace, coating marshmallows with chocolate. But Hannah's attention is elsewhere. I follow her gaze. Luke is sitting with a girl by Tom's studio.

I walk over to offer Hannah some distraction when I notice Luke and the girl are no longer sitting. Are they arguing? That twisty feeling in my gut draws me to take a closer look. Passing the vacant house next to Art and Annie's, I notice some empty glasses on the ground. After picking them up, I hide behind a bush lining the side of the house and watch and listen. The girl is wearing denim shorts and a lace bra top which parade more of her taut midriff than they cover. She obviously missed the black tie dress code.

'Quite impressive, isn't it?' Luke laughs as he holds his phone with the screen turned towards her. 'Who would have thought? Little Miss Perfect, A star student, Chelsea Clark.'

'Why would you do that?' Chelsea asks, continually tugging her side plait.

'Why wouldn't I?' Luke replies.

'I thought we were friends?'

'So did I.'

'Why are you doing this to me, then?'

'Don't you think it's more of a case of... why did you do this to yourself?' He peers at the screen. 'That's a more appropriate question.' He pushes the screen closer towards her until it's touching her nose.

She swipes it away. 'It's nothing to do with you.'

'It is now.'

She shakes her head, pulling her plait through her hands like a rope she's contemplating hanging herself with. 'Why? Why?'

A glass slides from my hand. Damn, I try to catch it, but it drops on the concrete tile, shattering.

They both jump as if I've caught them doing something they shouldn't. They simultaneously turn in my direction.

There's nothing I can do but come out of hiding. 'Everything OK here?'

Chelsea, tight-lipped, nods her agreement as she blows her fringe out of her eyes. 'All good, thanks, Eva,' Luke says with a wave. Chelsea throws him a look of disgust and marches off to rejoin the party.

'Friendly tiff,' Luke says. 'What smashed?'

'I was helping to clear up, and I dropped a glass,' I say pointing behind the bush. I know he knows I was snooping.

'Let me help you. We can use my torch.' He finds the right app on his phone and beams a light on the path. 'Here, hold this.' He passes me his phone. Bending down to pick up the shards of glass, he carefully collects them in his hand. 'It's gone everywhere. We need to sweep up,' he says. It's like he's a grown man, not a teenager still living under his parents' roof. 'I'll go and find a dustpan and brush.'

'Leave this with me,' I say, holding up his phone, 'and I'll keep looking.'

'No, I'll take it with me, thanks.' He snatches the phone out of my hand. 'Wait until I get back. You might cut yourself.'

Damn, damn, damn. I pick up the larger pieces, puzzled by what I've just viewed in the Luke and Chelsea performance. What was he showing her on his phone? He reappears within minutes and begins sweeping up the remaining glass, chatting about the success of the party. 'Everyone's having a great time over there. You should go and join them. I'll finish clearing this up.'

In the line of duty, detectives develop an intuition. Call

it a sixth sense. An inherent instinct that forewarns us when something or someone doesn't look, sound, or feel right. Or even *smell* right. It tells us when to delve deeper and ask more questions. My senses are heightened. 'Everyone seems to know each other well around here.'

He pauses mid-sweep and looks up at me. 'We've all lived here for a long time.'

'How long?'

'Sasha and Marc since before us. Pen and Pete too. And the couple who've just moved out.'

'What about you?'

'We moved here when I was eight, about ten years ago.'

'Where did you live before that?'

'Barnet, North London. My dad wanted to be closer to his parents, and he wanted somewhere he could work from home, so we moved here. His parents lived in the next road, but they both died a few years ago.'

'You'll miss it here when you go to uni.'

He shrugs. 'Not really.' He stands up and wipes his forehead. 'There, I think I've got it all. I'll come and have a look in the morning.' He waves and turns towards the party. I watch him go, shivering.

I find Jim helping Hannah and Grace man the chocolate fountain. Not that they need any help. I think people are sugared-out by now. 'Where've you been?' Jim asks. 'I've not seen you all night.'

As I slip on my cardigan, I give him the look. Our "I'll explain later" expression. We can have a whole conversation with these kinds of exchanges. 'I'll take over here, Hannah, for a while. You two go and enjoy yourselves.'

'You sure?' Hannah asks. 'Come and find me if you need help.'

The music is louder, the beat faster, and most of the teenagers are dancing now, jumping in a clustered group with their hands pumping towards the sky. Family, and family friends, congregate around the bar in small groups. Some are drinking beer and wine, chatting, while others are hunched over their smartphones. The couple I served earlier is letting off party poppers and shooters, showering the crowd in a cascade of metallic confetti and multi-coloured streamers. And someone has set off a bubble machine, unleashing hundreds of bubbles into the night sky. Above the roar of the music, I see Sasha, her hands covering her ears, mouthing to Hannah, 'We need to turn this down.'

'Top marks for the playlist,' I say to Jim.

He pulls me onto his lap 'I hope you're being careful.'

'There's something very odd about this lot,' I say and brief him about my evening so far.

'Why don't you take this to Arthur now?'

'I know what you're saying. Not sure what he'd do about it, though.' I massage his thighs. 'If Marc were missing, yes, he'd probably start an investigation. But technically Marc's not missing, and there's no evidence he's at risk.'

'What about the fact he was depressed?'

'That would have a bearing, but he has specifically said he doesn't want to be found. We've got nowhere to go.' I sigh heavily. 'I can just hear Arthur's voice: "We have drug dealers and murderers roaming the streets, and you want me to direct my already scarce resources at hunting someone down who has expressly stated they don't want us to." He'd laugh me out of the station.' I lean back, and he enfolds me in his arms.

The freakish commotion commences simultaneously in the night sky and on the dance floor, advancing from nowhere into an onslaught of pandemonium. A pull of wind tugs the air and the skies burst open. Rain starts to hammer down like we've been hit by a water cannon, and the music abruptly stops as if someone has ripped the power supply from the speakers. Screams fill the air, along with howls of, 'Fuck off, just fuck off!'

'Whatever's going on?' says Jim.

I hoist myself up, seeking a better view of the drama unfolding. The voice is male and familiar, but I can't place the owner. Is that Harry or Luke, or maybe George? 'Fuck off the lot of you!' The aggression in the tone intensifies. Panicking, people stumble and tumble in their hysteria to escape. Glasses are smashing and screams of, 'Help me. Help,' resonate across the chaos.

I pull away from Jim and grab an umbrella out of his bag. A necessity he keeps in there for occasions like this. I open it up and cover us. We sit there huddled together until the rain stops, almost as quickly as it started, filling the air with an earthy freshness. I jump up to investigate the disruption, but he hauls me back. 'For Christ's sake. Where *are* you going?'

'I need to see what's going on.' I try to shake my hand from his grip, but his hold is too strong.

'You'll get hurt.'

'I can hear Sasha.'

People are helping each other up from the floor. Others are running towards the exit of the close. Reluctantly, Jim lets me go, and I rush over to the mayhem. And there, in the middle of the frenzy, stands Harry, his hands tugging at his dripping hair. Strands stick to his face. 'Just go. Everyone, go.' Sasha is crying while trying to console him, but he continues his offensive barrage of abuse. 'How could you?'

Luke appears and grabs Harry's shoulder. 'Come on, mate, calm down, let's go inside.' Luke steers Harry towards the house, pushing willing helpers away and telling them they should go home, with such maturity it's hard to believe these two young men are the same age.

Harry wrestles with Luke's forceful grip, but Luke is too strong.

'Calm down, Harry,' Sasha says.

'Calm down! Calm down!' Harry yells, lunging for his mother. 'You fucking lied to me, so now you can tell me the truth. Where has my dad gone?'

SEVENTEEN

'Oh, God, help me,' Sasha cries, pressing her fists into her sunken cheeks. The rain has stopped but left its stain. Black splodges smear her face where her eye makeup has run. Harry lashes out, catching the side of her mouth. Blood thickens her lip. Sasha stumbles backwards, but I manage to catch her fall. The tiles below are a smudged rainbow of soaked party poppers and streamers.

'Cut it out, man. That's your mum.' Luke forces Harry towards the house as Hannah, her clothes wet through, comes bounding over.

'What's going on?' Her voice is high-pitched. She looks from Harry to Luke to her mum.

George appears, puts an arm around his sister and roars at his brother. 'I saw you belt Mum. You leave her alone; do you hear me?' He launches himself at Harry.

Luke holds his arm out, blocking George's attack. 'Don't make things worse, mate.'

Guiding George out of the way, Luke steers Harry into

the house. Sasha and the twins follow. They stand by the front door, a knot of confused people in disarray. Harry is hurling accusations at his mother while Luke is telling him to control himself so they can talk it through. Hannah is wailing, pulling at her hair, while George is yelling, 'Calm down!' at everyone.

Art and Annie, and Pete and Pen, have taken charge outside, ushering people homewards. Jim is helping. I catch his attention and wave, indicating I'm going into the house. He nods, and I mouth at him to come inside too.

I stand in the hallway, unsure of how much I should get involved. I've faced similar circumstances many times before, but not with people I know. It's not for me to meddle here, but Sasha thinks otherwise. 'Tell him, Eva. Tell him.'

It's time to defuse this situation before it blows into another storm they will all regret getting caught up in. I pummel my fist on the back of the door. 'Quiet!' Stunned, they all silence their outbursts and spin around to stare at me. 'Let's go into the kitchen and talk this through rationally.'

I corral them all into the kitchen, still arguing like primary school children. Sasha demands everyone take a seat at the dining table as she opens a drawer and pulls out a stack of clean tea towels. She orders everyone to dry their hair as she swipes kitchen roll from its holder. Wrapping it around her hand, she dabs her lip and barks an order for silence.

'You might want to put some ice on that,' I tell her, reaching for the freezer door.

Harry, Hannah and George follow her order to sit, scraping their chairs along the floor, but Luke steps backwards and stands with his hands laced behind his back, observing the situation like a security guard, ready to step in if needs be. Sasha, holding a piece of ice to her swollen lip, joins her troubled kids at the table while I fill the kettle and search for some sugar. A few spoonfuls are needed all round. I open the fridge for milk. The birthday cake sits on the bottom shelf, lonely and untouched.

Harry is the first to break the shocked silence. The whole ordeal seems to have sobered him up. 'I'll never live this down. The whole school will be laughing at me.' He shakes his head fast, scattering drops of water across the table.

'I wouldn't worry,' Luke says. 'You're leaving in a few days.'

Harry turns to Sasha. 'You have to tell me where he's really gone, Mum.'

'Where who's gone?' Hannah asks, frowning as she glances from one family member to another.

'How do you know?' Sasha asks her son, ignoring her fretful daughter.

'I overheard Art and Annie discussing it. Annie said Dad has walked out on us.' He turns to Luke. 'Did you know?'

Luke raises his hands. 'I haven't a clue what you're talking about.'

Hannah stands. 'Can someone please tell me what's going on? You're all scaring me.' Luke steps forward and guides her to sit back down, caressing her shoulders.

'Hannah and George, can you two leave your brother

and me alone, please.'

Harry reaches out and slaps the table directly in front of Hannah and George. 'No, you two stay where you are.' He turns to Sasha. 'They need to know the truth too, Mum. You can't lie anymore, to any of us.'

Sasha slides down in her chair, deflated yet again. But Harry is right. It's time to come clean and wash away the lies floating about in this family. Harry's outburst has made a start. She takes a deep breath. 'Your father walked out on Monday. I don't know where he's gone or who, if anyone, he's gone with. But he's made it pretty clear he doesn't want us looking for him.' Harry tries to butt in, but she silences him with a raised hand. 'He went to the police and told them if anyone comes looking for him, he doesn't want to be found.'

I could cry for her.

'What's all this about Scotland?' George asks.

Sasha sits up straight as if she knows she must swallow her suffering and find some bravery from somewhere for the sake of her children. She blows her nose in the bloody remains of the kitchen roll and sniffs loudly. 'I lied. I'm truly sorry to you all, but Harry, you're in the middle of your A levels, and I didn't want to stress you out any more than you already are.' She looks from one to the other of her children. 'I was planning to tell you the truth when Harry's exams had finished.'

'Why? Why would he do this?' Harry asks, his voice barely a whisper.

Sasha shrugs. 'I don't know. If I did, maybe I could accept it.'

'Dad would never leave us,' Hannah says, crying.

'Something's not right. He wouldn't do this to us. He wouldn't. You have to go to the police,' says Harry.

Sasha glances over to me with a look that conveys, 'See what I mean?' She turns to her children. 'I have been to the police, but there is nothing they can do.'

George calls out to me. 'Can't you find him, Eva? That's what detectives do, don't they? Look for missing people.'

'I'm afraid your father has clearly expressed he doesn't want to be found, so our hands are tied.'

'Oh, Mum,' Hannah says, shifting her chair along to cuddle up to her mother. 'You shouldn't have lied. You've kept all this to yourself when we could've helped you.'

'I'm so sorry, please forgive me,' she says, looking up to Harry.

George hauls himself up out of his chair and rushes to hug his mum too. Sasha curls her arms around her twins.

Harry is a different story. The pressure is too much. He explodes, propelling himself out of his chair and rushing from the room. Luke flies after him.

'Leave him,' Hannah says, taking control. 'Luke will sort him out.'

I deliver a tray of sweetened tea to the table. 'Drink these, and I'll take those two a cup.'

Upstairs, I knock on Harry's door. 'Go away. Leave me alone,' he barks.

I knock again. 'It's Eva. There're two mugs of tea out here for you. I'll leave them on the floor.'

The door opens before I've had a chance to put them down. 'Thanks,' Luke says, taking the tray. I peek past him.

Harry is lying on his bed looking as you'd pretty much expect for someone who has just been told his father never wants to see him again.

I can sympathise with him. My mother abandoned me and my brother when I was only four years old. The hurt and disappointment are a life sentence with no hope of parole. But if you are lucky enough to encounter a Gill in your life, you learn to cope.

'You go home. I want to be on my own,' Harry says to Luke, taking the mug.

'I'll come over in the morning. You still going to Robbins' class?' Luke asks.

Harry shakes his head.

'Come on, mate. See the next week out. You can't let all this ruin your exams.'

'Easier said than done. Just go now. I'll catch you tomorrow.'

I return to the kitchen with Luke close behind. Sasha is still comforting the twins. 'I need to get going. Jim will be waiting for me,' I say, gulping down my tea. A mouthful of bitter-sweetness.

'I'll see you out. Then I'm going to get these two to bed.' Sasha says, hauling herself out of her chair.

'I think people are chipping in out there,' I say as I walk to the door.

'I knew I shouldn't have told anyone about Marc leaving.' She screws up her eyes and shakes her head. 'How could Art and Annie be so stupid?'

'I doubt they did it on purpose. Get some sleep. I'll call you in the morning.' I give her a big cuddle. She needs it.

Outside Jim is helping people as best he can to clear debris. The rain has stopped, but the wind has picked up again, dispersing the smell of spilt alcohol.

'Why didn't you come inside?' I ask.

'I thought I'd be better off out here helping everyone clear up. I didn't know how long you'd be, so I cancelled the cab. Sasha's friend over there is going to give us a lift.'

I nod my agreement as I watch Luke slip out of Sasha's house and head to his own home. I shiver, but not from the cold. Is there something different about his walk? He's strutting like a peacock, parading a cockiness I haven't noticed before. As if he is in love with himself. It doesn't suit him. It looks horrible. My stomach twists. What is it about him?

'I guess it's all come out about Marc,' Jim says.

I update him as I squat down to pick up pieces of glass. I drop them in the cardboard box of rubbish on his lap. The glass clinks against an empty can. 'Was anyone badly hurt?' I ask.

'I don't think so. One girl had a cut on her arm where she fell, but I'd say people were more shocked than anything.'

I sigh heavily. 'What a complete mess.'

'Yep.' He takes my hand. 'You OK?'

'Thinking things through,' I reply as an upstairs light comes on in Annie and Art's house. I squint up, waiting for what instinct tells me won't take long. There it is. A jerk of the curtains and the shadow of a young man – Luke staring out at the aftermath of the party.

I've decided I don't like this boy at all.

PART 2

EIGHTEEN

LUKE

What a night! Deserving of a five-star review! I certainly didn't expect such a spectacular ending. Spot on! If only I'd acted quicker, I could have recorded it and enjoyed an encore. I'll have to rethink my staging for the coming week, though. That's a shame. Trust Harry to scupper my plans. He couldn't hold it together, could he? Exploding into his audience like a firework gone astray – on his eighteenth birthday of all days too! That's what happens when life has always been cosy fires and hot cocoa.

Oh, well, as they say, the show must go on.

I wander over to my bedroom window and pull the curtains aside. Just enough to follow the chaos. That woman, Sasha's friend, the pretty blonde one, is picking up the remaining mess from where everyone was dancing. If that's what you can call hopping and jumping up and down like a mob of kangaroos. Her husband is following her around, a cardboard box on his lap, helping her collect shards of glass, a snapped stiletto heel and crushed party popper shells from an eighteenth birthday party gone so publicly wrong.

People I don't know – Harry's family, perhaps? – and Pete are helping Dad clear the mess from the bar into black bin liners and recycling crates as my mum and Pen discard the remains of all that crap Hannah was serving up. Ah, sweet, vulnerable Hannah. I feel bad my plans had to involve her. She doesn't deserve it, but what could I do?

It's strange how, for so long, years in fact, while everyone lived such seemingly perfect, happy lives, I thought I was the fucked-up one. But now, I know, apart from Hannah, I'm the only sane one around here.

Where do I start? Take that prick, Pete, for one. Does he know his slapper wife is cheating on him with the ginger opposite? And what about all the others around here? Surely they've caught on too. I find it hard to believe not. I'm aware, and I don't even live with her. Not that it takes a member of Mensa to work it out. I mean, why would you regularly visit a dog grooming parlour when you don't even own a dog? And I've seen her trying to slip out of his house unnoticed after their weekly rendezvous. You'd think they'd be more discreet. Someone really should tell him that he needs to rearrange his trousers before he leaves her studio, not while he's walking back to his own house.

Maybe they don't care. Not that I blame her. If I were her, I'd be searching for an escape from the life with that prick she calls her husband. And I should know what an obnoxious moron he is. I have the damning proof from when that dreaded, toe-curling time arrived, in the winter of year twelve, when, as part of our school's careers programme, I had no choice but to undergo a week's work experience during my Christmas break, that my dad arranged with Pete.

It wasn't my idea. I've never had any intention of going into the City when I finish my education. I've always wanted to pursue my photography – but my dad insisted I give it a try. 'Get a job in that environment, and you'll never be broke. You're so clever, you could make a fortune in one of those banks or brokers,' he said, as if he were colluding with the haughty school careers adviser who agreed with him that I had the brains to make it big in the City.

'If you go into media, you'll always be poor. Precious few make it to stardom. Do it the sensible way. Make your fortune, secure your future, and you'll be free to do what-ever you want. The world will be your oyster,' Dad kept saying. After much resistance – I was a teenager, after all – I clammed up and agreed. Because all I wanted was to please him. That was before, though.

Before I found out the truth.

The small outfit that Pete the Prick worked for in those days occupied half the ninth floor of an imposing, glass-fronted high-rise, smack bang in the nucleus of the City. The building had at least twenty levels, maybe more, and on the outside, a lift travelled up and down all day, impressing its riders with extensive views of London. The panoramic sights did nothing for me, and I hate elevators.

So, I always ended up taking the stairs. He works somewhere else now – a similar type of operation, full of pricks, where I'm sure he fits in equally as well.

I hated every second of every day I spent there. The offices were nice, sleek and crammed with excessive luxury – from the marble floors and high-end everything, to the smell and feel of the expensive leather chairs. Pete explained how the acoustic environment, air-quality and lighting had all been designed to boost employee productivity. Even the coffee tasted gourmet. From his large workstation, composed of ten or so computer screens displaying yawn-inducing charts and graphs, figures and trends, you could vaguely see workers at similar desks in the surrounding mirror properties. A cluster of glass display cases with people inside screaming, 'Look at us, aren't we a cut above the rest?'

That week turned out to be an endless nightmare. That's what I thought at the time. As it turns out, it helped kickstart my plans this year. To begin with, the hours were long. I left and arrived home in the dark. Why would anyone want to live like that? I still don't understand. Then there was the crammed Tube journey, congested with suckers who believed the only way to success was to occupy their desks from dawn to dusk. Every morning, I had to endure that painful experience with Pete wittering on about how he anticipated the markets to behave that day while he ogled anything dressed in a skirt.

'So, tell me, boy, what kind of girl are you attracted to?' he asked the first morning of that miserable week. 'Blondes, brunettes, or redheads?'

I shrugged, cringing, not daring to answer that I didn't know if it were girls or boys I was attracted to. I thought it could be both.

The first two evenings, I suffered the return Tube journey with him, but on the Wednesday I was alone. 'I'm meeting clients tonight, so you'll have to make your own way home,' he said as we left the building.

'What a shame,' I said, punching the cold air with elation as he strutted off.

I don't know what came over me but, whatever it was, I'm thankful it did. I followed him. He walked for ages and ages, all the way up to the West End, through the tumult of passers-by and the squeaky brakes and honking horns of exasperated taxi drivers. I kept having to stop in shop doorways to cough out the mix of the icy winter air and choking traffic fumes tormenting the back of my throat – bloody asthma.

Despite falling snow, I was sweating by the time he turned left up Shaftsbury Avenue. Gathering pace, he marched on to turn right into Dean Street and stop outside an establishment that didn't surprise me in the least. He nodded at a hulk of a man who moved aside a rope barrier and waved him in. Pete glanced behind him before disappearing into the other side of righteousness.

'Good night?' I asked him the following morning as we walked to the Tube.

'Very good.'

'Where did you go?'

'Met a friend up West for a bite to eat. Nice place. I'll have to take you there when you're older,' he said with a smirk. He stopped and turned to me. 'You know what? I've got a client meeting today. I know the guys pretty well, so you can come along too. Wouldn't be fair not to show you the perks of the job. I won't bother ordering food in today. I'll give the guys a call, and we can make it a late lunch.'

Around two-thirty, he told me to get my coat, and we caught a cab up to the West End, stopping outside a Japanese restaurant near the club he'd entered the day before. I inwardly groaned. I'm not a lover of Oriental food. Too much salt, and noodles have always felt like eating worms. And who wants to endure that?

'This is going to be such a one-of-a-kind experience for you, lad,' Pete said, stepping out of the cab. How right he was. Much to my astonishment, he handed the driver a fifty-pound note and told him to keep the change. The guy's jaw dropped as if he couldn't believe his luck, and off he sped for fear his generous client might change his mind.

'So, how're you finding your work experience?' he asked as he led me up the street.

'Good, thanks. The work is fascinating,' I said with spurious enthusiasm.

He looked genuinely pleased.

Sometimes I really impress myself with my ability to say what people think they want to hear.

After a couple of minutes, he stopped outside an unassuming black door wedged between an upscale French eatery and a licenced sex shop. He pressed the gold-plated buzzer and stated his name into the intercom. The door clicked open. 'After you,' he ordered, and I entered a long, light hallway, empty save for an old-fashioned coat stand holding an array of brightly-coloured umbrellas, but little else. 'Move along. All the way to the end.'

I felt a little nervous. Where was he taking me? But I needn't have worried. At the end of the hallway stood another black door out of which burst a busty blonde, smartly dressed in a red trouser suit. 'Good afternoon, gentlemen,' she said and politely asked for our coats. A uniformed waiter appeared and led us through a lively, packed restaurant – the type with minimal food choice, but an extensive wine list. Invisible bank notes floated through the air – fivers and tenners, twenties and fifties – you could smell them in the fabric of the Savile Row suits and expensive leather brogues.

Manoeuvring through the crowd, we arrived at a glitzy booth with high-backed seating already occupied by two suited men who Pete introduced as James and Rupert. 'Ah, the schoolboy,' said James, smoothing his tie. They were odious energy traders, dressed in tailored suits and shirts with pound-coin cufflinks, who waffled on about the prices of crude oil and natural gas, in the most monotonous of tones, the entire afternoon.

Stiff white cloth covered the table, and the oversized cutlery had a new shine. Staff floated around, on-hand to deal with the non-stop summons of over-demanding pricks like these three men I was unfortunate enough to have ended up wasting an afternoon in the company of. The place was mobbed with them. I could hear their toffee-nosed chatter over classical music playing from speakers camouflaged in the unusual collection of artificial pot plants.

It did, indeed, turn out to be an interesting afternoon which spilled into the early evening by the time the waiter finished pouring their sixth bottle of champers, politely asking them if they wanted another. Pretending to be interested in what they had to say, I learned a lot. Most importantly, not only were my thoughts on not wanting a boring career in the City confirmed, but I learned about the type of person I never wanted to be. A dull knob who truly believed that frequenting those kinds of repugnant places signified the pinnacle of a successful life.

As James flagged down the waiter for the bill, Rupert kept trying to rest his head on his open hand propped up on the table, but his elbow kept slipping and shunting his floppy fringe into his glasses. James kept belching and apologising even though he wasn't remotely sorry. When the waiter arrived with a column of paper, folded several times on a silver dish, the pair of them bantered over whose turn it was to pay, shoving the dish backwards and forwards to each other until it toppled to the floor.

After we'd said goodbye to his tedious acquaintances, Pete opened his wallet, swung me two fifty-pound notes and told me to find a cab. 'I'm meeting up for one more drink with the boys. You can't come to this one,' he slurred and stepped out into the busy road to hail an approaching black cab. The driver swerved out of the way, waving his fist to Pete's unmerited bombardment of vulgar insults.

'You're OK,' I said, snatching the notes out of his hand. 'I'll make my own way home. See you in the morning.'

It was early evening, about eight o'clock, and the frost-covered pavements were glistening like sparklers in the glow of the streetlights. A few metres up the road, I turned to see him sway towards the club he had visited the previous night. Stealthily, I followed him. When he stopped to lean against the window of the neighbouring shop and light a cigarette, I slipped into a busy newsagent, pretending to browse through some birthday cards while eyeballing him. He removed his phone and made a call, his breath forming smoking clouds in the frozen air. When I saw him flick his cigarette butt on the ground, and carry on up the road, I boldly followed his clumsy footsteps.

He didn't know where he was going, it seemed. We moved in circles, around and around Soho, up past the Royal Opera House until, arriving at a backstreet on the edge of Covent Garden, he punched a code into a keypad and entered a block of flats. What was he going in there for? Intrigued, I jogged up the steps and peered through the glass panel. He disappeared into a lift, and I waited until the red light above the doors indicated he'd stopped in the basement. There was only one thing for it. I stood by the bottom stair, and when a couple approached and entered, I slipped in behind them before the door clicked shut. They pressed the down button for the lift, and I got out my phone and pretended to make a call until the doors closed. I looked around. With walls covered in greying flock wallpaper and the floor in swirly patterned carpets, it wasn't the most glamorous of places. It smelled of the medicated chest rub my mum used to put on me as a kid when I had a cold.

My stomach was turning, but my inquisitive nature urged me forward. I called for the lift again and pressed the

B button when a redhead in a long coat entered the lobby and hurried towards me, waving. 'Hold for me, please,' she called out in a low voice. It was the most uncomfortable half a minute of my life. She wouldn't take her eyes off me. When we bumped down at the basement, the doors slowly opened into a dark dungeon. Redhead winked at me, and I followed her into what I can only describe as an electrically charged sexual playground. A stark contrast to the lobby I'd descended from.

A man sprung out of the corner of the candle-lit room as if he'd been waiting hours for my arrival. 'I like them young. Want to come with me?' he asked.

'Not at the moment, maybe later,' I whispered as if I'd left my usually confident voice in the lift.

Removing her coat, Redhead grabbed my hand. I swallowed my astonishment to see she wore nothing but a leather chest harness with a lead attached like a dog. 'I like them young too.' I should have turned around, but the stimulating mix of perfume and naked bodies lured me to go with her. I was intrigued, to put it mildly. We tip-toed between the moans and groans of couples everywhere – on cushions scattered on the floor, chairs, L-shaped squashy sofas and up against the walls – changing positions and partners as fast as my stomach was turning.

A day of education that can't be taught in the classroom.

We passed through more shrills of sensual delight until she led me to a room where it took all my resolve not to vomit that five-course lunch over the carpeted floor. Much to my advantage, Pete had his back to the door as he wriggled on a giant sofa with a man and a woman while Guns

175

N' Roses belted out from an old-fashioned stacked music system in the corner of the room. I turned to Redhead, 'Not for me, thanks.' She tutted and stroked my cheek before wandering off to hunt down her next victim.

I had to be quick. Confident I hadn't been seen, I snuck out of the room, leaving the door ajar. Peering through the gap, I whipped out my phone and flicked the video switch. Never one to miss such an opportune moment, I crouched down, aimed it in the doorway and recorded myself a little film.

NINETEEN

DAY 7

'How long until Gill gets here, Mummy?' Joe asks. He is standing with Isabella next to the kitchen counter, scooping flour into a mixing bowl. They have raided the dressing up box already. Joe is wearing a triceratops costume complete with horns and beady eyes. Isabella looks equally as cute dressed as a winged fairy, waving a wooden spoon like a magic wand. I have said for weeks that I will teach them how to make pancakes, and when they woke me this morning, they wouldn't let me forget.

I yawn. It's only seven-thirty, but they insisted on getting up an hour ago. By the time we'd finished clearing up after the party last night, and Sasha's friend was ready to give us a lift, Jim and I didn't get home until gone one, so I've left him sleeping. Another night of pain will keep him there at least another hour.

'Anytime soon,' I say, kissing my son's perfectly smooth cheek.

'How long is she staying for?' Isabella asks.

'The whole week. I've already told you. While Mel is on holiday.'

'Yippee.' Joe claps his hands. Despite my head throbbing from too much alcohol and lack of sleep – not to mention the emotional upset – I share his excitement. It's been three months since Gill last visited, and that's far too long.

Joe cocks his head to one side and squints at me with the pensive look of a curious child. 'Why don't you call her Mummy?'

'Because she's not my mummy.'

'You love her more than Grandma.'

So cutely intuitive.

'Now make a well in the middle of the flour like this.' I take the wooden spoon from Isabella and hollow out the bottom of the bowl. She grabs it back to continue the task.

'Now we need to crack the eggs into the middle,' I say, mulling over the events of last night. What a disaster! But that's what lies and deceit do to a family.

'I'll do it. Let me. I want to,' Isabella says, bouncing up and down with her usual hunger for life. Like I can see Joe in Jim, my daughter is a mini-me in the personality department – always wanting to get involved, always seeking a solution.

'One each.' I pass them both an egg and out poke their tongues as they carefully crack the eggs into the bowl and fish out bits of shell. Once they have stirred until they can stir no more, they run off, leaving me to clean the worktops.

I pack a picnic ready for our trip to the beach, and, as I'm clearing up, the doorbell rings. I rush to answer it. There Gill stands, as always, with the same wiry hair and the same loyal smile. She hands over a generous bunch of flowers, and I fall into the familiar relief of comfort her hugs always give me. I swallow the lump in the back of my throat as I tell her it's been too long.

'I know, I know, but now I'm retired, life seems to have got even busier,' she says. 'How does that happen?'

'You keep going on holiday!'

She steps back. 'You feel thin. What's been going on?'

I carry her suitcase to the bottom of the stairs, smiling. She always tells me I either look or feel thin.

The kids come skipping down the hallway, calling out her name on repeat. She hands them both a package, and their breathless impatience overrides their manners. They drop to the wooden floor like they do when the music suddenly stops in a game of musical bumps. Eyes wide, they rip open their gifts as if they've never before received a present. Out falls a box set of books for each. I remind them of their manners.

I leave them discussing their stories. Shrills follow me to the kitchen where I flick the kettle switch and swing the patio doors open to the dazzling morning sun. Not a cloud in sight, the Bleu de France sky pledges another glorious day. 'Let's sit outside,' I say when Gill appears.

I find my sunglasses, and we take our tea over to the grey rattan table and chairs, and I fetch some cushions from the deck box. 'What a wonderful morning,' she says, helping me discard the cover of the garden umbrella. I push the umbrella up the pole until the ribs fully extend, and the fabric becomes taut, but it gets stuck as I try to lock it into position. This keeps happening. Another damn thing that needs fixing. We ditch the umbrella in favour of the shade from the out-of-control laurels, which provide the garden with cherished privacy from the neighbour's unsightly loft conversion. 'It's too early. You'll have to wait a couple of hours,' I hear Catherine, my neighbour, say to her children, arguing with her about what time they can fill their paddling pool.

We catch up on life as if it were only yesterday we discussed her plans for retirement and the increasing bouts of Jim's unexplained pain. She's the only person I can talk to about anything and everything.

'Excuse the mess of the garden.' I nod towards the duvet of weeds suffocating the uncut lawn. It's a garden with limitless potential for the green-fingered. Just a shame I'm not such a person. An abundance of trees – acers, willows and cherry blossom – and clusters of laurels line one side. A bricked pergola runs the length of the other, overspread with various foliage providing a covered walkway down towards a large oak tree and the kids' trampoline. A three-tier water fountain blights the area in front of the patio, a cast stone oddity left by the previous owners which Jim and I still squabble over now and again. He says it makes a nice feature. I say it's good for the tip. I think about the delphiniums, butterfly bushes, coneflowers and rose bushes galore that crowd Gill's cottage garden wondering what it would take to get ours in some kind of presentable order.

She shields her eyes with her hand and squints across the garden. 'I'll have a potter while I'm here.' There's something different about her. She looks younger, fresher, not so many lines and wrinkles surround her eyes. Retirement suits her.

'How's work?' She takes a sip of tea. 'Caught any naughty people lately?'

I brief her on what I've been up to, before moving on to tell her about the trouble with Sasha and Marc. 'Remember them? You met them when they were here last summer.'

'The chap who manned the barbeque?'

'That's right. He's walked out on her for no apparent reason. Made a statement at the station to say he never wants to be found.'

'Wow. He didn't seem the type. They looked so happy together.'

I nod. 'Totally. The problem is, because he has stated he doesn't want to be found, there's nothing the police can do.'

'So? What're *you* doing about it?' she asks with a twisted smile. She knows me so well.

'I've done something really bad.'

She raises her eyebrows.

'I looked him up on the PNC – the Police National Computer – which is a criminal offence. I've used police information for personal gain.' I sigh. 'I found out stuff I shouldn't, and I'm feeling incredibly guilty. Not only that, I disclosed the information to a third party, which is a criminal offence too.'

'We all do things we shouldn't at times, Eva. Put it behind you. Guilt is a wasted emotion unless you've done something really wrong. You had good intentions.'

'I can't seem to shake it.'

'Come on, you aren't dealing drugs, and you haven't committed murder, so move on.'

Joe and Isabella scurry over, voicing the state of their empty tummies. 'We won't be long,' I say and tell them to see what's in the fruit bowl.

Gill asks after my brother Ben.

'He's still travelling, expanding his business. I've not heard much from him since he left Bangkok a few weeks ago. We've had a few text exchanges, and he's tried to face-time a few times, but I keep missing him. I must give him a call. He and Emmy broke up.'

Her hand shoots to her mouth. 'Oh, no. I thought they were together for good. What happened?'

'She broke it off before he left. He hasn't even told me. I met up with her for a drink the week before last. She thought they were going in different directions, wanting different things. You know how career orientated she is. She's gunning for a consultant title. He wants a family.'

'Not like him to keep that from you. Perhaps he thinks they'll get back together.'

'He's not been the same since Mum died, you know.'

'Really? After all this time?'

'It'll be three years in December.'

'Gosh, is it really that long? Any chance of them getting back together?'

'Not according to Emmy. I thought they'd stay together

forever. It's painful to think of them apart. I love them both so much. At least they didn't have kids.'

'I'm sure you'll still see her. You've been close for so long. And how's Dan?'

'The same as ever. Chasing every woman he meets as long as they aren't English,' I laugh. 'Jim spoke to him a few nights ago. He's been offered a new job here, in London.'

'So, he's moving back from New York?'

I nod. 'It won't be until the end of the year, though.'

'That'll be great for Jim to have his best friend back in town. And for you. Dan's always been a great support for you when he's around.'

'It sure will be.'

'Has he got somewhere to live?'

'He'll stay here until he gets himself sorted. I can't wait.'

We chat and smile, debate and laugh until I can no longer bribe the kids to give us another five minutes. 'Can we make the pancakes now?' Joe asks for the fifth time. 'It's been ages.'

I wake Jim while Gill supervises the kids. All I can hear is their laughter and cheer. I try to persuade Jim to get up, but it's another bad pain day. Are they getting more frequent? When the pain throbs this badly, there's little I can do to make him discard the duvet. Leaving him in bed is the only option, with the hope that the next hit of painkillers will dose him with the strength to enjoy what's left of the day. Perhaps the thought of the beach will entice him.

'Do you remember when I taught you to make pancakes?' Gill asks me as we sit down to the misshapen mounds which the kids serve with lashings of pride. I douse their efforts with maple syrup and chopped banana, surprised at how great they taste.

'How could I forget?' I laugh.

'Why?' asks Joe.

'They kept falling apart.' I suppose one could say a bit like me, back then.

'Why?' Joe, always so curious.

'They needed some TLC,' Gill says.

'What's TLC?'

'Tender loving care,' Gill and I say in unison.

'How old were you Mummy?' Isabella asks.

'Sixteen.'

'That's old.'

'Well, that's when I first went to live with Gill.'

'Why?'

'Because Grandma wasn't very well.' I don't tell him that Grandma hadn't been well for several years before that, and I had lived with a succession of foster parents. Some things can be saved for when your kids are older.

'Dead Grandma?' she asks.

I half-smile and nod.

'Why did she die?'

'Don't you remember me telling you? Because she had cancer that kept coming back and, in the end, she couldn't fight it anymore.'

'I don't remember her. What's cancer?' Joe asks.

'A terrible disease.' That's all I want to tell him. He's too young to learn about chemo, clinical trials and the metastasis that travelled from my mother's breast to her spine and eventually drove her up to heaven. She fought like a warrior for six years, but the continual battle defeated her in the end. I take solace in the special bond we managed to develop in the years before her death.

'Right, who's ready for the beach?'

Gill and I poke our fingers in our ears as shrieks of delight threaten to deafen. 'You two clear the table, and I'll go get Daddy up.'

Jim's not good. I can tell by the way his head droops a tad to the left as if the pain is pulling it down. 'I think I left my phone there last night,' he says, combing his wet hair. There's a slight tremor in his hands. 'Can you check with Sasha, please?'

'Whereabouts?'

'I don't know. I can't find it, though. Unless it dropped out in the car on the way home.'

'Are you sure you're up for coming today? I could take the kids with Gill,' I say, trying to relieve him of the guilt I know he feels because we've been promising the kids the waves all week.

'I can't let them down,' he says, his pale face showing the agonising pain he's in.

After a quick shower, I call Sasha, but there's no answer. I leave a message asking if she can look for Jim's phone and call me as soon as she can.

'Do you think this is a good idea?' I ask after I've loaded the car with overpacked bags, beach balls, buckets and spades.

He winces and shifts in his seat. 'Go,' he whispers.

During the drive to Brighton, Gill occupies the kids

with games of I-spy, number plate bingo, and who packed what in their suitcase. Jim sleeps the whole way, allowing me to reflect on the events of last night. There are some dubious characters living in Napier Close, that's for sure.

When we arrive, the cloudless sky presents a stunning candy-blue. It's crowded, as if every family in London decided to visit the beach today. The kids, their eyes alight, their little bodies loaded with buckets and spades and our beach bat set, skip and squeal to an empty spot along the lower promenade. 'Here, here,' they shout, plonking their toys on the concrete alongside the beach, where I get us all set up. Once settled, I slosh their bodies with suntan cream, ignoring their strops and screams of protest.

'Come onto the beach and build us a sandcastle, Mummy,' Joe says.

'Please, please,' Isabella says, jumping up and down.

'You've got your hands full, haven't you?' Gill says, as we kneel on the beach filling castle buckets with gravelly sand.

'And Jim wants another one!' I shake my head as I swivel the bucket one-eighty.

'And you?'

'I've always wanted a big family. You know that. The one I never had.' I sigh as I bash the top of the bucket with a spade. 'But that was before the accident.'

'Sometimes, we need to adapt our plans to suit our circumstances.'

'I don't want the accident to define us,' I lower my voice, 'because then the fuckedupness of it all wins.'

TWENTY

After we've munched ham sandwiches, crisps, and fruit, Gill drags her cotton, striped bag from under her deckchair. 'Who fancies ice cream?' she asks, searching for her purse. 'Let's give Mummy and Daddy a rest.'

I smile at her unending generosity, thankful for some peace if only for ten minutes. You wouldn't think she was in her late sixties, the energy she always has for the kids. Jim is snoozing, so I reposition my towel next to his chair and stretch out. The gentle breeze sweeps through the labyrinth of my mind, clearing a path to allow me to think a little straighter.

I need to suss that Luke out. And Pete. And Annie and Art. Perhaps Pen too. All of them!

Opening my eyes, I check on Gill and the kids. The queue to the kiosk curves past the gift shop next door. I watch for a while as they shuffle along the line. By the look of Gill's hands flying around, she is telling them a story, and they are listening intently. I rest my eyes, the hum of bathers inviting me to doze, but not for long. The family in front of us leave. Another immediately arrives, cramming a collection of beach bits and bobs into the vacant space. I watch them. The father is battling to get the two five-or-so-year olds into their trunks. They are moaning incessantly about being too hot, stressing their father even more. One runs off. The father swears and races after him. The mother, nursing her fussy newborn – trying to conceal the fact under a sarong – shouts at the remaining boy to do as he's told. Her raised voice sets the baby off wailing. So much for the peace. How can Jim even consider a third?

My phone rings. I fish it out of my bag. It's Sasha. 'I found Jim's phone this morning,' she says, her voice brittle.

'Thanks. We're at the beach. Can I pop in later to collect it?'

'I'm driving back from Cambridge. I won't be home for an hour.'

With everything that happened last night, I'm surprised to hear she still went. That's what desperation does to you. It leads you headlong to places you shouldn't visit. 'How did it go?'

Her voice breaks. 'I'll tell you later.'

'I'll text you when I'm about to leave.'

Jim wakes, a lot brighter. Sleep and sunshine have blushed his cheeks and done away with the glassy look in his eyes.

'You're looking better,' I say.

'That's what sea air does for you.'

. . .

After dropping everyone home, I drive to pick up Jim's phone. Parking up, I think what a good job everyone did in clearing up out here after Jim and I left last night. You'd never believe a party took place. I glance at my watch. It's seven o'clock, but the early evening sun is still warm in the unclouded sky. I can hear screams and squeals from children playing in nearby gardens and smell smoke from sausages and burgers charring on barbeques. Hannah answers the door, mumbling a hello. 'Mum's upstairs. She said she'll be down in a minute.' Usually, Hannah would join me for a chat but today doesn't even ask after the kids.

Inside is not so tidy. It seems every unwashed glass and item of crockery used last night is stacked by the kitchen sink. How did she walk out on this lot? She's not thinking straight. I open the dishwasher. A rush of steam and a beeping sound indicate a finished load. Grabbing a pair of Marigolds draped across the washing-up liquid dispenser, I turn on the taps, filling the bowl with hot water while I empty and restack the dishwasher.

'No way, you've done enough,' Sasha says when she glides in looking like a ghost of the woman I know and love. She places Jim's phone on the worktop. She is so pale and has clearly lost weight in the past week. The spaghetti straps of her long, tiered, print sundress drop off her shoulders every time she pulls them up.

'Update me while I make a start.' I soak dirty items in the filled sink. 'I can't stay long. How're the kids?'

She fakes a smile, her dimples appearing for a split second. 'I haven't been able to get Harry out of bed. He should be revising, but I don't think he's done a thing. And he was meant to go to a maths revision class this morning at school.'

'On a Sunday?'

She nods. 'They've had such a committed maths teacher this year. He arranged some extra revision classes because some of the kids were panicking. Luke came over to try and persuade Harry to go, but he had as much success as me. Harry's so angry with Marc. He reckons he's having an affair.'

She opens a drawer, whips out a tea towel and starts drying. 'George and Hannah aren't as bad. George stayed here with Harry, and Hannah came to Cambridge with me. We distributed the leaflets around all the market stallholders, but no luck. They all said the market closes at four each afternoon and none of them would have been around when he got that cash out at six. We went round all the surrounding shops too. And the church.' She shakes her forlorn head. 'On the way home, Hannah suggested we ask the local shops to look at their CCTV.'

'You could try, but I doubt they'd show you. They only have a legal obligation if you are asking to see footage of yourself. And you have to do that in writing. They have a month to comply. I wouldn't waste your time.'

'What about the police, can't they demand to see it?'

I exhale deeply. 'We've been over this. He doesn't want to be found, Sasha. They won't do a thing unless you can prove he is at risk. And you know they interviewed him and deemed him not.'

'What about everything I'm finding out about him?'

'I know it's shocking and hurtful for you, but he hasn't done anything illegal.' I still can't bring myself to mention the coke.

When I've cleared the sink of washing-up, I remove the gloves and slap them back over the dispenser. 'Look, I'm sorry, I must go. Are you sure you still want to do Jim's physio tomorrow? Why don't you take a few days off? It must be so stressful working and dealing with all this and now the kids, too.'

'I can't afford to take time off. That's the downside of being self-employed.' She leans back against the worktop and folds her arms across her chest. 'If Marc never comes back, both financially and emotionally, I'm going to need my business to survive.'

'I'll see you tomorrow. Call me if you need me.' I squeeze her arm. 'Anytime.'

'I need to tell you something quickly.' She walks over and closes the kitchen door. 'I went over to Pen and Pete's earlier. I've debated about getting Pen involved, but thought what the heck? I pretended I thought the five grand came from both of them, and I asked why they transferred it to Marc's account last week.'

'And?'

The stress is audible in her strained and confused voice. 'Pen didn't know anything about it. I could tell. She was shocked. Pete said it was a short-term loan. Marc told him he was cashing in twenty-five thousand pounds worth of shares, but he wouldn't get the funds straight away and needed five grand urgently. He said he would pay Pete back this week.'

'And you have no idea what this urgent need was?'

'No. No clue at all. What I do know is…' she pauses to swallow, 'we've never owned a single share of any kind.'

TWENTY-ONE

LUKE

An extra class? My arse!

Any excuse to see her, the dirty perv.

They must have found it difficult meeting up since study leave scuppered their afternoon break and lunchtime trysts. Probably after school sessions too, not that I would know. Sufficient evidence fills my phone for me not to have wasted my precious time spending another minute in this place. I'm done with learning now.

So, what better excuse than to offer some extra revision classes? Round Robbins' Sum Ups, he titled them. He thinks he's so smart, that man. Mr Timothy Robbins. A man of letters and Maths Teacher of the Year to his credit, too. He didn't account for my astuteness in his calculations, though.

He's known all along I'm not attending these extra

classes because I need to. I mean, come on, I'm predicted four A stars, why would I? Even two Sundays ago, when I turned up with Harry for the first of his two-hour classes, I think I put a fraction of uncertainty into that mathematical mind of his. 'Luke, what're you doing here?' he asked, his eyebrows rising a notch. Did I also notice panic in his voice? Or was that his excitement at seeing her again?

'Every little helps, sir,' I replied, staring into his questioning eyes longer than he could stand.

'Not sure what extra I can teach you, lad. But you're more than welcome. Take a seat.'

So, I did, in the first row, next to Chelsea Clark. And, for extra amusement, I flirted with her, complimenting her on the pretty dress she was wearing. A floral one that stopped mid-thigh and did nothing to disguise the generosity of her chest. I shuffled my chair as close to her as I could get away with – all the time holding my gaze on Robbins – and I kept lightly touching her arm and nudging her shoulder with mine.

'What's with you today, Luke?' she asked during the break. She was snacking on a granola bar and sipping a homemade drink of a disgusting shade of green – such a goody-two-shoes. 'You're acting all strange. Creeping me out. What's up?' But I brushed her questions off with some sweeping comment about geometric progressions.

So, again today, I'm attending this last class for nothing other than sheer enjoyment. I stroll along, thinking about how much I am looking forward to it.

I couldn't persuade Harry to come along. After Sasha called me this morning, asking for my help, I tried. But when I went up to his room, he was lying in bed, his face as white as the walls, staring at the ceiling. 'Come on, Harry, it's Robbins' last class today. Don't ruin things for yourself now. We've got less than a week to go.'

I was half expecting him to tell me to get lost, but after five minutes of incessantly slagging off his parents for the liars they are, his message was loud and clear. 'Leave me alone.' So, I did. No use wasting time trying to steer a ship that's gone off course at this stage of my journey. I need to keep a clear head. Don't want the captain going overboard, do we?

All the way to school, I wonder if Chelsea has already been in contact with Robbins. Has she warned him after our informative little chat at the party last night? But, as soon as I stroll into the classroom, I know he knows. The guilt and shame are furrowed in his glistening forehead and fill the beads of sweat trickling down his temple. Everyone else probably thinks it's the heat of the day, but they don't know what I know. His shoulders are sagging from the punishment of his crime. I stifle a giggle. They will be sagging a lot more by the end of this session.

'OK, everyone. Today is our last…' He drops his pen. He bends to pick it up, catching my smirk like another kick in his oversized incisors. I do wonder what Chelsea sees in him.

Robbins continues. 'As agreed last week, we'll cover the remaining topic of quadratics before going on to review the answers of the 2015 paper. Listen up.' He usually speaks with such fluidity, gracefully even, as if numbers and equations flow without him having to think. Today, however, his words keep getting stuck in his dry mouth, emerging with a nervous croak. I'm dying to laugh, but come on, Luke, you need to keep it professional. This will be a business transaction, after all.

He goes to write on the board, his clammy hands twitching, ruining his usually impeccable writing and the perfectly formed curves of his graphs. Oh, what fun it is to see them both squirm. Robbins keeps twisting from side to side, his head twitching, as he writes on the whiteboard and Chelsea fidgets and wriggles in her seat. The pair of slimy snakes.

It's such a shame. He was my favourite teacher until I discovered his involvement in Chelsea's extra-curricular activities. Not only my favourite, but he was also the best, and I've always held him in such high regard. He even manages to make mind-bending differential equations and 3D vectors a stroll through the playground. He's one of those motivating teachers too. He tells each cohort at the start of every September, 'Set yourself high standards, people. I'm all about creating a culture of self-efficacy. You can do this. You just need to believe you can. Then all that's left is the hard work.' And he begins each sacred lesson with the words, 'Listen up, lovely people. It's a great day to solve mathematical problems.'

Halfway through today's two-hour lesson, he rewards us all with a break. 'Refuel those brain cells, team. Be sure to be back in ten minutes. Luke, would you mind staying behind.'

Not at all, Robbins. Not at all.

I kick out a foot, breaking Chelsea's dash from the

classroom. 'You too, Chel,' I say, gripping her arm way too tightly. Carefully does it, Luke. You'll bruise her skin. There's no point in attracting unnecessary attention to yourself.

With everyone out of the room, Robbins speaks, his voice a feeble echo of the confident man he usually portrays. 'Chelsea told me about your little conversation last night.'

Little? I don't think so. You've got your calculations wrong this time, sir. There's a pause which I refuse to fill. I'm not the one who has to explain myself.

'She told me about the videos.'

Carry on, sir, please do. I need to see him squirm some more before I show him what I know he wants to see with his own eyes. I've got the videos ready. No use wasting time. I always have been given full credit for my organisational and planning skills.

'Do you care to show me?'

'You're forgetting your manners, sir,' I say, my scornful voice teeming with the contempt he deserves.

His lips purse to the side. Chelsea is clenching her jaw, flaring her nostrils. Not a sight that suits her; I should tell her so, but can't be bothered.

'Sorry, sir. I didn't quite hear you.'

'Pleeeeeease,' he seethes through gritted teeth.

I leisurely remove my phone from my pocket and slowly tap in my passcode, unable to restrain myself from smirking. I press play on one of the many appropriate videos and turn the screen to face him.

For at least thirty seconds, his eyes don't blink as he

stares at Chelsea straddling him with her school tie and shirt half-undone. Talk about breaching a position of trust. In the small store cupboard which houses books and stuff needed for different parts of the younger kids' syllabuses, of all the places.

'I hate you, Luke Walker.' Chelsea's voice is barely a whisper above Robbins' grunts of pleasure from the video. I turn the sound up. Chelsea Clark, eh? Who would have guessed? Months of letting everyone think she's the teacher's pet when in actual fact she's been the teacher's whore.

He tries to grab the phone, his hands trembling like a user without sight of his next fix. 'What're your plans for that?' he asks.

I arrange my most charming of smiles. 'That all depends on the two of you.'

'Us?' they say in unison, exchanging glances of helpless despair.

I tell them that if they play by my rules, I'll reward their good behaviour and delete this and all such similar filth.

'Stop the games, Luke,' Chelsea says. 'What do you want from us?'

'Ten grand. Each. By Tuesday.' I delve into my jeans pocket and hand them each a Post-it note detailing where to send their funds.

Robbins gasps painfully like someone taking their last breath. 'I can't get hold of that kind of money.'

'And how do you expect me to?' Chelsea starts to cry. Poor little love.

I point at Robbins. 'You can get a loan,' I say, then jab a

finger at Chelsea. 'And you can get down to the bank and make a transfer from that generous savings account Daddy set up for his precious pampered princess on her eighteenth birthday.' I tut several times. 'You really shouldn't boast about these things, Chelsea.'

'And if we don't?' Robbins asks.

I take great pleasure in delivering my reply. Great pleasure indeed. That at nine o'clock on Tuesday night, the five videos in my possession are set to circle around social media channels faster than a cyclist in a velodrome.

'That's blackmail,' Robbins says. 'You'll ruin my career. I'll never get another teaching position.'

I wink and give him the thumbs-up sign. 'Full marks, sir.'

TWENTY-TWO

DAY 8

On the way to work, Rob calls. 'Are you planning on making an appearance any time today?'

'If you bothered to read your texts, you'd know I was going to be in late.' I called Arthur this morning and told him I had to meet with the kids' headteacher. Jim was going to come, but we woke up late, so he wouldn't have been ready in time. Besides, I've done so much overtime in the past year, if I were to take it all off in lieu, Arthur wouldn't see me before Christmas.

I sit on a moulded plastic chair outside Mrs Miller's room, watching children file in to start their school day. Some kids stare, making me feel like a naughty child. After a quarter of an hour, Mrs Miller appears, flustered, apologising profusely for her tardiness.

She leads me into her room, a busy shrine to her many

pupils. Their work plasters the walls from the skirting to the ceiling. Drawings and paintings, certificates of achievement and a collection of posters depicting the school's ethos and values: respect, learn, aspire and care for one another.

'This constitutes bullying in my books, Mrs Miller, and something needs to be done about it,' I say after explaining my little chat with Isabella.

'Rest assured, now I have your side of the story, I will tackle this with utmost urgency. Bullying is not something I will tolerate in my school. Can I just mention something else while I have you here?'

Her tone suggests I am not going to like what she has to say. 'When I spoke to Isabella about this incident on Friday…'

I interrupt her. 'She never mentioned that you'd spoken to her.'

She nods. 'We had a good conversation. I'm pleased she felt she could open up to me.'

'What did she say?' I ask, curious. I can't imagine Isabella opening up to anyone else. A pang of resentment perturbs me.

'I've debated whether to tell you this. Being a working parent myself, I know how difficult things can be at times, but she got very upset about not seeing you very much.'

Her words repeat themselves in my head for the rest of the day.

. . .

Sasha calls when I get to work. As soon as I hear her high-pitched voice, I know she's had news of Marc.

'A lady called me this morning. She owns a B&B on the outskirts of Cambridge. Near the hospital. I gave one of my missing leaflets to a friend of hers when I was there yesterday. She was visiting that friend and recognised Marc on the leaflet.'

'That's encouraging.'

'She said he booked into her B&B last Monday night, for two nights, but get this. He used a different name. Hastings.' Her voice breaks. 'He really doesn't want to be found.'

'You know anyone with that surname?'

'Nope.'

'How sure is she that it was him?'

'She has CCTV.'

'Will she let you look?'

'She said she would.'

'That's surprising.'

'She said her friend told her how desperate I was. I've arranged to go up there tonight. I need to know if it was him. If he's still alive.' Her voice dips. 'I need to know, Eva.'

'Do you want to leave Jim's physio for today?'

'Definitely not. He's seeing Art too, don't forget.'

I arrive at Napier Close mid-afternoon. Luke and Harry follow me in. They must have just finished another exam. 'Hi, you two,' I call out as I click my car shut. Harry doesn't acknowledge me. Stomping towards his front door, he looks already done with the day, his cheeks flushed, and his mouth twisted like a taut red knot. Luke waves.

I nod over to Harry. 'Not a good day, I take it?'

'We've just come from another maths paper. He thinks he's stuffed it up,' Luke says.

'Poor guy's not having a good time.'

'Shame he missed the revision class yesterday. A question came up on today's paper that the teacher went through in some detail. Typical, eh?'

'How did you find the exam?'

'Good, thanks. I'll go over and help him later. We've got another maths paper tomorrow. I'll run through the other stuff the teacher went over yesterday.'

Ralph is laying outside Sasha's studio, panting, beside his empty water bowl. Luke takes a bottle out of his rucksack and removes the lid. 'Hey, buddy, you thirsty?' He bends down and fills the bowl with water, encouraging Ralph to take a sip. Luke looks up at me. Despite what I felt about him on Saturday night, his dark, puppy dog eyes display nothing sinister today. 'This hot weather isn't good for them.' He strokes Ralph's coat. 'You should be inside, little fellow, where it's cooler. Finish that, and I'll take you in.'

Ralph laps up his drink as if he'll never get another one. 'Take it easy, buddy.' Luke caresses the dog's tail. 'Don't worry. I'll pour you another one when this is finished.'

I can't stop staring at him. There's something oddly mesmerising about the way he's stroking Ralph. Sasha opens the door, interrupting my thoughts. The murky cloud that has been hanging over her usually sunny face for the past week is even darker today. 'I thought I heard voices. Ah, Luke, you're back. Did Harry come home with you?'

Luke scoops up Ralph and holds him in his arms like a baby. 'He's gone straight in. I'll take Ralph in too.'

'You're such a sweetheart. Tell Harry I'll be about twenty minutes.'

'Sure thing, Mrs O. See you later.'

Mrs O? Does he always call her that? I've not noticed before.

'You coming in, Eva?' Sasha asks.

I hear her, but her words don't register. I'm too busy watching Luke carrying Ralph away, wondering why my guts are twisting. I lean a hand against the studio wall, feeling nauseous. The taste of cheap coffee and salty, smoky pig shoots up to the back of my throat. I knew I shouldn't have eaten that bacon butty Rob bought me for lunch. He's got friendly with the owner of a greasy café just off the High Street, near the station. The type where Formica tables and battered chairs meet the waft of fried food and over-brewed tea. Sometimes, when I'm really stretched and haven't brought anything in from home, I succumb to his offering to buy me a sarnie. I don't know why I bother. I never fail to regret it for the rest of the day.

'Eva? You OK?' Sasha asks.

'I think this heat has got to me. I need a drink of water.'

'Pop into the house. I'm about halfway through Jim's session.' She glances at her watch. 'We'll be done by quarter past.'

In the house, raised voices flow from the kitchen.

Leaving the front door open slightly, I inch my way up the hall, knowing I shouldn't be snooping, but that's me. I seem to be doing it a lot lately. Through a gap in the door, I can see Harry and Luke and just about hear them over the sound of the radio.

'It's all right for you. Your mum and dad aren't liars,' Harry says in a voice hissing with venom. A missing father accompanied with exam stress, let alone the embarrassment of Saturday night, must have fuelled his anger.

'Come on, mate. You've got to keep your shit together. All parents are dicks. Mine included,' Luke says. He is scooched down beside Ralph. The dog has rolled onto his back, his paw sticking up in the air like a beetle.

'Yours? What've they ever done to you?'

Luke is gently kneading Ralph's belly. 'Another story for another time, but they're not the saints everyone thinks they are.'

'How about a story for now?'

'Look, we can't allow parents to ruin our futures. They're not worth it.'

There's silence for a while, just the clink of ice cubes, and water filling glasses.

'Do you reckon my dad has hooked up with another bird?'

Luke stops doting on Ralph and stands up, brushing hairs off his jeans. 'Not something that would've ever crossed my mind. I'm confused about his departure as much as everyone else. I'm gutted in fact. Your dad has been more of a father to me than my own.'

His words don't match his expression, and a disturbing

glow lights his eyes. I shiver, despite the perspiration from the sweltering day creeping down my spine.

'I can't think why else he would've left. You know him well. Of all the dads we know, would you've put him as the one to have done this?'

Luke pulls out a stool from under the breakfast bar. 'He'll probably be back soon. Let's get through these exams, and I'll help you trace him. No one can go undetected for long in today's world. You want me to go over this maths stuff Robbins went through with us yesterday?'

Harry remains seated at the breakfast bar, chin propped up in his hands with a "woe is me" expression shadowing his tired and pained face. Luke pulls a file out of his rucksack. He opens it and unclips some pages. 'If we're lucky, one of these questions will come up in tomorrow's paper, the same as today.'

I sneak back to the front door, open it wider and slam it shut. 'It's Eva.' I call out as I walk back to the kitchen.

Luke acknowledges me with a friendly smile, but I catch the way he stealthily pokes Harry in the ribs. I find a tumbler and turn on the tap as they collect their things and disappear upstairs.

Draining the glass, I pour myself another. As I'm drinking the second, I stop midway as the radio announces the news. This morning, two college students discovered the dismembered remains of a body by the river Cam, along The Backs in Cambridge.

TWENTY-THREE

I carry on listening, not wanting to think the worst. The body has yet to be identified. Police have cordoned off the scene, and forensic officers are combing the area. There is a mention of police dogs too, but Sasha barging into the house interrupts me hearing anything further. Her stricken face tells me I don't need to ask if she has also heard the same news.

'Sit down,' I tell her, flicking on the kettle. More sweet tea is required here; perhaps something stronger.

'They've found a man's body in Cambridge,' she whispers.

'I heard.'

'It could be him.'

'And it probably isn't.' It takes me five minutes to calm her down. I'm convinced that it's a coincidence, even though I can't be sure.

'I need to get back to Cambridge,' she says, throwing her car keys into her bag.

'What good will that do?'

'I can identify him.'

'But you don't know it's him. Anyway, they wouldn't let you do that straight away, Sasha.' My heart goes out to her. I know what it's like to tread the fear that you could become a widow.

Not much I say can convince her. It's as if she has already organised her husband's funeral in her head, chosen the coffin, written the eulogy. She raises her voice, her cheeks reddening. 'Go and take your husband to Art. Leave me to find mine.'

I step back as if she has shoved me. All I've tried to do is support her. But I know she's not thinking rationally. It's the stages she's going through. The shock has subsided, and now the anger is intensifying. I try and console her, but she's adamant she wants to be left alone. Sometimes that's all you can do. I've been here umpteen times. People need time to make sense of how they are going to clean up the mess that has been catapulted their way. I squeeze her shoulder on my way out. 'You know where I am.'

'Eva!' she calls out as I leave the kitchen.

I turn around.

'Sorry. I didn't mean to speak to you so harshly.'

I give her a straight-lipped smile before leaving her to her thoughts.

I'm still feeling queasy as I walk over to her studio. I glance over my shoulder and look up to Art and Annie's house and the window where I saw Luke looking out on Saturday night. I don't know why. No one is standing at the window today. My phone rings. It's Rob updating me on a potential lead on Shane Baker. We discuss tactics for a couple of minutes. Before he hangs up, I say, 'Do me a favour, will you?'

'Another one?' he asks. Humour underlies his playful sarcasm.

'A body has been found in Cambridge. Chopped about by the sounds of it. See what you can find out about the victim.'

'Drugs related?'

'I don't know anything other than what I've heard on the news. Check it out for me. See what you can find out.'

'Leave it with me.'

'Oh, and, Rob,' I say as I smile and wave at Jim who is waiting for me outside the studio. 'Don't listen to me in the future when I place an order for that crap food you don't seem to be able to live without.'

I end the call and walk over to Jim. He looks so well, his sun-kissed face glowing from yesterday's trip to the beach. A far cry from the pale pained face of yesterday morning. 'Good session?' I ask, bending down to kiss him.

'Great,' he says, 'I feel better today than I have in a long time. Minimal pain. A day at the beach did me good.' We continue next door to Art's studio. Expecting a sweaty atmosphere, I'm quite surprised by the calm and airy room. It has a citrusy smell, like a glass of freshly prepared lemonade. Floor to ceiling mirrors cover two of the walls which exaggerate the size of the space, and, apart from an extensive set of free weights, there's surprisingly very little equipment. I look around. In the corner stands a state-of-the-art treadmill. The type that appears more complicated to operate than the police national computer after an upgrade. Being another scorcher of an afternoon, and still feeling queasy, I'm relieved to find air conditioning pumping throughout.

'Glad you could come now,' says Art. 'It's a quiet time of day.' He slides one of the mirrors attached to rails to reveal a cupboard stacked with more fitness bits and pieces. There is a row of different sized kettlebells and medicine balls, foam rollers, boxing gloves and other equipment I can't even name, let alone describe how they could possibly be used to better the human body. Art rolls two large gym balls into the middle of the room. They hit an exercise mat, and he signals for me to take a seat and for Jim to wheel himself over. He fills two plastic cups from a giant water bottle by the door and brings them over to us. 'I ask my clients to bring their own reusable bottles to each session. It's important to stay hydrated, especially in this weather.'

Art fetches his bottle and a clipboard then balances himself on the other ball. 'I'm not sure how much Sash has told you, but I work holistically by creating a bespoke programme for each of my clients.'

He looks so different from the guy I met on Saturday. There's something rogue about him today which I can't explain. Maybe it's his unkempt hair, or his gym attire – black shorts and a blood-red T-shirt. It shows off his muscular physique and is such a striking contrast to the tuxedo he was wearing on Saturday night which disguised his thick, bull-like neck.

'To do that I need to gain a comprehensive under-standing of you, both present and past. This allows me to set workable targets. There's nothing less motivating than unrealistic goals.' He bends over and reties his laces. 'So, to do that, I need to know everything about you.'

This isn't an understatement.

As soon as he starts enquiring into every microscopic fact about Jim's medical background, I know this will take more than the half-hour visit I had anticipated. Jim reluctantly spills the details about the accident. Of what he can remember anyway. I butt in to complete the sentences he can't finish because he doesn't know how they end. He moves on to describe the extensive surgery that followed, when optimistic surgeons tried to put his broken body back together again. It takes a while.

I peer around the room. Behind me, a fascinating poster covers the entirety of the unmirrored wall like wallpaper. It details all six hundred and fifty muscles in the intricate machine better known as the human body. No wonder it stops working properly if those muscles are not all kept in sync. I peep at my watch. Joe has to be back in his classroom by six for his school play. I wanted to get home to take him myself, but the way things are moving, that's not going to happen. Texting Gill, I ask her to take him and meet us there.

'This is all going to be about building up your strength and core stability,' Art tells Jim. 'I think I'll include some intense massage in your programme too, to begin with, if that's OK with you. Get the knots out of those tight muscles.' He goes on to explain what else his plans entail. He knows his stuff. I've always thought having a personal trainer outrageously self-indulgent, but I'm surprisingly impressed by this well-informed man. Before this meeting, I was sceptical about whether this was the right path for Jim. Is there a better direction for him to take? Countless tests have proved there is no medical explanation for his pain. All I know is, he can't go on suffering, so we have to try something.

'For the first month, can you fit in three sessions a week? Two here where we will work on the physical programme, and one down at my other gym where my massage room is set up. I'll also write up a daily plan for you to do at home.'

Jim asks for my acceptance with a glance. I nod. I don't think we have much choice. I make a mental note to call Mick. We're going to need some help with transport to and from these gym sessions. Art drops his clipboard and pen on the floor and puts his hands above his head, stretching out like a thick elastic band. His T-shirt rides up, exhibiting an abdomen exceptionally toned for a man of his years. 'Three times a week it is. That's great. Believe me, you're going to feel so much better when we get going. You'll wish you'd done this years ago.'

I slip my hands behind my back and cross my fingers.

'So, I'll see if I can slot you in for your first massage tomorrow. If not, I'll–'

A high-pitched scream stops him mid-sentence. Crying that turns to sobs like a child in a shopping arcade who has lost their parents. We look at each other curiously.

'Is that Hannah?' I ask, despite already knowing that it is. I race outside with Art on my heels.

Sasha bolts out of her studio. She opens her arms to a

distraught Hannah charging towards her. George is close behind. 'Whatever's happened?' she asks her daughter. 'What is it?'

Hannah stutters and splutters. 'Dad was waiting for me when I came out of school.'

TWENTY-FOUR

LUKE

I'm taking the rest of the day off. Another exam ticked off, and I've done my good deed for the day and shown Harry everything Robbins went through yesterday. There's no need for me to revise for tomorrow's exam – no point at all. Whatever I look at, I already know. Who do I have to thank for my photographic memory, I wonder?

Now it's time to do what I do best. The folks won't be back for a while. It doesn't happen often, but tonight I fancy a beer, so I grab a can from the fridge and a family-sized bag of crisps from the cupboard. All set. Time to get to work.

I park myself at my desk and fire up my Mac. This is going to be the most enjoyable of evenings. I smile and run my fingers along the top of the screen, admiring the cutting-edge machine. I bought it last year, along with a-top-of-the-range editing keyboard, with money saved up from Christmas and birthdays. While waiting for the editing software to load, I pull the tab on the can of beer. Editing these snippets of delight will be the best fun I've had for weeks.

Well, nearly. Let's not go forgetting Robbins' face on Sunday.

It will calm me down too. Hannah's outburst at seeing Marc has unsettled me. And that's not what I need at the moment. I'm the director here, and I call the shots. Was it really him she saw? Surely not?

Yesterday morning, I couldn't sleep after the fracas at the party. So, I got up early and downloaded all the photos and video clips ready for this post-production process – no need to waste any time. I always have been complimented for my proactive nature and coordinated approach. It's been in every school report since I can remember: *Luke has such exceptional organisational skill for a boy his age. This, coupled with his analytical mind, will reward him with a bright future.*

How right they were.

I made a copy of each photo and sorted them into two groups – one, in time order – the other, by people. That way I can pick them out much more easily, as and when required. That's the way I work best. With the videos, I left them in time order ready to go through one by one.

Now, time for the part of the job I love best. Getting rid of all the flawed and unwanted content to construct the story I want to tell.

And, man, do I have so many stories waiting to be told.

Don't get me wrong, shooting this stuff is fun – getting the right people in the right places and poses – it's an art form. But the real creativity comes at this stage. The manipulation of the raw material into something aesthetically pleasing and dramatically compelling. There are so many things to get right: creating perfect scene transitions, selecting the best music to complement the material, choosing the best visual effects. It involves tons more than a bit of cutting and pasting as most people seem to think.

There are six hundred and ninety photos and forty-seven video clips in total, spanning nearly fourteen hours. I'm glad now that I organised them all yesterday morning. I start with the videos as they will take a lot longer. The first one stars the O'Sullivans, minus Marc, of course. I press play. Sasha, Harry, Hannah and George appear, setting up for the party on Saturday morning, with Ralph pootling amongst them all. They are carrying tables out to the front of the house, putting up the banners and blowing up the balloons. Sasha pins bunting to the trees. She flashes a smile. It's fake of course, but all the same, let's give credit where credit is due. Her face brims with the determination to deliver a party to remember for her eldest's coming of age.

Little did she know.

Little does she know.

I beaver away for a few hours – three, to be precise. Time flies and all that. Until I hear a car pull up and keys turn in the front door. As usual, she bolts up the stairs to check on me, 'Luke, you there?' She sticks her head around my bedroom door. 'How was your day?' she asks, pretending to care. 'Why didn't you answer my call? Exam go well?'

'All right,' I reply, grinding my teeth. Hearing her voice has vexed me.

She starts to walk into the room, although my body language tells her I wish she wouldn't. I toggle to the BBC news website and pretend to be engrossed. My peripheral vision and sense of smell inform me she's in her clammy workout gear. Why oh why, does she spend so much time in the gym? Hasn't she got better things to do? I've never understood it – how has Dad made such a success of getting people into that sweaty, smelly place, including her?

That is, until recently.

'Can you even spare one minute to look at me?'

No.

'Luke!'

I huff and puff and turn to her. Come on, Luke. Keep your crap together. There's not long to go now. My raised eyebrows ask her, what now?

'I've bought some cold meats and salad from Marks and Spencer. Please go and prepare them and lay the table and get drinks ready while I take a quick shower.'

'I'm busy.'

'Luke!'

'Why can't Dad do it?'

'He's not coming home until later. Just get down there, will you?'

She flounces out of the room, asking God to give her

strength. I snigger. Oh, what fun it is to ride on the wave of her indignation.

It's called getting my own back.

I toggle back to my video creation, save the latest files and head downstairs – no use in riling her at this late stage.

What I still can't fathom is how she still doesn't know I know. Neither does Dad. All these years of bragging to everyone who will listen about how highly intelligent their only child is, and they still think they can keep their dirty collection of secrets hidden from me.

It's getting on for two years now since I started to guess. One Saturday, when Dad and I were out with Marc and Harry celebrating our GCSE results. Even I was chuffed with my clean sweep of grades.

The four of us took a trip up to town, starting at the Photographer's Gallery in Soho. Purely for my benefit, although, to their credit, Marc and Harry did try and show some interest. Dad wandered around, nodding and commenting, "Impressive, impressive" even to the exhibits that didn't deserve such adulation. I remember watching him and thinking, what a knob, how can he not see the difference? It was so transparent to me.

There was an exhibition on that day titled *Divided Self* by Tom Butler. An artist's work has never intrigued me as much – how he manages to manipulate images to create such distorted and disturbing scenarios. While I viewed the exhibition a second time, Harry, Marc and Dad went to the café for coffee. They had to drag me out after their second cup.

Lunch followed in some pizza restaurant near London

Bridge that makes their own dough with fresh seawater from the Mediterranean. The minerals make it lighter, apparently. Everyone else stuffed theirs down, but I couldn't eat. Why can't people learn to eat properly? It's not hard. One bite made me gag as I watched Dad gorge a slice of pizza down his thick neck.

We visited the Clink Prison Museum afterwards, England's oldest prison. I'd never heard of it – that was Harry's choice. He's always been interested in history, and it's the only subject in which he managed to achieve top marks in his GCSEs. The three of them enjoyed it far more than the gallery. I thought it more akin to a haunted house at a funfair.

It was while Dad was browsing around the reproduction torture devices, the metal mask and thumbscrew in particular, that it occurred to me how different he is to me. We don't look alike, we don't sound alike, and we certainly don't think alike. He was laughing with Marc. 'Don't you wish that sometimes you could get hold of some of these contraptions to use on the missus?' His maniacal laugh unnerved me the most. As if he had once been an inmate in that prison. I'd never noticed it before. He creeped me out more than the gruesome artefacts.

It was at that moment I knew.

There is more to him than he allows the world to view.

It disturbed me for many months – nineteen to be precise. Until April this year when, as part of her annual ritual, Mum asked me to help with her yearly clearing-out stocktake. She sorts all unsold items she doesn't think she has a chance of shifting in a sale, and I load them onto eBay. It marks the start of the school Easter holidays. From opening to closing, I hide in her stockroom at the back of the shop and list all the shite for auction. I scribe a short paragraph on each, price them up by researching how much similar items are selling for, before uploading them to her selling page. The following week entails packing and posting all the items that sell – which is pretty much all of them. It's tedious and boring, but the upside is I get to bank twenty per cent of the sale price.

This year, I finished by mid-afternoon on the Thursday. I must have got quicker because there was roughly the same number of items as in previous years. Mum was busy with a couple of customers who had come in to try on the new lines she had displayed on the dummies in the shop window. I didn't want to go out while they were umming and ahing about which colour best complemented their skin tone. So, I sat at her small desk, in the corner of the stockroom, nosing through her annual tax return spread out on top of a cluster of fashion magazines. I did the maths. It wasn't hard, and it didn't take long. I'm no accountant, but even I could see there was no way that shitty business of hers made that much annual profit. No way at all.

What was she up to?

I opened the drawer to the filing cabinet next to the desk and pried through the drop file marked TAX AFFAIRS to find six plastic wallets. Each one contained a tax return. Trying to be quick, before the stupid women out the front made up their fickle minds whether to purchase which stupid whatever, I scanned the contents of each file. While flicking through all the paperwork, my jaw dropped further and further as it became evident this wasn't the first year she had paid out an extortionate sum of tax for her underperforming little show.

And that wasn't all I found.

TWENTY-FIVE

Sasha eases Hannah away, her hands still grabbing her daughter's slumped shoulders. 'Calm down. What did he say?'

Hannah sobs uncontrollably. Tears cascade down her face in an unbroken stream as if they're trying to extinguish her pain. I fish in my bag for a tissue and hand her the whole packet. 'Nothing... he... gone... time.'

'You have to calm down!' Sasha says, shaking her daughter's shoulders. Her voice trembles along with her bottom lip. Her growing troubles sprouting into fear. 'What did he say to you?'

Hannah removes a tissue from the packet and blows her nose. 'He didn't say anything,' she says as she tries, but fails, to wipe her nose clean.

'Nothing at all?'

Hannah sniffs loudly. Fresh tears spring out of her eyes and onto her cheeks. 'I went to go over to him, but it was busy. The bell had rung, and everyone was leaving. He was standing by the entrance to the music block where you always meet us when you come to sch... school. But by the t-t-time I got over there, he'd disappeared.'

Sasha glances at me, confused. 'What? You didn't even speak to him?' She shakes Hannah's shoulders harder than she realises.

'Mum, he wasn't there when I got to where I saw him.'

Sasha swings around to George, who has remained silent the whole time, trying to decipher Hannah's words like the rest of us. 'Did you see him?' Sasha asks.

'I had to go and collect a book from my locker for homework, so I was about five minutes later coming out. All I saw was Hannah crying by the music block.'

'Are you sure it was him?' Sasha asks Hannah.

'Don't you believe me?'

'I'm asking if you could've been mistaken, that's all.'

'It was him, Mum.'

'Are you sure?'

'More than sure. He had that blue top on. The one we bought him for his birthday.'

Sasha wrenches her head back, and her glassy eyes stare to the sky. Her lips move as if mumbling a prayer.

We can't miss Joe's performance. He'll never forgive me, and I'll never forgive myself. 'I'm so sorry to leave you in the middle of all this, but it's Joe's school play,' I say. 'I'll call you later.'

I start the engine. 'I'm going to have to put my foot down to make it there on time in this traffic.' I say to Jim. We can't be late. We can't. Especially since Joe has got the main part. I feel a prickle of panic. Joe will be looking for us in the audience. I imagine him centre stage in his amazing technicoloured dreamcoat, standing on tiptoe, scanning the audience for his mummy and daddy. He will be flustered if he can't see us. I know all too well what it's like to land the lead role in your school play only for no one to turn up to watch. I rarely cry at anything, but the thought of putting my Joe through this is killing me.

'The fun never stops around here, does it?' Jim says, sarcastically, as I pull out onto the main road.

'Do you think it was him?'

'Sounds like it.'

'You missed the commotion about the body found in Cambridge when I went to get a drink of water.' I fill him in.

'I heard it on the radio in the studio. This is getting more complicated and more abstruse by the day. You sure you can't go to Arthur?'

'Maybe.'

'What's Marc doing outside the school if he doesn't want to be found?'

I shrug. 'If it was him.'

'She was quite specific about the blue top. Watch it!'

I slam on the brakes as red lights blaze from the back of the car in front of us.

'You're doing a lot of slamming of those brakes lately,' he says, the palm of his hand pressing against the dashboard.

'This is all we need, a damn traffic jam,' I say. I open

the window and poke my head out to try and see what's going on, but I'm none the wiser. My fingers tap on the steering wheel, forcing myself not to look at the clock. 'She only saw him from a distance. Maybe it wasn't blue. Maybe it wasn't him. Just saying.' The car in front starts moving, but slowly. I can only crawl behind it. 'Damn congestion.'

'I keep saying it. We need to move out of London.'

'Where would we go?' I ask, irritated.

'Somewhere quieter.' He points to the windscreen. 'Somewhere with less traffic.' His hand reaches across and squeezes my knee. 'Someplace where you are not constantly rushing around. The beach.'

I turn and stare at him. 'Where did that come from?'

'Let's move somewhere where we can spend the time you usually waste seething in traffic jams, taking daily walks along the beach instead.' He takes his hand off of my knee and reaches for his phone. 'Let me see where the hold-up is.' He pulls up Google maps. 'I'm serious, you know.'

'Whoa.'

'What do you mean, whoa?'

'What about my job?'

'You could get another one anywhere.'

'But our home. I love our home. I couldn't leave it.'

'We could make a new home.'

'What about our friends?'

'We can find new ones.'

What about our support network? The Mels and the Micks, and all the special people in our lives who form our backup plan, take time to find. I couldn't trust just anyone with the kids.

'Think about Joe and Isabella,' says Jim. 'Do we really want them growing up in London?' He elbows me. 'Here, turn left up the next road, it's a shortcut.'

'Yep, I know. I've got it.' I slow to make the turn before picking up speed again. 'Harry, Hannah and George are doing OK.'

'They're at private school. We could never afford the fees. At least give it some thought.'

No. No, London is my home. I've lived here for most of my life. Most people want out by the time their kids reach school age. I'm not one of them. Things bug me about it, that's for sure – the constant traffic slowing me down all the time, the stress, the pollution – but I love the anonymity of London. I can't imagine living in some small town where everyone knows what time you get up in the morning and where you do your weekly shop.

I navigate the alternative route. One of the benefits of being a copper in London is knowing all the backstreets better than I know myself. The road is empty. I look at the clock. We've got eight minutes. I break the speed limit. The thought of Joe's face if we fail to arrive on time drives me to put my foot down.

'Steady on.' Jim puts a hand on the dashboard again. 'I remember the days when it was you telling me to slow down.'

'What do you think of Luke, Harry's friend?' I ask, tapping the brake.

'You're pulling that face.'

'What face?'

'The "I think he's a wrong'un" face, like this.' He tightens and raises the corner of his lip, glaring at me.

I laugh and slap his leg.

'What's your hunch?'

'He gives me the creeps.'

'Seems like a nice lad to me. I spoke to him for a while at the party on Saturday. I was interested in his camera. Can't fault him – he was polite and took the time to show me how it works.'

'There's something about him I don't like. Probably my imagination,' I say, although I know it's not.

Luckily there's a vacant disabled parking spot in front of the school. Even so, we're last into the crowded hall. I emailed reception this morning to say we were coming, so they've reserved us a couple of chairs and a wheelchair space. Gill and Isabella are already there, waiting for us.

'Mummy, Daddy, you're late,' Isabella shouts. I cringe as eyes turn to stare and stifled giggles dishing out shame ripple around the hall.

'That was close,' Gill says removing her bag from my chair.

I fan myself with the programme. 'Tell me about it.'

As soon as we seat ourselves, the show begins. I close my eyes as they draw back the curtain, and silently pray my little boy won't forget his lines. I open them again to see the children file in one by one. Some are smiling coyly; others stride in with confidence way beyond their seven or eight years. A few, like Joe, aren't looking where they are going. He is searching for us like I knew he would. I wave and give him our sign which tells him he's got this – three sways backwards and forwards of the thumbs-up sign. There's a crash of drums, and a flash of lights as the little actors and actresses burst into song.

The play lasts less than twenty minutes, but with eyes swimming with tears the whole duration, that's a damn long time. Joe proves a little superstar on that stage. Jim leans over and whispers in my ear. 'Don't tell me seeing him up there doesn't make you think about having another.'

TWENTY-SIX

DAY 9

I get up at five and pull on shorts and a T-shirt. An early shift today means I need to get a run in first. Everyone is still asleep, so I creep downstairs and find my shoes. I check my phone. Several missed calls from Sasha last night dominate the screen. As soon as Rob phoned me when I got home from Joe's play last night, I called her. She didn't answer, so I left a message to tell her the body found in Cambridge couldn't possibly be Marc because Rob fed back that it belonged to an Asian man. Several stab wounds covered the victim's remaining torso, and both feet and hands were discovered within the immediate vicinity – minus both index fingers. I didn't mention where they were found.

I tie my laces and head out onto the streets. It's my favourite part of the day to go running. When the temperature is not too hot, and London hasn't quite got going. Time is not on my side, so I opt for my Tooting Common three-miler, choosing en route to head back via Balham to add an extra stretch.

After a quick shower, I kiss everyone goodbye and drag myself away from Isabella who is determined not to ease her grip from my thigh today. When I get into the car, I phone Sasha. She doesn't answer, so I leave her a message to call me. The roads are rammed when I hit Balham High Road, and I sit in a hold-up for ten minutes before the traffic reports announce an incident near Clapham South Station. I slam my fist on the steering wheel. I'm going to be late again. Debating the next best route, I pull a U-turn and spend the next twenty minutes worming my way through the backstreets to join the road through the Common. I sprint into work, half an hour late, breathing a sigh of relief when I remember that Arthur is away on some training course. Sasha returns my call before I've even managed to grab a coffee.

'It wasn't him.' The relief in her voice is immense.

'No, it wasn't.'

'I mean in Cambridge. I went there last night, remember? The man who booked into that lady's B&B. It wasn't Marc. She showed me the CCTV.'

'Sorry, I thought you meant the body found yesterday. Are you sure?'

'One hundred per cent.'

'Perhaps Hannah did see him yesterday?'

'She's been distraught ever since. I'm keeping her off school today.'

'Probably not a bad idea. You've all been through a lot.'

'What now?'

'I don't know, Sasha.'

'The police must be able to do something.'

My heart goes out to her. The emotional attachment makes this such a difficult situation. Arthur's words ring in my head once more. "Don't get involved in their story." I tell her again that the police won't do anything at this point.

'Even if I call them myself?'

'I can't stop you, but I don't want to give you false hope. I'm off on annual leave from tomorrow. It'll give me time to think about things.'

When Rob arrives, I tell him not to sit down, we're going out for coffee. We head out to a cafe up on the High Street. One which always seems to smell of burnt toast but is far fancier than the greasy spoons he likes to frequent. It's not a particularly relaxing place. The sound of clinking cutlery, plate scraping and clanking from the kitchen is over-stimulating, but the aroma from the coffee machines draws a crowd. We take the only spare table by the window, and order coffees from the young waitress whose body language suggests she would rather be somewhere else.

Rob tells me about a witness in the Shane Baker case and a possible connection to Jason Harper while we wait for our drinks to arrive. When the waitress plonks them on the table, slopping coffee into the saucers, Rob rips open three sachets of sugar and asks, 'Why are we really here?'

I open up about Marc. And not before time. If I were

him, I would have been asking a lot more questions as to why I was being asked to sit outside someone's house and wait for him on more than one occasion.

'No chance. Arthur will never spare scarce resources to chase after someone who has explicitly stated they don't want to be found.'

'I know. That's what I keep telling Sasha, but I wanted to pass it by you in case you can think of anything.'

'What's your gut feeling?'

'There's too much weird stuff going on. I mean the computer being wiped, the whiteboard in his office too, the depression, the meeting with the lawyer, Hannah – the daughter – seeing him outside school yesterday.' I mention the drugs but keep the driving ban to myself. Certain things, I've learned, are best kept to yourself. Especially actions you've taken that constitute a sackable offence if you were ever found out.

'Nothing solid to go on, though.'

'Right.'

'Have you looked him up on the PNC?'

'What do you take me for?' I say calmly, despite the wave of shame rising to redden my cheeks. 'We'd better get back.' I grab the bill. 'I'll get these. And don't forget I'm off early today and on annual leave for a week.'

'Such a slacker,' he says, dodging the slap on his arm I send his way. He grabs my elbow and looks seriously into my eyes. 'Do you want me to do some digging?'

'No, you're alright. Thanks, though, Rob.'

The ever-increasing admin that loads into my inbox on an hourly basis eats the rest of my morning. I pick up the

Jason Harper file but get nowhere. Mr and Mrs Shirley are proving tricky to get hold of by phone. I leave them another message to call me. At two-thirty I ring Jim to make sure Mick has arrived to pick him up and take him to the gym, then mouth to Rob, who's on the phone, that I'm leaving now. He puts his palm over the mouthpiece and mutters something about keeping part-time hours before reverting to his call, stealing my opportunity to retaliate.

Art's gym is far from what I expected. It's more of a body-builders' haunt than your average place for people wanting to keep fit. For the time of day, it's busy. Mostly men crowding nearly every workout station, but a few women are also going for the burn. Where do all these people work that allows them a mid-afternoon workout session? High-energy songs I could never name pump through the floor as vibrations radiate through my body. Industrialised fans are positioned in all four corners of the windowless, warehouse-like structure, providing a continuous flow of warm air, but it still smells of vinyl and BO. Art could do with investing in some air condi-tioning.

I spot Jim at a rack of dumbbells where Art is demon-strating how to properly perform a bicep curl. I weave over to them, through the grunts and groans of what appears to be a circuits class. Art has his hands on Jim's shoulders, easing them back to straighten his spine. 'He's done here,' Art says. He lifts the dumbbell from Jim's grip and slots it in its space amongst the rows of metal.

I swing the car keys around my finger. 'You've been working out too?' I ask Jim.

'No, just the massage. Art was showing me a couple of techniques while I was waiting for you. I'm ready to go.'

Art chats with Jim while I peer around the place. Men dressed in shorts and sleeveless T-shirts, and women in Lycra pants and bra tops, are flexing and lifting and pumping and pressing. A trio of men occupy the far corner, taking it in turns to pound a heavy punchbag which is barely swinging despite the force of their strikes. 'He's all yours, Eva,' Art says after a couple of minutes. He firmly pats Jim's shoulder as he looks towards the entrance. 'See you Saturday as planned.'

I follow Art's gaze to see a spaghetti-thin man with a mass of dark curls entering the building. I can't help but stare at him. Dressed in jeans and a canvas jacket, he clearly doesn't fit amongst the tribe of lifters working out here. He and Art exchange nods before Art swiftly bids Jim and me goodbye. The man approaches the reception desk. A modular unit with a till and various tubs of supplements for sale. He leans against it, drumming his fingers on the surface. He has that cold, dead look; "nobody's home" eyes. My skin turns cold despite the heat of a summer's day in a stuffy gym.

I hear Art mutter to him, 'Be with you soon.'

'What's wrong?' Jim asks, when we get in the car.

I put the keys in the ignition and start the engine, but the detective in me drives me to go back inside. 'I need the loo. I don't think I'll make it home. I won't be long.'

I walk over to the reception area. Behind it stands a

cooler unit packed with bottles of Evian, sports drinks and flavoured electrolyte water. And next to that, commercial shelving filled with more tubs of power shakes and jars of capsules claiming this and that to dramatically improve performance. I scan the building. Art and the skinny man are nowhere to be seen.

A red-faced woman with sweaty hair scraped back in a ponytail is walking towards me. Beads of sweat glisten on her temple. She wipes her forehead with a towelling wristband.

'Excuse me,' I say. 'Could you tell me where the toilets are?'

She lifts an arm, winces and laughs about having overdone things today, then points towards the back of the building. I thank her and wander over, fully alert.

The toilets are situated next to a storeroom with its door ajar. I burst in, startling them both. Art is kneeling at a large open safe located in a cupboard to the rear of the room.

'Sorry, I thought this was the ladies,' I say, pretending not to acknowledge the wad of cash Art is handing over to the skinny man who is holding out a package of something. I spin around, dazed, and steam back outside.

'What's wrong, darling?' Jim asks when I return to the car. 'You look troubled.'

'Art is not the squeaky clean neighbour Sasha believes him to be.'

TWENTY-SEVEN

LUKE

Alisha Davies. A common surname for such a unique lady. She is smart, that one. Way smarter than any woman I've ever met, and not only in the head. Every aspect of her radiates sophistication. The chic way she dresses, the eloquent way she talks, and even the way she walks – briskly, with her head held high – as if she belongs on the cover of one of those voguish magazines lying around her stylish house. Everything so immaculate, spotless.

What is she doing with that loser of a husband, then? The man with the charisma of an out-of-date ham sandwich. She's not stupid. She's a lawyer for heaven's sake. She must know he has been shagging one of the neighbours for the past year. It could be even longer. I first caught Penelope Price and Thomas Davies at it twelve months ago during Harry's seventeenth birthday party. I didn't actually catch them in the act, per se. No, it was the video clips I was browsing through a few days later that aroused my attention. So much so, I found myself rewatching certain bits several times over. Pen the dog groomer and Tom the graphic designer, however did those two get it together? What amused me the most was how they tried to pretend nothing was going on. But the frequent glances in each other's direction and Penelope's childish giggles failed to slip *my* attention. I have a lot to thank those two for. They were the start – the start of my lucrative future. They planted the idea in my mind.

I nearly gave up gathering evidence on the two of them. The opportunity rarely arose, and when it did, something always seemed to get in the way. Most annoying. But one thing my dad taught me from an early age is never to quit. "Quitting is for the weak, boy. If you want something bad enough, you'll succeed in the end as long as you hang on in there."

I suppose he's been good for something.

I felt like someone was looking down on me from heaven when Alisha popped around here Monday last week and asked if I would be interested in shooting an introductory video for her new website. 'Hell, yes,' I wanted to shout, but suppressed my eagerness with a polite, 'What did you have in mind?'

'I've prepared the script. I need someone with decent videoing skills.' She gave a slight flip of her head. Her silky hair, as lustrous as onyx stone, swished away from her face. 'You've come highly recommended.'

'Whom by?'

'The neighbours.'

'I'm sure I could manage this. I'm free to come over tonight.'

'Would it better to wait until your exams are finished?'

No!

'Not at all. It won't take me long. Around seven?'

So, when I was at her house that evening, shooting that video for her, I was orchestrating a way of gaining access to her bedroom. When the chance arose, I thought to myself, it's now or never, Lukie-boy, take it. Chances are for taking, are they not? Her phone rang at the opportune moment. 'I need to take this,' she said.

'May I use your toilet, please?'

Little did she realise how easy she made my life when she said, 'There's a problem with the downstairs toilet. You'll have to nip upstairs.'

Thank you, Alisha. Thank you very much.

I took her stairs two at a time to gain as much advantage as possible. Although a replica in build, her house felt so different from ours. Its luxurious ambience ran from bottom to top like the cream, deep-pile carpet. At the top of the stairs, I didn't turn right to the family bathroom she said I could use. No, I had other ideas. Living in a house with exactly the same layout, I knew precisely where I was going. I marched towards the master bedroom. From the loft room at the top of my house, I can see into that room. Penelope Price should be more careful and stay away from the window. I've seen her in there on several occasions; most Wednesday afternoons to be exact. You'd think they'd be more discreet, she and her lover. I mean, come on, having an affair is one thing, but they could surely show a little decency and not be conducting it in either of the marital homes.

There are such lowlifes in this world.

I nipped in there as nimbly as a sleuth and removed my little piece of magic from the pocket of my jeans, scanning the room for the perfect spot. First, I positioned the tiny camera on her dressing table in amongst her umpteen pots and tubes of cream and gels, all claiming a more youthful complexion. Then I thought better of it. Too risky, the bookcase would prove a far safer option and a more impressive camera angle. So I concealed it amongst their collection of designer never-to-be-read hardbacks. Slipping my phone out of my back pocket, I checked the camera was paired correctly, waving my hand in front of the spy hole. Abracadabra, there it was; the magic performing its trick to perfection. I couldn't wait to view the footage on this one.

No time to waste, I legged it back downstairs to pick up where I'd left off.

'How long before you can transfer the video for my website?' Alisha asked when I'd finished.

'I'll have to go home and edit it. Then I'll come back and load it onto your website for you.'

'Oh, no need. I can get my website designer to do that.'

Think, Luke, think. 'Probably best I do it myself. Sometimes there are issues with buffering. How about I come back on Friday and get it all sorted for you. I can have it done in no time.'

'Can't you do it remotely if I give you the passwords?'

Think, Luke, again. Think.

'Doesn't always stream right, and it's never wise to share passwords. Best I upload it straight onto your computer. Do you have a Mac?' I knew she did. I'd seen it in her study opposite the front door.

She nodded.

'Perfect. Always easier.'

She bought it, thank God.

I couldn't wait for Wednesday to come around. At two-thirty, which was the usual time for Tom and Pen's rendezvous to begin, I clicked the app. The pair of cheaters disgusted me so much, I had to decrease the volume and turn away when they got to it. But there was no need to watch it all. It was sufficient to know that I had enough for my plans to come to fruition.

On Friday I returned, only to be challenged yet again when asking to use the toilet. Alisha said, 'Plumber's been, you can use the downstairs one now.'

Think. Think.

But I couldn't this time. There was no way I could get away with nipping upstairs to collect my belongings. I would never be able to get back down in time. But I am never one to give in so easily. So, when I was in the toilet, I banged my head against the mirror. One, two, three. *Bang. Bang. Bang.*

I returned to her study with a plan. I'd have to come over another time. I sat at her glass desk which ran the length of the room, clicking away on the keyboard of her Mac, faking irritation with each click of the keys.

'Something wrong?' she asked from the sofa where she was tapping away on her laptop.

'There's a problem with the beginning of the video. I'm sorry, it seems to have corrupted. We're going to have to reshoot.'

She tutted. 'Really?'

'Won't take us long. We know what we're doing now. Twenty minutes, half an hour tops.'

She sighed in irritation. 'Let me go and get changed and sort my makeup.'

Ten minutes later we had recommenced filming when the doorbell rang. Alisha rushed to answer it, returning with Sasha and her friend.

They started yakking away, asking me questions I didn't particularly want to answer. Boring questions about where I was going to uni and what I was studying. I kept my cool, though, and, when I was finished, I left them to it and went back to Alisha's study to work on the upload. And that's when I took my chance. While they were rambling on in the kitchen, I darted upstairs to the bedroom, whipped my button camera from the bookcase and slipped it in my pocket.

Job done.

I can just hear my dad's voice. "See, if you hang tight, you get there in the end."

TWENTY-EIGHT

'Steady on,' Jim says as I screech out of Art's gym car park. 'What's happened?'

I open the car window, trying to dispel the nausea burning my throat. Of all the sights I've witnessed in my career to date, why has what I've just seen affected me so much? Hell, I've been subjected to far worse. I cast my mind back to my first year in the force, when I attended a stabbing on the Lindley Estate in Peckham. Boy, that was a rough one. It was the first time I witnessed death firsthand. A man had stabbed his wife in both eyes. One eye was hanging out and the knife remained embedded in the other like something from a Halloween movie. The wife's brother had turned up before we arrived and pummelled his brother-in-law who died at the scene. The image of the hanging eye tormented me for days after.

That man in Art's gym reminded me of the wife's brother. Was that it? No. He reminded me of my brother, Ben: the slight frame, the mass of curls, the lost-soul look.

That's it. He didn't even flinch when I barged into that storeroom. He turned to me. But here's the thing. He didn't look at me. Rather he stared right through me as if I weren't there. He didn't appear to be a user, though – no bloodshot eyes or dilated pupils.

'I think Art's dealing drugs.'

'Drugs? But he's a fitness freak.'

'What've I told you before? Don't judge a book by its cover.' I relay what I've observed.

'You sure they were drugs?'

'Pretty sure.'

'Not one hundred per cent sure?'

'I know what I saw.'

'Why didn't you arrest him?'

'I need to think about this.'

'What's there to think about if he's guilty? Shouldn't you arrest him?'

Jim. You're always so black and white.

Thoughts of Art's reported involvement with Marc over the past few weeks are unnerving me.

Jim nudges me. 'Eva?'

'What?'

'Shouldn't you arrest or report him?'

I sigh. 'Probably.'

Gill is ready to dish up dinner when we get home. The table is set, and Joe and Isabella are belly laughing at the jokes they are instructing Alexa to tell via the Echo Dot. Jim uncorks a bottle of white wine, laughing with them. I fix the kids a glass of apple juice, and the five of us sit down to a helping of shepherd's pie. Watching Gill dishing out spoonfuls of her homemade delight makes me realise how much I love it when she is around. It strikes me that there's something about five of us around the table. Usually, Joe's place is beside me, and Isabella next to Jim, but while Gill is here, she sits with Jim, and the kids sit with me on the bench. I find comfort in their bodies squashed up close to me.

Jim goes for a lie down afterwards, and Gill offers to put the kids to bed.

'I have some work to catch up on,' I say. 'Why don't I do that, and then we can finish that bottle of wine from dinner?'

'You're meant to be on holiday,' she says.

'I know, but I left early to pick Jim up from Art's, and there's a few things I need to finish. I only need half an hour.'

Joe and Isabella kiss me goodnight, and I go to the lounge. I log on to my laptop and deal with a document Arthur has been chasing me for. It can't wait until I'm back at the station next week. My inbox is chocka, despite me having spent most of the day at my desk. Damn admin! I answer a few important emails and type an out-of-office message.

Next, I pull up the website for Art's gym. Its homepage heavily focuses on promoting nutritional supplies for bodybuilders – whey powder, energy bars, protein shakes. I browse through the gallery showcasing the onsite equipment captioned with glowing testimonials. There's a short introductory video. It's only three minutes long. I press play and watch Art speak about everything his gym has to offer. I play it again but find nothing untoward. Clicking on the Facebook icon, I wait to be redirected. It's an active page with lots of engagement. Three thousand followers with several regularly sharing their workout achievements and posting pictures of their bulging muscles. I scroll through them, knowing what I want to find, but unsure if I will.

Gill interrupts my thoughts. 'The kids are both asleep.' She walks over to the coffee table and shuffles some blocks of Lego into a plastic tub. 'Wine in here or the kitchen?'

I drag myself away from the screen. 'Let's have it in here.'

She plumps the sofa cushions before going to fetch the wine, and I go and check on Jim. He is laying on the bed, snoring. A cool breeze, refreshing in the evening heat, blows through the open window. I grab the chenille throw from the end of the bed and cover him.

I feel the need to go and check on the kids. Isabella is lightly snoring, her body shrouded in her princess-design duvet. The glow-in-the-dark stars I decorated her ceiling with last Christmas twinkle in the darkness. Kissing her forehead, I whisper how much I love her.

Tip-toeing next door to Joe's room, I repeat my actions. The planet stickers I stuck up for him transform his ceiling into outer space. His pyjama bottoms stop mid-calf, I notice. He has grown so much this year. I make a mental note to order him the next size up. Perhaps he even needs to skip a size? Sliding down the side of his bed, I rest my head beside his sleeping body, inhaling the familiar smell of apple shampoo and thinking how swiftly the years are slipping by. Before I know it, we'll be buying uniform for secondary school. I draw my legs up to my chest, surprised by how much this saddens me. I sit like that for a while, thoughts of secondary school uniform, homework planners and exams loading my heart with heaviness.

On the way back to the lounge, I text Sasha to ask her how they all are. I've quit asking if there's any news. I'm sure I'll be one of the first to know when there is.

Gill is waiting in the lounge. She hands me a glass of wine. 'I'm not going to last long after this. Those kids have run me ragged today. They insisted on a game of hide-and-seek before I read them a story.'

I laugh. 'You're too soft.'

'I'll be asleep before my head hits the pillow.' We chat about work and she tells me a funny story about the kids at the park earlier today.

My phone beeps. It's Sasha answering my text.

Not good here. Harry and Hannah have both lost it. I think I'm about to as well! X

I place my untouched wine glass on the table.

'I'm going to pop into town tomorrow. Would you like to come? I'm meeting Derek for lunch, but you could join us.'

'Not for me to disturb a romantic engagement!' I pick up a packet of gummy bears squidged down the side of the sofa. There's one left. I squish it between my fingers before popping it into my mouth.

She shakes her head. 'How many times have I told you. There's nothing going on between Derek and I.'

'I know,' I tease. 'And there will never be another Michael.' Widowed at an early age, she has always sworn that no one will ever come close to replacing the love of her life, however hard they try.

'And on that note, I think I'll retire for the night,' she says.

'I think I'll go over to Sasha's. Jim's out for the count. Could you listen out for the kids, please?'

The roads are clear, and I arrive at Napier Close in no time. Sasha is standing at the door when I get out of the car, raising a waving hand to acknowledge my arrival. Shoes and trainers clutter the usually tidy porch. She kicks them out of the way.

She appears to have shrunk since this nightmare of hers began; the overwhelming weight of her burden drags her shoulders down. Circles have darkened the skin beneath her eyes. Stress attacking her in every form. 'Thanks for coming over. You didn't need to, but I'm glad you did,' she says in a flat voice that doesn't sound one bit like the bubbly Sasha I know.

I step inside and follow the waft of red wine down the hallway to the kitchen. Is it my imagination, or is she staggering? As we pass the lounge, Sasha calls out to the twins, who are sprawled on the sofa, glued to their phones, 'Carry on without me, kids.'

'No, Mum, you've got to see the ending,' Hannah cries out.

'You can update me later.' Sasha turns to me and whispers, 'I wasn't watching it anyway.'

In the kitchen, a strong waft of leftover Chinese food hits me. Discarded foil cartons litter the breakfast bar along with used cups and glasses. Dirty plates and cutlery fill the sink. Such a contrast to the organised Sasha from before this saga began, but she seems oblivious to the state the place is in.

'Can I get you a drink?' she asks. She pulls her shoulder blades together, sighing, as she reaches her hands to rub her lower back. Her face scrunches up.

'You sit down. I'll make it,' I say, collecting the dirty crockery. 'Where's Harry?'

'Over at Luke's. Art was here when he and Hannah lost it. I think Art took pity on me, so he took Harry back with him. I don't want tea. I'm going to continue with the wine. Fancy joining me?'

'I'd better not. I had a glass at dinner. I'll have some tea.'

'Do you want some birthday cake?' she says, pointing to the remains of my effort for Harry on the counter. 'The kids said it was delicious.'

'What did the kids lose it about?'

'Harry started it. He said Hannah had imagined seeing Marc. Then it all kicked off. You should have seen them. They ended up fighting.' She drops her head in her hands, shakes it, then looks back at me with her fists supporting her chin. 'Harry slapped her, and she punched him in the face. No word of a lie, I think he's on for a shiner.'

'What was Art doing here?'

She fetches a glass and fills it with the remains of a bottle of Chianti from the table. 'He popped over to tell me about a new client he's sending my way. And to check on me, I suppose. I don't know what I'd do without him. He's been such a good friend this past week, and he's responsible for half of my client base.'

'From his gym?'

She nods. 'They do things they shouldn't.'

'What do you mean?' I ask, sharply.

'They can't see that they're wrecking their bodies. He should stick to the more structured personal training he does from his studio, but the place earns him too much.'

'I went there today to pick Jim up from his massage.'

'Understand what I mean?'

I pull a chair out from under the table. 'I need to talk to you about Art.'

'Nothing sinister, I hope.'

'This is between you and me.'

She frowns. 'Go on. Hit me with it. Things can't possibly get any worse, can they?' She takes a gulp of wine. Drops dribble down the side of her mouth. 'Blast! How did I miss?' She wipes them away with the palm of her hand.

'How much do you know about what goes on in Art's gym?'

'In terms of what?'

I don't hold back. 'I think he's dealing drugs from there.'

She lets out a shrill cackle. 'Not Art. He's a fittie. He wouldn't touch the…'

The slam of the front door interrupts her, and Harry

wanders in with Art behind him. 'I'm sorry, Mum,' Harry says and bends over to hug Sasha.

'It's not me you should be apologising to. Your sister's in the lounge.'

'I know, I know. I'll go and apologise to her too.'

He starts to walk away, but she grabs his hand. 'Things will be OK,' she says in a tone suggesting she only half-believes it herself.

When Harry's gone, Sasha gets up and pulls another bottle from the wine rack wedged between the fridge and a cupboard. She pours herself another glass as Art comments to me on his session earlier today with Jim, as if what I witnessed afterwards never happened. 'How's Jim after his massage?' he asks.

'He fell asleep straight after dinner.'

Sasha bursts out laughing. She raises her glass, slurring her words. 'Hey, Art, guess what? Eva thinks you're a drug dealer.'

I stare at her, incredulous at her out-of-character outburst. What's got into her? Too much red wine, that's what. I need to have a strict word with her in the morning.

Giggling, she takes another sip and coughs and splutters. Red wine spurts across the table.

'Steady on, Sash,' Art says. He slaps her on the back to quell her coughs.

'Sorry, Eva,' she says. 'I shouldn't have said that.' She starts cackling like a hen that's just laid its second egg of the day. I grit my teeth. No, you shouldn't have Sasha. I want to tell her not to drink anymore. I need to end this conversation now. The mood she is in, she will blurt out what I discovered on the PNC.

Art turns to me. 'Are you talking about this afternoon?' he asks.

I bite my lip, unsure how to handle Sasha's unexpected display of disloyalty. This wasn't meant to happen.

He bellows with laughter. 'You thought JJ was passing drugs to me?'

I bite my words to let him finish, knowing for sure whatever he's going to come out with next is going to be a lie.

'You couldn't be further from the truth. JJ is a rep. He's trying to get me to stock a protein powder new to the market.' He continues laughing. 'The size of him, you think he'd try taking some himself!'

TWENTY-NINE

DAY 10

'Mummy. Mummy,' Joe cries out as he launches himself on top of me.

I sit bolt upright, disorientated. I slept fitfully, a night of twisting and turning as I tried to make sense of Art. Not to mention the added burden of Sasha blurting out things she shouldn't have. My bucket of worry is starting to overflow. When I finally managed to drop off, Gossiping Gloria from the office admin team kept appearing in my dreams wagging a finger in my face, telling me what a naughty girl I have been. I must have a word with Sasha today.

'You're late, Mummy.'

Dressed in his school uniform, Joe already has his shoes on. 'You said you'd take us today. It's time to go. But don't worry, Gill said to let you have a lie-in, and she'll take us.'

'Absolutely not,' I say, leaping out of bed and throwing

on the jeans I left on the floor last night. Or should I say this morning? It was gone midnight by the time I'd finished listening to a drunk Sasha apologise for the hundredth time.

'Get Isabella and your bags by the door, and I'll be there in one minute.' He jumps up and down, his cute little face a ball of excitement as he turns and bounces out of the room yelling his sister's name. 'Make sure you are ready to go,' I shout out after him.

'Not like you to oversleep,' Jim says.

'I can't believe it!' I pull on a T-shirt and dash into the bathroom to give my teeth a quick brush.

'What happened to you last night?' he calls out.

'Sasha's. She was in a right old state,' I sputter through a mouthful of toothpaste. 'Too much red wine got the better of her.' I brief him on the night's events before he once again questions my involvement, frowning with disapproval.

Gill has left for town when I get back from dropping the kids at school, and Jim is in his study working. I filter some coffee and take him a mug. 'We really should've arranged to go away while you're off,' he says, stretching his arms. 'A couple of nights break would've done us good.'

'Then I wouldn't have got anything done here.'

'Are we going to book something for the kids' summer holiday?'

'Let's do that today. I'm going to make a list of everything that needs doing around the house and all the admin still outstanding. And I must sort those weeds out the front. And mow that damn lawn.'

I take my coffee to my desk and grab a piece of paper from the printer. The events of last night have stolen my concentration, and I find myself doodling faces around the perimeter of the blank sheet. I know Art was lying. It was the way his eyes blinked a little too fast.

My phone beeps with a text from Sasha, apologising profusely for last night.

I reply straight away:

Forget it. You're under a lot a pressure. X

She replies:

You're wrong about Art, you know. I've known him for years. He's not the type. He's too into his fitness. I'll see you after school. X

When I first started working for Arthur, he told me I had been pointed out as one to watch. 'You've got that little bit extra,' he said. 'True detective's intuition and an eye for the truth.' I'm not wrong, Sasha.

I finish my coffee and, opening the desk drawer, gather all the scraps of paper that have been mounting up since New Year. I note every job that needs doing around the house: sort out the cupboard under the stairs so that every time we open the door, half the contents don't spill out; weed, front and back; descale the showerhead; sew some buttons on clothes so they can be worn again; put a new bulb in the security light out the back. The list continues with all the admin and paying outstanding bills. I cringe at the things that shouldn't have made it to the list in the first place: arrange a smear test; book dental appointments.

Feeling unusually flat, I tackle a few quick wins, before heading upstairs to start on Joe's room. It's a complete mess without Mel's daily dose of efficiency. Gill is brilliant, a real diamond, but she's not Mel in the tidying department. I kneel and start clearing toys off the floor into the wicker baskets I bought at New Year in an effort to keep more on top of things. As I'm sweeping a pile of Lego into a box, I swear when I see the state of the radiator that Joe climbed on top of a couple of months ago when, in his childhood innocence, he thought there was nothing wrong with using it as a step to get a better view of the garden. His weight snapped the bracket and dislodged the radiator from the wall. I did a bodge job on it at the time with some cable ties as my mind had been preoccupied with a trial I was helping Arthur prepare for court, but when I crawl over to it, I find one of them has snapped. 'Damn.' It needs fixing before it gets any worse. While there, I notice a wet patch on the carpet. It's not coming from the radiator. I look up to the ceiling and see a brown stain. The paint has started to bubble. A leak. I bet that's from the roof tile I found on the patio a few weeks ago. I knew I should have sorted it out before.

Standing up, I lean against the window ledge and peer into the garden, which is still in serious need of my undivided attention. Gill hasn't managed to get out there. We really should get a gardener. A small tree that lost several branches in the April gales needs sorting too, I notice from up here, and the kids' old trampoline that I dismantled a couple of summers ago, in favour of a newer model, lies stacked by the fence waiting to be taken to the tip.

I stare at the new trampoline and think of Marc. He came over to help me assemble it. I managed to get the frame up, but when it came to attaching the springs, I wasn't strong enough. Jim had already called him because he knew I wouldn't be able to do that part myself. His "We'll get this done in no time," attitude and repertoire of humorous jokes turned it into an enjoyable afternoon. Probably helped by the six-pack he had arrived with, tucked under his arm. He only drank one can because he was driving later that day, ferrying the kids to their Saturday evening jollies. He brought a tool bag with him, too. 'These trampolines can be dangerous in the wind. I saw a video clip of one blow across a garden.' He removed a box from the bag, rattling the contents. 'These U-pegs will make sure it doesn't happen to you.'

When we finished, he pulled the tab on another can of beer, handed it to me and told me to relax on the sun lounger. He joined the kids on the trampoline for over an hour while I snoozed to the sound of uncontrollable giggles and shrills of overexcited kids with a new toy.

He's such a good person.

I look around the garden, a sense of foreboding hanging around me like a cloak I can't take off.

Where have you gone, Marc?

Never one to feel sorry for myself, my despondent mood unsettles me. Perhaps Jim is right. Maybe it is time for a change.

. . .

The kids are so happy when they spot me waiting at the school gates. They scuttle over, flinging themselves at me. As I lift them up for hugs, they raise my mood. 'Ice creams?' Joe asks, and I laugh as I tell him I'm sure Hannah will make them one of her dinner-skipping super specials.

When we get into the car, I search for the times table app I downloaded onto my phone a few weeks ago. Gossiping Gloria from work recommended it as her son had struggled with maths until she discovered this gem. It's a compilation of times tables sung to pop stars' songs, which is a hit with my two. I turn the volume up loud, and we roll off the nine times table at the top of our voices all the way to Sasha's place.

When we arrive, the kids are out of the car and darting over to Hannah before I've even switched the engine off. I open my window and call out to Hannah. 'I'll stay in here until your mum's finished.' She nods and welcomes the children in.

The phone has rung three times since we got into the car, and I want to listen to my voicemail. I'm hoping it's the plumber who I called earlier about Joe's radiator. As I press voicemail, a woman's cry grabs my attention. I look up and around to see Pen standing at Pen's Parlour door, crying after a white-faced Tom storming away.

THIRTY

LUKE

I spent all morning in two minds as to who to go to first. Tom, then Penelope? Or Penelope, then Tom? Or perhaps I was better off targeting only one of them. Decisions, decisions. All the way to today's exam, I pondered my options. Sasha offered us a lift, and Harry sat in the front banging on about failing today's exam, too.

I'm many things. I know that, but aggressive is not in the collection. However, the desire to smack him around the head, tell him to man up and stop bloody moaning overcame me. He was really starting to scratch at my nerves.

The exam went as expected. Easy-peasy. I didn't bother waiting around for Harry afterwards. I'd had enough of his ear-bending on the way here. I couldn't hack another ton of his bleating all the way home, too. I called in at Domino's on the way home and picked up a large hot and spicy stuffed crust, along with a double helping of potato wedges.

It came down to money in the end. Most things do, don't they? Not who, out of the two of them, would have the most, but which of them would I be able to extract the most from. As I chucked the last potato wedge into the air and caught it in my mouth, I decided it had to be her. I washed the grease from my hands and went upstairs to study the video clip one more time. Perfect. Just perfect.

I waited until three-thirty – fifteen minutes before the usual time for her to slip out for her weekly sinful visit to her neighbour – grabbed my phone and wandered over to Pen's Parlour. Pressing her buzzer, I had to stop myself from laughing. It was time to be serious, after all. I knew about the *Lassie* theme tune that amuses her visitors, but I'd not yet heard it in person.

Pulling open the door, the surprised look on her face said I was not who she was expecting.

Of course not.

'Time for a chat, Penelope,' I said, barging past her. She smelled like she'd just stepped out of a bath of cheap perfume. Her surprised look morphed into one of confusion. I leaned against the reception desk and pinged the pink service bell several times for no other reason than to confuse her further.

She flicked her hands over the top of her high hairdo. 'What do you want, Luke? Why're you here?'

I laughed at her standing there in her pink outfit. I couldn't help myself. She looked like an enormous stick of seaside rock. 'Luke?' Her hands dug into her hips as her chin jutted out. Her voice rose. Did I detect a hint of fear? 'Get out of here.' Her dog, a pug with a pink bow clipped to its collar, waddled over from its bed by the door and rested at her feet.

Slowly, while staring at her with contempt, I propped my phone up against a box of tissues on her desk. 'I've got something to show you, Penelope.'

The frown lines on her face deepened as she glanced from me to the phone several times. I stood still for a minute so I could draw out our meeting that little bit longer. I was having fun, so why not? She gritted her teeth. 'What is it?'

I raised my eyebrows up and down.

She folded her arms across her chest and let out a big sigh. 'I don't have the time for games.' She nodded towards the door. 'Please leave.'

She's a few spuds short of a roast dinner, this one. Has she not worked it out yet? I pressed play. Colour drained from her painted face as she stepped forward, squinting, and her bottom lip started moving. Small quivers turned to tremors, as I turned the volume up as loud as it would go.

'Dear Lord.' Her hand flew to cover her mouth as she mumbled more words I couldn't make out.

'Take your hand away from your mouth, so I can properly understand what you've got to say for yourself. There's a good girl,' I said like a headmaster to a child. Was I having fun or what? 'What do you think Pete and Alisha will have to say to all this?'

She stood there in defiance. Or was it denial? One of

the two. I picked up the phone and held it closer to her so she could get a better look. Wouldn't want her to miss anything.

'What do you want, Luke?' she asked, her breathing laboured.

I dug out the scrap of paper I'd prepared earlier and handed it over to her. 'Ten thousand pounds into this account by nine o'clock or this little montage goes to your husband and your lover's wife.' I nodded at the screen. 'And all the loyal dog owners who use your services.' I gave her the biggest smile my lips would form. 'Have a nice day, Penelope,' I finished, before strolling towards the door.

She hurled herself after me, screaming high-pitched like something out of the wild. 'You won't get away with it!'

'Won't I?' I waved the phone at her. 'Oh, and if you try any funny games, this will upload to all the contacts on your phone as well.' It wouldn't, but she'd not know that.

She held her hands together, the tips of her fingers touching her lips as her tacky façade began to crumble. 'Please, Luke.'

'It'll be fine. Calm down. Transfer the funds, and I'll delete this.' Oh, the satisfaction in using a derogatory tone. It wasn't as much fun as when I faced Robbins and Chelsea, but I was still enjoying myself. Immensely.

'How do I know you will?'

I scrunched my features into my hurtful face and traced a fake tear from my eye to my jaw. 'Oh, Penelope. Come on. Honestly, do I look like the kind of guy to play silly games? I've been pretty straightforward and fair with you, don't you think? I mean, I've given you every chance to stop me exposing your grubby little secret to all your friends and family, have I not?' I swung out my arm and swept it around the room. 'Not to mention all your clients.' I opened the door and stepped outside. 'Nine o'clock, don't forget. And that's nine o'clock tonight, to be clear,' I said, waving. 'Cheerio, for now.'

'You'll pay for this, Luke Walker. You won't get away with it.'

I stifled my laughter all the way to the road. It was only fifty metres or so, but it felt like heaps longer. When I was out of view, I let it out – a hearty roar of satisfaction which jiggled my shoulders the entire walk to the Tube.

The second part of my plan for the day was yet to be executed so, once in the station, I regained control. Luckily, a train pulled in straight away. I positioned myself at the end of the carriage where the door met that of the adjoining one. Steadying myself with the handrail, I closed my eyes and ran through the next stage. This one was going to be trickier. But being such a tenacious individual, I'm a firm believer that nothing is insurmountable.

The journey was straightforward – only twelve stops and zero changes. I skipped off at Goodge Street, my head swimming with the spiel I was about to drown Pete Price with. His firm dominates the top two floors of a building above an ostentatious retail outlet for the older man. The kind of place where Pete kits himself out with handmade suits and expensive shirts. I'd done my homework. The exclusive global brokerage firm he now works for specialises in over-the-counter derivatives in the commodities market. So, he's still a trader at the end of the day. Like Mr Patel, who owns the small, indie supermarket on Balham Hill. Both of them selling coffee or electricity, but on differing scales.

I wanted to keep things simple. There was no benefit whatsoever in causing any commotion. Not at this stage. So, in accordance with my intricate plans, as soon as I was sitting in the café opposite his work, and had ordered an Americano, I called him.

'What can I do for you, Luke?' he asked before giving me the chance to say hello. 'Looking for a job now you've finished school? I knew you'd come around in the end.'

Such arrogance. So unattractive. 'Kind of. Well, it's more like payment than a job. I'm in Café Bacoli now, opposite your work. I need to speak to you as a matter of urgency. Get here, now.'

I felt and heard him shuffle uncomfortably in his seat. Now that was fun. He tried to argue with me. The man tried to argue with *me*. Who did he think he was? Actually, it was more of a negotiation. Spilling the names of a couple of nearby pubs, he told me to make myself comfortable with a pint, and he would join me within the hour.

'Not possible, Pete. You need to come now.'

'I can't leave work at the moment.'

'Oh, yes you can, because I'm telling you. You don't want me coming over there because you'll find yourself leaving and never going back. I'll see you in five minutes.'

He got it at that point. 'What is going…?'

I stabbed the red cross on my screen. There was no point in prolonging the situation. I'm not that evil.

He arrived out of breath with a flushed face and an

uneasy smile. I felt sorry for him for a second. But only a nano one. He pulled out a stool opposite me and climbed onto it. Was that a faint rankness of body odour I could smell?

'What's going on? Are you in trouble?' he asked.

Me in trouble? *Me*? I didn't answer. The guy needed to show a bit more intelligence.

I'm sure I saw him trembling. A tiny spasm in his neck twitched his jawline. Then the nervous leg-bounce started, which rewarded me with an inner sense of achievement. His shoes, polished to a high gloss, kept catching the light as his leg jounced. 'Luke? What's going on?'

I huffed and puffed. 'No, Pete. I'm not the one in trouble here.' I swivelled my phone around so I could deliver his ultimatum. 'I thought you'd like to see this little collection I've assembled for your enjoyment. It starts in Covent Garden a few years back. Do tell me what you think of it. I love hearing feedback on my work.'

He caused less fuss than his wife. After asking me what I wanted, he left in a hurry with the departing words of, 'You're gonna pay for this.'

'No, Pete,' I called after him, 'You're the one who's going to pay.'

THIRTY-ONE

DAY 11

Jim's tone is unusually forceful. 'You need to stay out of this. I'm worried about you. Nothing good can come from you being involved.'

'I'm telling you. The dog lady is having an affair with the redhead who lives opposite.'

'What proof do you have?'

I can't answer him. 'Something's going on. I've seen him coming out of there too many times now, minus a dog.'

'What does Sasha have to say about it?'

'I haven't mentioned it. She's got enough on her plate.'

'You're spending a lot of time over there.'

'She needs me.'

His voice lowers. 'So do we.'

I sigh heavily. 'I know. But they've been so good to us. Think of all the things they've helped us with over the past few years.' I mention when they looked after the kids last summer so we could take a long weekend in Spain, the number of times Hannah has babysat, and the problems Marc has fixed around the house that would have cost us a packet to a pay a professional to do. 'The least we can do is be there for them in their time of crisis.'

'Still no word of him?'

I shake my head. 'Nothing at all. Just a load of strange goings-on.'

'What are your plans today? The boys are coming over tonight, don't forget. It's Mick's birthday.'

'Fine by me. I'm going to carry on with my list of jobs. Gill is off to meet her friend again for lunch. I'll cook an early dinner. Fancy a stir-fry?' He nods his approval. 'I'll drop in to see Sasha this evening once Mick arrives.'

'Let's go out to dinner tomorrow.'

'I don't feel we can do that to Gill. It'll be her last night with us. What about lunch today?'

'Deal.'

After dropping the kids at school, the morning passes in a blur of mundane jobs between showing a plumber and roofer the areas that need fixing. If Marc were around, I wouldn't be bothering. He would have fixed these problems for us. An hour before school pickup, Jim and I head up to the High Road for a late lunch. To a family-owned Italian restaurant we often visit on my days off. I love it here, sampling their freshly prepared pastas and salads and browsing around their onsite deli. I never fail to leave without one goodie or another: a tub of their special stuffed olives or an exotic cheese we've never tried before. Isabella is in the same class as Aida – the owner's great-granddaughter – and they have the occasional play date together.

Two salads and a slab-sized herb focaccia arrive when my phone rings. I glance at the screen. 'It's Rob,' I murmur. What does he want?

Jim tuts. 'You're meant to be on annual leave.'

I lift the tab on my can of drink.

'He shouldn't be bothering you when you're on holiday.'

'It must be urgent otherwise he wouldn't.'

He rolls his eyes, giving an understanding smile. 'Go on, take it.'

I reject the call. 'It's fine. I'll catch him another time. Let's eat.'

Later, at home, I'm playing with Isabella when Rob tries to catch me again. But I miss the call, and then he doesn't answer when I phone him back. I wonder what he wants to speak to me about.

Gill arrives, rosy-cheeked from her lunch uptown. The kids beg her for a story. 'Baths first,' I say, only to receive a volume of abuse about how unfair I am.

'Leave them to me. You have the evening off,' Gill says.

'This is becoming a habit.' I smile. 'I did want to go and see Sasha for a while, if that's OK. I won't be long.'

'Fine by me. I'm beat, to be honest. We can spend the day together tomorrow.'

Mick arrives with a face full of smiles and a mouthful of optimism. 'Happy birthday,' I say, handing over a card and a bottle of whisky Jim and I picked up on the way home from lunch.

'How's my favourite copper?' he asks, the same as he always does. 'Tell us about your latest arrest.'

'I would, but I'd have to kill you,' I tease him with my standard reply, pecking him on the cheek.

I tidy up the kids' toys – clearing away astronauts and robots from Joe's Playmobil space station and stuffing the pieces of Isabella's Spirograph set back into their box – as I listen to Jim belly laughing at one of Mick's filthy jokes. I smile. It's good to hear the joy in his mood. The sessions with Sasha and Art seem to be doing some good.

When I get into the car, I text Sasha to tell her I'm on my way before trying Rob. It goes to voicemail. I sing along to a Lady Gaga playlist, entirely out of tune. When I'm nearly there, along Balham Hill, the traffic slows, and I notice a young man shrugging off a large backpack. He throws it into a black cab. He's holding his jacket hood over his head but releases it before stepping inside. He looks like Luke. I wish I could afford the luxury of using black cabs. I swerve as a blue Mini Metro pulls in front of me. It slots into a space behind the cab. Why are the roads so full of idiot drivers?

When I arrive at Napier Close, I find a police car blocking Sasha's drive. My heart beats double time.

Marc?

I divert my car to the empty space in front of the neighbour's studio and run to Sasha's house. I bang on the front door, desperate to know what's going on. Sasha appears. 'What's happened?' I point to the police car.

Her eyebrows squish together. Signs of confusion, her constant companion of the past eleven days. 'I haven't a clue.'

What is it doing here? Which house are they in?

As I debate what to do, two uniformed officers exit Art and Annie's house. I don't recognise them. It's not like me to dither, but I don't know what to do for the best. I am off duty, after all. They jump in the car and drive off, and the commotion begins with screaming and bellowing resonating from the house.

Sasha's questions mirror my thoughts. 'Whatever's going on in there? Do you think we should go and see?'

I shrug. 'Sounds like a marital row to me.'

Annie comes running out, hysterical tears staining her usually perfectly made-up face. Art follows, lunging to grasp her arm. She tries to shake him free, but his hold is too tight.

Sasha runs over to them. 'Hey, hey, what's going on?'

In two minds, I follow her.

Annie succumbs to her husband's strength. He pulls her into his arms, catching her wails in the crook of his neck. His hands cradle her head, but she swings around as Sasha asks. 'What's wrong?'

'Luke's gone!' Annie cries.

THIRTY-TWO

'Gone? Where?' asks Sasha.

'We had a massive argument, and he walked out. I've tried calling him, but his phone is switched off,' Annie replies.

'Is that why the police were here?' Sasha asks.

'Routine enquiries. Nothing to do with you,' Art says in a firm voice. Sasha looks taken aback. Art drags his fretful wife by the arm. 'Come on, let's go inside. The neighbours don't want to listen to our rendition of EastEnders.'

'Can I do anything for you?' Sasha calls after them.

Annie forces her arm from Art's hand. She directs her question at me. 'Where do you think he's gone?'

How would I know?

'I could be mistaken, but I think I saw him getting into a cab on my way here. What did he take with him?' I ask.

A phone rings. 'Quick, quick.' Annie shoves Art towards the house. 'That's yours. It could be him.' Art tuts and runs in.

'Do you want us to go?' Sasha asks.

'No, no. Come in. Come in. Art's not being rational. We need someone rational to talk this through with.'

My shoulders shudder as I walk in. It's the first time I've been in their house, and I can't identify the exact reason, but an eerie sense of foreboding hangs about the rafters. The aromatic smell of lavender wafts about, but there's nothing calming about this place. I'm not the tidiest person, the semblance of order in my house is solely attributed to Mel's presence, but even so, when she's away, it's never this messy. Stuff lies everywhere. A coat rack, overloaded with jackets and hoodies, sweatshirts and bags, crowds the space by the door, along with a set of free weights, a football and a cycling helmet. We follow a trail of trainers and sports bags into the kitchen, where Art is ranting on the phone. It sounds like a problem down at the gym. He inflicts upon his wife a dirty look, clearly indicating his irritation at our presence. Annie snatches several tissues from the box on the centre island and wipes her cheeks, smearing them with red and black from her makeup. She dabs the swollen skin beneath her puffy eyes. 'I must look such a state.'

Art finishes his call. A deluge of expletives floods from his mouth. 'I've got to pop down the gym. There's all kinds of trouble going on. Angelo hasn't turned up, again, and that bloody JJ hasn't delivered.'

It seems these protein powders are more important than Art would have me believe.

He grabs his jacket from a chair. 'As if I need all this crap at the moment.' I catch a look between him and his wife, a knowing glance of a married couple. He slings the jacket over his shoulder and bounds out.

Sasha looks confused, as if she is seeing a side he's never allowed her to view before. I must admit, it's a complete opposite to the friendly one I've observed too. 'Shall I make us some tea?' Sasha asks.

'There's some gin in the fridge. Want some?' Annie looks from Sasha to me.

'Not for me,' I say. 'I'm driving.'

'I'll join you,' Sasha says. Opening the fridge, she grabs a bottle of gin and some tonic and takes them to the table. 'Do you want to tell us what's going on?'

It takes Annie a while to regain her composure. 'You know I've mentioned how difficult Luke has been this past year – more so since Easter. I haven't told you the half of it. He's been secretive and so defiant.'

Sasha loads a couple of glasses with ice and plonks them down in front of Annie. Shaking her head, Annie fills them with equal amounts of gin and tonic, takes several gulps of one then slides the other across the table to Sasha. Not the best medicine for either of them in the circumstances, but who am I to prescribe their beverage intake?

'We've come to the conclusion he's got serious issues. We thought it was normal teenage behaviour. You know – him expressing himself as an adult. Well, today we discovered the real reason.'

Sasha wriggles out of her cardigan and arranges it over the back of the chair. 'And?'

Annie pauses as if mulling over what to tell us. 'I suppose it'll come out at some point.' She pauses to wipe her eyes again. 'We adopted Luke when he was a toddler. At twenty-two months to be precise. And he recently found out.' She glances up with a look of shame.

Sasha gasps. 'I never knew that.' She takes a long sip of her drink. She's making me edgy. I don't want another outburst like with Art the other night. 'Does Harry know?' Sasha asks.

'I don't know.' Annie shakes her head as if she can't believe her predicament. 'Luke may have told him.'

'So what happened?' Sasha asks.

'He found the adoption paperwork at Easter.' Annie smacks the palm of her hand into her forehead and clenches her jaw. 'It was tucked away in a filing cabinet in my stockroom at work. I was stupid. I never thought he'd go through my stuff.' She necks the remaining half of her drink, wipes her mouth with the back of her hand and reaches for the bottle. 'He didn't have a good start in life, poor boy. His father had issues. He beat Luke and his mother.' Her bottom lip quivers. 'When Luke was taken into care, he had welts across his back and was showing signs of malnutrition.'

'That's awful,' Sasha says. 'You'd never guess he wasn't yours, though.'

I think I'd have to agree. They aren't identically alike, but there are some similarities. Not physically, although they both have dark hair, but more so in their mannerisms.

'Art and I couldn't have children.' Art's problem, not hers, she hastens to add. 'So we decided on the adoption route. And when the opportunity arose to adopt Luke, I jumped at it. Art wasn't so keen. He said children with such disturbing beginnings develop problems later on in life. "Who knows what else went on?" he used to say. But I couldn't walk away. Luke was such an endearing child, and I felt desperately sorry for him. I had to give him a home. There was us, childless, want-to-be parents, and there was a child desperate for the kind of home and love we could give him.' Two tears drop from her eyes. Sasha pushes a handful of tissues across the table. 'This evening, when we came home, Luke went ballistic. He wasn't expecting us. We were meant to see our accountant after work, but the meeting got postponed until next week, so we were much earlier than we said we'd be. Luke started shouting, wanting to know why we'd kept details of his adoption and birth parents from him.' She shivers. 'He called us all sorts of names. Said we were fraudsters as well as cri–'

'As well as what?' I go to ask her, but Sasha gets in first.

'Why tonight? Why did he wait all that time to confront you?' Sasha says.

Annie shrugs. 'Art always said from the beginning that we should tell Luke about his real parents, but I've always refused. He's my son, not theirs. They never cared; they didn't deserve him.' She lifts her glass to her lips. The ice cubes chink. She reaches for the bottle of gin and pours herself another drink.

'Where do you think he's gone?' Sasha asks.

Annie shrugs again. 'He left in a hurry. He took a back-pack he'd organised before we got home this evening. It was waiting by the door.' She shakes her head. 'Art's been saying for years that something's not right about him, we should get him "seen to". I should've listened to him, but I didn't want to admit it to myself. He's always been too wise for his years, that boy. His parents' evenings have always been exemplary. But every day, a different child walked through our door at home time. So defiant and uncooperative, and he's got some kind of OCD, that's for sure. Whenever I've tried to talk to him, he clams up.' She nods, her features despondent. 'Yep, I should have listened to Art, but you don't want to believe the worst in your child, do you?'

'I would've never guessed. He's always so charming when he's round ours. Marc was always singing his praises.'

'He got on better with Marc than he did with Art. They had a special bond.'

'That's the computer geekiness in them both.' Sasha frowns. 'Maybe Harry does know something.'

'Harry's his only friend you know,' Annie says. 'Harry and Marc.'

'The guy I saw getting into that cab earlier had a backpack. Did he take his passport?' I ask.

Annie's jaw drops. Her hand flies to cover her open mouth. 'I didn't check. He wouldn't be going abroad, would he?'

'What makes you think that?' Sasha asks.

Words slip out of her mouth but don't form a sentence. She stops speaking and shrugs again.

'Where do you keep your passports?' I ask.

'In my workroom upstairs.'

'Does he know that?'

She nods. 'I'll go and check.' She takes another gulp of her drink before disappearing.

'I bet you wish you'd never met us lot,' Sasha snorts. 'Where do you think he's gone?'

I don't know why she thinks I would know the answer to this question. I've noticed over the years that people think because you're in the police, you have all the answers, but how would I know where her neighbour's tempestuous teenager has taken off to?

'That's a silly question, isn't it?' she snorts again.

I don't need to answer her.

Annie runs back into the kitchen, panting, shaking two passports in her hand. 'He's taken his. He must be thinking of going abroad. I need to stop him. You have to help me find him.'

'Luke's an eighteen-year-old man. He has every right to go abroad without your say-so. You can't stop him. Have you checked his room?'

'What for?'

'Clues. See what else has gone. The type of clothes he has taken.'

She pauses at the door. 'Come and help me look.'

Sasha and I follow her up to Luke's bedroom. It surprises me. 'However do you manage to make him keep it this tidy?' Sasha asks. Unlike the rest of the house, everything is meticulously in place. Apart from a Mac, and a modest row of books arranged in size order, the desk is clear. Even the bed is made as neatly as you would find in a hotel room, with a row of scatter cushions neatly arranged below the pillows.

Annie opens the wardrobe. 'He's always been like it. Ever since he was a kid.'

'I remember you saying,' Sasha says. 'I never realised he was this tidy, though. I'm surprised Harry has never said anything. Harry's wardrobe compared to this is like a Marie Kondo before and after.'

Being the mother of a son, I think there's hope that Joe will choose not to live in the mess that he does. Clothes hang perfectly here, all facing the same way, the hangers lined up. On a shelf above, jumpers and sweatshirts are folded impeccably and stacked by colour. Rows of footwear line the floor like something out of an upmarket shoe shop.

'You know he's always preferred it over at yours. I always thought it was because it was too quiet here. On the odd occasion when Harry does come over, they never come up here. Luke insists they hang out in the office downstairs or the kitchen. It's like this is some kind of sanctuary. A shrine to Luke.' She sighs. 'Even when he was little, he never allowed kids up here to play, which wasn't often because he was so bloody horrible to other kids, they stopped coming over. And God help Art and me if we dare step past the threshold.' Her bottom lip protrudes as her arm presents the contents of the wardrobe. She looks from Sasha to me. 'This isn't normal, is it?'

It's a bit late to be asking this question.

Sasha's eyebrows rise a rung on the ladder of surprise. I can understand why. Teenagers are not like this. Kids' bedrooms are never this tidy. Even the rubbish in the bin appears to have been placed in there neatly. I tried to put bins in the kids' rooms a few months ago. Isabella gets it, but with Joe, I still can't work out if it's his poor aim or his

277

laziness that results in rubbish accumulating around it, rather than in it.

'What do you think he's taken?'

Annie scans the contents of the wardrobe, swiping the hangers of clothes. 'Not a lot.'

'If he were to hide something, where do you think that would be?' I ask.

'What're you looking for?'

'Nothing in particular.' This is the truth. I don't know what I'm looking for, but there's something to be found for sure. 'Let's think here.' I peer around the room but return my focus to the wardrobe.

'Perhaps under the bed,' Annie suggests. She walks over and lifts the valance. It's as immaculate as if a cleaner had sneaked in and spring-cleaned under there only this morning. 'Perhaps not.'

The wardrobe is built-in, with several drawers and space-saving compartments. I pull open the drawers and shift tidy piles of clothes aside, searching for that something. And there it is, under a pile of immaculately folded T-shirts on the top shelf – a laptop and a plastic file crammed with papers. I slip my sleeves over my hands and hold them up. 'Are these Luke's?'

Sasha gasps as she lunges to empty my hands. 'That's Marc's laptop.'

THIRTY-THREE

LUKE

Pete played his part with admirable speed. As soon as I arrived at the Tube station, my phone buzzed – a text from the man himself:

How do I know you'll destroy the evidence?

I wasted no time with my reply:

I won't. I'll leave that job in your capable hands. Once you transfer the funds, I'll send you all the files I have, and they'll be yours to do what you want with.

Can't say fairer than that!

Despite threatening him with the fear of shame and humiliation, he still tried to barter with me. Some people! As I approached the ticket barrier, my phone vibrated in my pocket. I fished it out to see his name flashing on the screen.

'What do you want now, Pete? I'm busy.'

'Look, you fuc…'

'Pete, Pete, stop! There's no need to swear. Let's be civilised about this.'

Shallow breaths sounded in my ear. 'I'm not transferring any funds to you until you hand over everything you've got.'

I thought for a while, to annoy him more than anything. 'You probably won't agree, but I'm a reasonable guy at heart.' I let out a chuckle to provoke him further. 'I'll transfer your performance with those bimbos you regularly meet with. You cough up the funds, and I'll send your entire portfolio.' I paused for longer than was necessary. 'See, I told you I was a decent chap.'

I didn't hear the rest of what he had to say. I wasn't interested. I turned the phone towards the crowds surging towards the escalator and stood there for a minute or two until his ranting stopped.

Arriving home, I filled a glass with ice and fetched a Diet Coke from the fridge. All this diet crap my mum buys. I keep telling her it's doing her no good. Perching on one of the breakfast bar stools, I sent Pete a WeTransfer of his shenanigans with a woman he hooked up with last year. The one where they had their tongues down each other's throats in the lobby of some shabby three-star hotel a few streets from Oxford Circus.

I tapped into my emails. A couple of new flight deals had come in. One, leaving Friday night, piqued my interest. I flagged it for me to return to later when a text pinged telling me to check my bank account. Logging into the one earmarked for Pete, I smiled. My reply, short and sweet, thanked him for his prompt payment. A call came in. 'Hand over the rest of what you have.'

Of course I'll hand it over, Pete.

But I hope you are not daft enough to think I won't keep a copy for myself.

I spent the evening fine-tuning the plans for the rest of the week. Around eight-thirty, I started to get twitchy. Penelope had not been as efficient as her husband. Silly woman. I debated what to do. Go over there or text her? I settled for a text:

Half an hour to go.

She didn't reply, but at three minutes to nine, the funds appeared in the account I had set up for her transfer. Why do some people like to play so close to the edge? Especially when falling off comes with such dire consequences.

Today, I take my final exam. That's it. I will never sit another one in my life. I won't need to.

'Coming for a beer?' Susie asks, afterwards. I like Susie. Not many others do. She's one of those unfortunate teenagers with acne and a squeaky voice, and people bitch about her behind her back, mimicking the way she speaks and calling her volcano face.

Why do such nasty people exist in this world?

If it weren't for Susie, I wouldn't have had any competition during my secondary education. So, for that, she deserves my time. She sailed close to my results many a time. Not that she ever managed to steer past me. I never let her.

'Sure, why not?' I reply. I have spent seven years with most of these individuals, after all. Is Susie blushing?

A group of us laugh and joke our way down to the Bricklayer's Arms – a pub where the upper sixth sometimes hang out in the evenings. You can feel the relief in the laughter of sixth formers officially done with school. Walking straight to the bar, I remove a card from my wallet and order the first round.

'That's very generous of you, Luke,' a voice whispers in my ear as I shove my credit card into the terminal. 'Come into some money, have we?'

I swing around to see Robbins sneering at me, his jaw tense and nostrils flared. Winking, I offer him a drink.

'I'm not that desperate,' he says. 'Watch yourself, boy. Just watch yourself.' He punches my upper arm before wandering off to speak to some of his students.

I rub my arm.

Slightly perturbed, I scan the bar. Where is Chelsea? She made a swift exit after the exam, but surely she is here if Robbins has made an appearance. I can't see her. Shame. It would be fun to wind her up one last time too. 'One more pint of lager to add to the bill, please,' I say to the barmaid, smirking because I know Robbins drinks ale. I even deliver it to him in person, thanking him for being such a fantastic, generous teacher. Seems rude not to.

'Where's Harry?' Susie squeaks.

I stare at her. Her hair is greasy. No wonder she has so many spots. 'Gone home. He has an exam tomorrow.'

'Of course. Final history paper. I remember him saying. What're you doing for the summer, Luke?'

'This and that,' I mumble, turning my stare to Robbins, waiting for him to look back at me so I can wink at him one last time.

'We should meet up.'

'Maybe.'

'I'm working in my dad's accountancy firm to save up for uni. What is "this and that"?'

Thankfully someone shouts out, 'Who's for another?' as, simultaneously, someone hands me a pool cue saying, 'Your turn,' saving me having to explain "this and that" to Susie. I wouldn't want to lie to her.

I only hang around for one game and one more beer. Far more than I usually drink. Unlike this lot, I have plans to put into action, a new life to start. After solemn vows to stay in touch and a final wicked wink for Robbins, I bid them all the best.

Arriving home, I knock together a fry-up, with hash browns and sausages. I even find some black pudding and mushrooms at the back of the fridge. I need something to negate the effect of the two pints from the pub earlier. I shouldn't have gone, but it was the last time I was going to see that lot; besides how could I resist one final dig at Robbins?

I savour my meal as I flick through all the deals I have been monitoring the past month. Some of them are no longer valid, or the flight times unsuitable, so I go to my room and carry on searching until I find one leaving early tomorrow morning.

Perseverance, that's all it takes.

Doubt writhes into my thoughts, clenching my fists, shortening my breath, and I have to give myself a little pep-talk. Last-minute nerves can't sabotage plans at the final hurdle. I won't let them. I take the leap and confirm the booking.

The beginning of my new life.

I go to pack. What to use? I don't want to be seen rolling a large suitcase down the drive. I need to be more discreet. So I opt for a backpack Mum bought me for a school trip last year. A stream of emotion ripples through me. A thickness coats my throat. What's got into me? Is this guilt? Surely not. Fear more like. 'You've got nothing to be fearful of, Luke,' I say out loud. 'Your plans are rock solid.' They are too. I've been working on mapping out the next stage of my life practically twenty-four-seven for a long time now.

I don't pack much – I don't need to – only sufficient clothes to see me through until I land. It's summer over there now, and I intend to treat myself to a whole new wardrobe. No one deserves it more. I load my toiletry bag, plug adapter, phone, laptop and charger and some books.

That's it. I'm ready to go. I carry the backpack down-stairs. At the front door, I debate whether to take one more trip to the loo. Yes? No? I decide, yes – don't want to go getting caught short on the journey. I'm taking a pee when I remember the other laptop. I knew there was something. How could I forget? I haven't finished with that bloody thing yet. Concentrate, Luke, concentrate. Too much going on. My flow stops to the sound of my mother's voice. Here we go, the Monday morning alarm call of my life. Have you ever grated a fingernail on a cheese grater by accident? The same grim feeling is exactly what the woman's voice does to me, permeating through each and every pore of my body until I shudder.

I didn't plan a row. I wanted to slip out of here unnoticed before they got home. But they weren't meant to be back for another hour. I had it all planned, but she had to start, didn't she? And when she starts, I can't stop. I let them have it, both of them. Every ounce of anger I feel towards them catapults out, as I hurl insults and accusations so rancidly bitter, I even surprise myself.

I storm up Balham Hill to the taxi rank; no more messing about with Oyster cards and Tube trains for me anymore. It's not until we join the M4 that I remember the laptop again. The bloody laptop. Bloody hell! Oh, well. Nothing I can do about it now. A wry smile crosses my face. I've got what I need. They'll find what they find.

Arriving at the airport, I check into the hotel. My room is clean and spacious, and the water pressure impressive. Small bottles of luxury toiletries line the shelf below an ornate mirror in the bathroom. I take a long, hot shower, sampling the sweet aroma of the cedarwood body wash. Afterwards, I lounge around in a fluffy white dressing gown, sipping a beer from the fridge and flicking through the numerous channels on the large flatscreen.

Later, I wander down to the bar and locate a wing back chair. It sits beside a sprawling palm in an enormous wooden planter. Waiters coast around with drinks and bowls of sea salt almonds and stuffed olives, while smooth music plays. Boring, but I guess it fits the scene.

A gangly waiter appears carrying a silver tray and a menu. Having already browsed through what's on offer earlier in the room, I wave it away. 'A bottle of Krug Grande, please.'

'Shall I bring one or two glasses for you, sir?'

'One will do. And a portion of tempura king prawns, followed by a club sandwich, please.'

He places a coaster on the table, and I log onto my laptop to finalise arrangements. Within minutes he returns with the bottle of bubbly and pours me a glass. 'Your prawns will be with you shortly, sir. Would you like chilli or soy dipping sauce with them?'

'I'm not sure. Which would you recommend?'

'The chilli,' he says.

'Bring them both.'

'Very well,' he says, laying a crisp white serviette on the table followed by a knife and fork. 'Enjoy your drink, sir. I will bring your food along shortly.'

When he's gone, I sip the champagne as I scroll through my emails, having a good tidy up as I go along. I set up a mailbox, titled, 'BEFORE' then add several folders under this heading, dropping emails into appropriate subheadings.

Time to start afresh, put this all behind me. Phase one of my life complete. I'll have my inbox clear before I finish that club sandwich.

My tempura prawns arrive. I lay the serviette over my knees and sample the sauces. The waiter is wrong. The chilli sauce is too hot. It adds fire to each bite, and I've had enough heat these past few weeks. Settling for the soy sauce, I dip a prawn, thinking how well I have managed to link it all up in the end. At times, I didn't think I'd make it. But you have to carry on. And slowly, the threads tie up perfectly.

I persevered, until I got there.

You've just got to believe, kiddo!

THIRTY-FOUR

I swipe the laptop and file from Sasha's reach. The file drops to the floor, causing the press stud closure to break open. Pages covered with mathematical formulae flutter to the carpet.

'Give that here. It's Marc's!' Sasha screams, trying to grab the laptop.

Annie reaches for it. 'It can't be. What would it be doing in here?'

'That's what your blasted son needs to tell us!' Sasha is losing control, widening fissures threatening to expose the despair beneath her solid wall of strength. Having desperately tried to hold herself and her family together for so long, she is cracking.

'Go. And leave this with me.' Annie catches me unaware and snaps the laptop from my grip. 'This isn't Marc's. It's Luke's. I'm sure of it.' She bends down and gathers the file and its contents. 'And these are Luke's revision papers. See.' She slips the laptop between her thighs and fans the pages in our faces. 'All of Luke's school notes.'

Sasha drops her head. 'I'm sorry,' she says, but something is missing from her tone, suggesting her apology is not authentic.

I give Annie a sympathetic smile and tug on Sasha's sleeve. 'Come on. Let's take a breather.'

'I can't. I need proof that isn't Marc's laptop.' Sasha shoves her hands on her hips. 'Please show me, Annie, switch it on. Marc has a screensaver of us with the kids on holiday in Spain last year.'

Annie glances from me to Sasha as she stuffs the maths papers back into the file. She pauses before walking over to Luke's desk and placing the laptop and file on the surface.

Sasha holds her breath, so do I.

Sitting down, Annie pulls open the screen. She pauses halfway. 'I know this is Luke's. He has a map of the world as his screensaver.' Undaunted, she spins the laptop to face us, but darkness meets our eyes. Annie glances at the screen and tuts. She stabs the return key. 'The bloody thing's out of battery.'

'Where's the charger?' Sasha asks, clenching her jaw.

'Hang on. Hang on.' One by one, Annie opens the desk drawers. No need to rummage, they are as tidy as every other space in the room. She retrieves a laptop charger from the bottom drawer. 'Let's try this.' She unravels it. Dropping to her knees, she reaches under the desk to find a socket. She tries to plug the other end into the laptop. It doesn't fit. 'This must be an old one,' she says.

'Has he got any others in there?' I ask.

Annie searches the drawer and shakes her head.

'What about the wardrobe?' I suggest. 'Here you go,' I say, pulling a charger from the back of the shelf where I found the laptop.

Annie plugs it in.

We wait in silence. Sasha is chewing the nail of her little finger. Annie is staring at the screen, clenching her jaw.

The machine makes a grinding noise as if it's struggling to start. Annie bangs her fist on the desk. A smug smile surfaces on Sasha's face as a sunny picture of the O'Sullivan family on a beach appears before our eyes.

THIRTY-FIVE

Annie gasps and stares at us both. 'This can't be happening.' She shakes her head so fast, her cheeks joggle.

'Well, it is,' Sasha says. 'Now hand over my husband's laptop.'

Annie pushes the chair away from the desk, raising her hands as if in surrender. 'Take it. Take it.' She fumbles under the desk to unplug the charger and throws it at Sasha.

'This is why the police were round here earlier, wasn't it?' Sasha says, backing out of the room, the laptop firmly in her grip.

'No, no. That was to do with Art. He's got trouble down at the gym.' She slaps the sides of her face, encasing her head in her hands and squashing her lips together.

I'm not at all sure she's telling the truth. I've been studying her since we arrived. Usually, I'm good at spotting even the smartest of liars, but she's proving a challenge.

Sasha runs from the room. 'Hang on,' I call out. She is

heading for the stairs. I tail her into the kitchen where she snatches her cardigan.

'Wait. Calm down. This is a matter for the police now,' I whisper.

'I've tried telling you that since he went missing, but you said the police couldn't help us.'

'But things have developed. There's some proof now that things might not be as they seem.'

'There you go again, Eva, "Might not be as they seem". *Might* – I've told you from the minute he disappeared that something is dreadfully wrong. No one else is going to help me, so I'm taking charge.'

'I'm on your side, Sasha. Believe me.'

The anger on her face takes a momentary pause. 'I'm sorry. I'm wrong to blame you.'

Annie is racing down the hallway. 'I need to get back into Luke's room. We can't leave here yet,' I say to Sasha. 'We need to find out what that boy is up to, and stop him.'

Annie bursts into the kitchen. 'Don't go. Help me find out what's going on, please.'

'We won't leave you. Sit down. Let me get you another drink,' I say, throwing Sasha a look. She is shaking, her arms guarding possibly the only clue to her husband's whereabouts. I go over to her and place my hands on her shoulders. I ease her into the chair and push between her shoulder blades, a prod of encouragement asking her to trust me.

'There must be some reasonable explanation.' Annie sloshes gin into their empty glasses. 'Marc must've given Luke his laptop for a reason,' she adds, picking at any splinter of hope that her son is the innocent young man she believes him to be. She holds a glass up to me. 'You want one now?'

'I think I'll make some tea, if that's OK,' I say, my mind racing to formulate a plan to get up to Luke's room.

'Help yourself,' Annie says, pointing to the corner of the kitchen. 'You'll find everything you need in the end cupboard.'

I fill the kettle. Sasha has taken my hints and is engaging Annie in conversation. 'Just popping to the loo,' I say, and leave them to it.

As I pass the toilet on the way to the stairs, I turn on the light and shut the door, leaving the integral fan humming away. Reaching Luke's room, I start searching. For what, I don't know, but I'm confident I'll find more than Marc O'Sullivan's laptop. I start in the wardrobe. Cautiously, I hunt through the entire contents, careful to preserve the perfection of every item, but with no success. I crouch down and take another look under the bed, but find nothing. One by one, I open the bedside cabinet drawers. There's nothing out of the ordinary in any of them. I step over to the desk. His Mac hollers out for investigation, but time is not on my side. A medium-sized TV unit sits by the window, perfectly positioned for bedtime viewing. I open the cupboard beneath. Ten or so DVDs sit neatly stacked on each of the three shelves. I take a closer look but find only run-of-the-mill films you'd expect in a teenager's collection.

I spin around, scanning the room. A small bookshelf built into the side of the desk piques my interest. Rushing over, I kneel down and scan the titles. They are mostly reference books on photography and videography: *In the Blink of an Eye, The Filmmaker's Handbook, How to Shoot Video that Doesn't Suck.* I pull each one out and thumb through the pages, searching for that something. And there I find it. A handful of photos slipped between the pages of *Hollywood Producers Directory.* I pull the pictures out and flip through them. Each image makes my eyes bulge. There are a few people I recognise – Pen and Tom passionately embracing. That doesn't surprise me. I pick up the next of a young woman straddling an older man. Is this the girl Luke was arguing with at Harry's party? Chelsea something? They are in, what appears to be, a cupboard. Shelves of labelled boxes surround them. I stare closer to read the labels: trig sorting cards, measurement units, 2D shapes, 3D shapes, geoboards. It looks like a maths teacher's storage cupboard. There's one of Marc and Sasha lying on their bed. I recognise the patchwork throw. Sasha has a nightie on, but, apart from a pair of boxers, Marc is naked. What the hell is Luke doing with these? Another one displays Pete the Prick in a dark room. Is that a male or a female he's with? I'm not sure. All I can say is, it is certainly not Penelope.

I lay the photos out side by side on the carpet like pieces of a jigsaw begging to form a picture, tell a story. There's only one certainty here, though. It isn't going to be a charming one.

What has Luke been up to?

I slip my phone out of my pocket and click on the

camera, taking snapshots of all twelve of the images. As I get to the last one, I hear a car pull up and a door slam.

Art must be back.

Hurriedly, I return the photos to where I found them. As I'm replacing the book on the shelf, my elbow overturns the wire bin. Neatly folded bits of paper, Amazon cardboard wrapping, and a crisp packet spill out. As I place them back in, two tiny pieces of green paper fall from the crisp packet onto the carpet. I turn the packet upside down and shake it. More green pieces fall out, orange ones also. They look like pieces of torn-up Post-it notes. I shake the crisp packet some more. Wafts of salt and vinegar hit me. Checking the bag is empty, I gather the tiny pieces and slip them into my jeans pocket along with my phone and head for the stairs.

The front door opens, and bangs shut. Art's voice bellows out. 'Annie, I need you.' As he bounds up the stairs. I hear him mutter, 'What're those bloody women still doing here?'

My heart pounds. I sidestep into the nearest room and dart behind the door. Piles of clothes and discarded polythene garment covers are strewn over a sofa beside a sewing machine. Dresses on hangers line the curtain pole. It must be Annie's workroom where she carries out minor repairs and alterations. The smell of lavender is powerful in this room, more so than the rest of the house, but I'm far from relaxed.

Art heads up the hallway, mumbling something about Luke. My heart hammers, drumming in my ears. I'm sure he must be able to hear it. I stare through the crack in the door. It appears he's looking straight at me. My heart beats even faster. He comes closer. A phone rings. Stopping to pat his jacket, he removes his mobile from the breast pocket and thumbs the screen. He glances up. I turn away, not daring to look anymore.

'Reg!' he bellows.

Silence follows. I force myself to peep through the crack of the door again as his voice fades.

'Where are you?' He hisses, leaning on the bannister. 'Get down to the gym straight away. Shit has hit the fan.'

He turns and comes towards me, shoving the door I'm hiding behind. I press myself against the wall to stop it smashing into me. Taking a deep breath, I hold it in. He enters the room and heads straight to a stack of floral storage boxes in the corner. I can see him in the reflection from the mirrored wardrobe on the opposite wall. I will him not to turn the light on.

He muscles the boxes aside. With his passage clear, he kneels and pulls up a section of carpet. Metal creaking follows a clicking sound. He removes some packages. What's in them? Money, drugs? Damn, I can't see. Both? He marches towards the wardrobe. Still swearing, he slides open one of the doors. It is jam-packed with clothes wrapped in plastic and on the floor a vast selection of designer handbags and shoes. He pulls out a holdall from the top shelf, stashing the bundles inside. I silently beg him not to look around. My heart is beating so fast, I can hardly breathe. He removes something from what looks like a clutch bag and slips it in the holdall. Is that a gun? Sliding the door closed with a crash, he returns to the corner, slams the safe shut and replaces the carpet with haste.

Annie appears. The gin slurs her words. 'What's going on?'

He grabs the biggest floral box and shoves it to cover the safe in the floor. 'We're in real trouble. We need to get this out of here.' He waves the holdall in her face. 'That bloody JJ Harper. He's got a lot to answer for. He's dead meat.'

JJ Harper? Harper? Have we found our Jason Harper?

He pushes her out of the room. 'I could've done without you getting pissed tonight.' They argue all the way down the stairs. I hold my breath, straining to hear their heated exchange but can't figure out what has happened to cause such a commotion.

When the front door crashes shut, I wait for Annie to return to the kitchen and my heart to return to a reasonable beat. I need to get Sasha out of here now. Returning downstairs, I hear them arguing and walk into the kitchen to witness Sasha strike Annie across the face with a cold hard slap. I wince. That was one almighty strike.

Annie's hand flies to her cheek as a disbelieving gasp gapes her mouth wide. 'What was that for?'

'For your son,' Sasha bellows.

'But you don't know what's happened,' Annie says. She retaliates, and it isn't pretty. She possesses more strength than she realises, and her counter-attack unbalances her opponent. Sasha steps backwards, trying to steady herself against a chair, but loses her footing and falls into the breakfast bar. Balancing herself, she rushes towards Annie.

They start scrapping like teenagers fighting over a boy. Hair is pulled and faces scratched. I can't believe the performance before me. Sasha gets hold of Annie's shirt and scrunches it up in her fist, shaking her backwards and forwards. Annie slaps her. They won't stop. Like boxers in a ring, they both seem hell-bent on throwing the winning blow. I knew neither of them should have touched that gin.

I attempt to break up their undignified scuffle. 'Cut it out. This isn't helping anyone or solving anything.' I prise them off each other like a couple of pieces of stubborn Velcro. 'What's got into you two?'

Annie shakes her shirt back into place. She straightens the collar and rubs the scratches on her neck. 'Get out of my house. Both of you.' Her voice is shrill, piercing like a whistle. 'Get out.'

Sasha grabs the laptop and rushes to the front door, peering over her shoulder as if frightened Annie might chase after her. 'Hang on, Sasha!' I call out. But she's not listening.

I follow her into her house and Marc's office, where she plugs in the laptop and asks it, 'What else are you hiding?' She looks at me. 'We might find a clue on here about what's happened to Marc.' With hands shaking as much as her voice, she lifts the lid. The screensaver of her family smiles back at her. A pitiful whimper escapes her mouth. 'I hope he uses the same password as his computer.' She enters 7June2001. 'Thank God for that.' She sighs. 'I don't even know what I'm looking for.'

'Here, let me look,' I say.

She slides the laptop over to me. It hasn't been wiped

like the computer, but it certainly appears to have had a good clean-up. Desktop files cover the family holiday screensaver. I open up several of them. Nothing untoward arouses my interest. I click on Finder and have a browse. There's surprisingly little saved. Clicking on Trash, I find nothing. Strange?

'Mum.'

Sasha mutters, 'Not now, Hannah.'

'Mum, where are you? I need your help.'

'You go,' I say.

'I'll be straight back.'

I open Outlook and browse through the emails. There are only twenty or so sitting in the inbox. Someone has had a good tidy-up of them. Who has been busy? Luke? Or perhaps Marc has been accessing his emails from another device? I scan through them, picking out a series of autoresponders from a place called the Green Tree Clinic all delivered within the last week. They have all been opened. I click on each to find a welcome to their online mental health counselling.

Sasha returns as my phone buzzes. I remove it from my back pocket. It's Rob. 'I need to take this,' I say, stepping outside the room to take the call. He needs to know about JJ Harper's involvement with Art.

'Finally. I was getting a bit bored of telephone ping-pong,' Rob says.

'It may have slipped your notice, but I am on annual leave.' I stare at Sasha through the doorway. Her fingers stab the keyboard.

'I know, but I needed to ask you where you've filed the

Carlisle report. Arthur wanted me to make some amendments. Don't worry, I found it. And now something else has come up I thought you'd want to know about. Your friend, whose husband walked out.' He pauses.

I turn my attention to my colleague. 'What about her?' I whisper.

A high-pitched moan sounds. I pop my head around the office door. Sasha, ghostly-white, grabs hold of the desk to steady herself as she stumbles towards me.

'Don't go anywhere. I'll call you straight back,' I say, and end the call.

I step into the office. With her mouth gaping open, Sasha stares at me as if she's just witnessed a car crash and proceeds to vomit gin-smelling liquid across my trainers.

I do a double take at the laptop, unable to believe the image before me. Sasha reaches out, grabs the bin beside the desk, and continues to retch. I step back against the wall, unable to release my gaze from the image smearing the screen of a half-naked Marc in bed with an equally half-naked Luke.

THIRTY-SIX

'This can't be real. It can't be,' Sasha says, wiping her mouth with her wrist.

I stare at the screen. Marc and Luke are lying on their sides, facing each other as if deep in a conversation no one else should hear. Along with the smell of vomit wafting up from my trainers, the image cramps my stomach. Luke has his hand on Marc's chin as if he is stroking it. Sasha and Marc's blue patchwork throw covers them both from the waist down. No wonder Sasha has been sick.

How could you, Marc? You are a happily married family man.

Were – *were* a happily married man.

I sigh heavily with the ever-increasing realisation that rarely do we truly know anyone.

'In our bed too,' she whimpers. 'Get rid of it. Destroy it. I never want to see it again.'

'Mum? Where are you?'

'When will they ever leave me alone?'

My eyes dart from her to the screen. I rush to click the laptop shut as Harry appears. He steps backwards. 'What *is* that smell?'

'I'm not feeling well,' Sasha says.

He sniffs. 'It stinks of alcohol. Have you vommed?'

'Harry, not a great choice of words,' Sasha says.

He bends down and puts his arm around her. 'Come and sit down, Mum.'

She shakes him off. 'No, I'm fine.'

'Mum, you're not well.' He tries to make her sit down, but she worms away from him.

'I've got stuff to do. What is it you want?'

'I feel bad asking you now.'

'I'm fine. What is it?'

'Can you pick me up from town tomorrow evening? A group from school are going out. I said I'd go for a while.' He looks at me, then at Sasha as he registers the laptop. 'You found it. Where was it?'

'In the filing cabinet.' Sasha's pale face flushes.

'It can't have been. I checked there when Dad first disappeared.'

'It was. I was looking for some paperwork and found it.'

Confusion squeezes his temple. 'I went through those drawers one by one. You were standing there. Don't you remember?'

She takes a deep breath, her nostrils flaring. 'You didn't look hard enough. It was there.'

'I know what I saw.'

'You are mistaken.'

Oh, how people weave webs of lies. Each one threaded

so tightly around the next until the mess they've created becomes impossible to unravel. I've seen it so many times.

Sasha closes her eyes and slowly breathes out. 'Please, Harry. Go and carry on with what you were doing.'

He rolls his eyes. 'You've never got time for me anymore.'

'I need to sort some stuff out with Eva.'

'What stuff?'

'Please, Harry, leave it. I'll be with you soon. That's fine about picking you up tomorrow night.'

'Whatever.'

He storms off, and Sasha stares at me with desperation, the strain on her face bulging her eyes. 'What has happened to my life?'

'Let's take a look at what else is on here.' I reopen the laptop.

She reaches forward and slams it shut. 'I don't want to see any more.'

'You need to involve the police now. At least get them to look into it.'

'I can't let anyone see this. It'll kill the kids. Their dad is having an affair with the neighbour's son. Harry's best friend.' She shakes her head, totally bewildered. 'How can this have happened and me not have a clue?' She perches on the side of the desk, grinding her knuckles together. 'I can't believe it.' Her breathing quickens.

'We need to take this down to the station.'

'No way. I don't want this out in the open. No one else must ever find out about this except us. It's going to destroy me. I can't have it destroying what's left of my family too. Promise me you'll never to say a word about this to anyone. Not even Jim. Promise me.'

'Sasha, listen to me. Something isn't right here. Your husband has disappeared without a trace, and his laptop has been found in your neighbour's son's bedroom with a photo of the two of them on it. Did Luke take the laptop from here before or after Marc left?'

She shrugs.

I point to the computer on the desk. 'And what about this being wiped? Was Luke in here after Marc disappeared?'

'I can't remember.'

I think for a moment. 'Well, I can. Luke was with Harry, Hannah and George after school the day Marc disappeared. Luke was discussing climate change with Hannah. Thinking about it, I've seen that boy here a lot. How often does he come over?'

'He's spent loads of time with Marc and Harry over the years on the computer. Marc was teaching them to code, or something like that. We used to tease them, call them geeky nerds.' Her head shakes from side to side. 'But Harry's attention span for the stuff they've been looking at recently has been that of a gnat. He lost interest and used to leave them to it. Harry did start to get the hump, though. I could tell. He used to say Marc treated Luke more like his son than him.' Her upper body crumbles into a ball as she whispers she wants to be alone.

I pat her shoulder twice before leaving her to go and call Rob. He really needs to know about JJ Harper and Art. Damn, he's not there. I leave another message, telling him to call me urgently. I return to the kitchen, planning my next move. Under the sink, I find an old sponge and a bottle of anti-bacterial spray and attempt to clean the rancid smell from my trainers.

Hannah's voice startles me. 'Is Mum OK, Eva?'

I walk over to her. She is flopped on a beanbag. Her feet are elevated on the sofa, her phone resting in the dip between her hip bones, and she is staring out of the patio doors into the garden. The angle of the light from the hallway accentuates the hollowness of her tear-stained cheeks. Marc's disappearance has signed its initials across the face of every member of this family. She's still in her school uniform, her hair in two plaits, looking far too young to bear the grief her family is suffering. I sit on the sofa and ask her how she is. We chat for a while. She reveals her anger about no one believing she saw Marc at school the other day.

'I believe you,' I say, truthfully.

'Do you really?' she asks.

I nod.

'Do you think Dad will come back?'

I consider my reply. 'I wish I could give you a definite answer to that.'

'He will,' she says with the innocence of optimistic youth. 'That's what I keep telling myself, anyway. We have to believe, otherwise what's the point?' She folds her arms, dismissing me in true teenage fashion.

I slip outside to try Rob again. 'That was a quick call back,' he says sarcastically. There's a pause. 'You OK?'

I drop down on the doorstep. 'Sorry, something came up. I did try and call you again.'

'Your friend whose husband walked out? I have to tell you something.'

'What about?'

'Their neighbour's son. You know him?'

'Luke? Why?'

'He's been accused of blackmail.'

'By whom?'

'A schoolteacher, a bloke called Timothy Robbins.'

I try to marry his words to my thoughts but can't quite make a connection.

'He walked into the station earlier. There was no one else free, so I saw to him. He reported that a Luke Walker has been blackmailing him. It's only when he relayed Luke's home address, I realised he was talking about someone who lives in that development we've stopped at.'

'Blackmailing him for what?'

'An affair with a pupil. Caught them shagging in a school store cupboard, apparently.'

'What?'

'You heard me.'

Chelsea? Is that what Luke was threatening her with on Saturday night? 'Male or female?'

'Who?'

'The pupil the teacher was caught with.'

'Female, why?'

'Never mind, carry on.' I need to hear this.

'Luke got video footage of the teacher and the girl. Threatened them both to pay him ten grand each. Pay or show. He told them he'd circulate the videos across social media if they didn't cough up. They both paid. The girl is from some rich family and had the money from her eighteenth. We tried to get hold of this Luke, but he wasn't there when we called at his house earlier. His mother said he was out but would be back later. His phone is switched off.'

Thoughts buzz around my mind like wasps in a jar – confused and unable to make sense of the situation. Has Luke been blackmailing Marc as well, with that image on his laptop? Is that where Marc's cash withdrawals went? Into Luke's bulging pockets?

I brief Rob on Jason Harper and Art Walker. 'There's a connection there, I'm sure. He's known as JJ Harper.' I tell him about the guy and dubious exchange I witnessed at Art's gym. 'We have to find Luke. I saw him getting into a black cab up on Balham High Street earlier. He's taken his passport. My guess is he's trying to get out of the country.'

'Leave it with me. I'm right on it. I'll give Arthur the heads-up.'

'We need to tread carefully here. I've been doing some snooping.'

'Gotcha.'

I return inside, unsure of what to do. I don't want to leave Sasha, but she needs time to absorb the misery the evening's events have inflicted. I pop my head around the office door. She is sitting at the desk, staring at the wall. 'I'm in the kitchen if you need me,' I say, softly. She waves a hand in the air. 'Go home, Eva. I want to be alone.'

Looking at her, my mind is made up. 'I can't leave you like this. We need to talk about what's going on here.'

'There's nothing to discuss. We're going to pretend we never saw that obscenity.'

Denial. A stage she needs to endure before anger takes the spotlight.

I leave her to it and go to the kitchen. Sitting at the table, I dig out the shreds of florescent green and orange Post-it notes I found in Luke's bin earlier. Each is torn into tiny pieces. Starting with the green, I line up the top edge, guided by the sticky, straight line, and work from there, slowly piecing them back together. Grease from the crisp packet smears some of the details.

It takes about ten minutes for numbers and three-letter mnemonics to take shape:

104 HIL,113 RAD, 79 REN, 169 <u>SOF 5*</u>

Leaning forward, I stare intently, trying to figure out their meaning. Several minutes pass before I crack the code. Grabbing my phone, I google hotels in close proximity to Gatwick airport but don't have any luck. I swap Gatwick for Heathrow and scan the page. The price of a room for a night at the Hilton hotel displays at £104. I scroll down to see a price of £113 for the Radisson, and finally see the figure of £169.

I tap Rob's number, but he doesn't answer. I leave him a message. 'Call me ASAP. I think I know where we can find Luke Walker.'

THIRTY-SEVEN

LUKE

I consume the last prawn as the waiter arrives with the rest of my supper. 'Can I get you anything else, sir?'

'Another portion of these. And forget the chilli sauce.'

'Was it not to your liking?'

'Far too hot.'

'I'm sorry to hear that,' he says, his neck twitching like a chicken. 'I'll bring you some more of the soy.'

I bite a chunk out of the club sandwich, then, placing it back on the plate, I carry on sorting my emails until there is only one remaining which contains my flight details. Clicking it open, I scan through, double-checking I have everything clear in my mind. My plane leaves at six in the morning. I wish I'd booked the direct flight now and taken an internal transfer to Sydney, but a two-night stopover in

Singapore seemed a good idea at the time. I always have fancied drinking one of their slings.

I click on the project plan I've been slogging away on since Easter.

Marc shouldn't have been so greedy. I'll give him his due, it was his idea, and he was the one who came up with the name, *Marc O's Magic Marker,* of course. He could have included me with the branding, but there you go. What gets me the most is that I've been the brains behind this operation. I sourced the know-how to progress the rough sketches to 3D models. I cracked the code. And I was the one who schemed up the means to finance the next stage while he was wallowing in self-pity. I've spent far more time on this than he has. Night after night, I've burned the midnight oil until dawn. But I'm a generous kind of guy. I saw it as a team effort. Shame he didn't share my opinion.

Shame. Shame. Shame.

What has he done since he was made redundant? Jack shit, that's what, when he could have done so much more. He's had all the time in the world to accelerate our plans but, instead, he's left it all up to me. Every time we've met up, all he's done is moan about not being able to find another job. 'By the time we've got this to market, you won't need another job,' I kept telling him.

'I don't have the finances to fund taking this to market,' he said. 'I have a family to feed.'

I kept reminding him there would be plenty of people willing to back a project with such revolutionary potential, but he wouldn't listen. Couldn't listen. His spiral down the gloomy hole of depression had spun out of control since he lost his job. He denied it with the fake smile colouring his face every day for the sake of his family. But I know the real Marc. He often opened up to me when we were working on progressing our project. I listened to him for hours and hours. The bloody mood swings started to get to me though, and he really disappointed me. Buying coke from my dad, of all the people. I was still prepared to support him, though.

Until he double-crossed me.

It was a little over three weeks ago. I was telling him to relax. 'I've sourced the funds to move things forward. We need to be patient until the money comes in. It won't be long.'

'I'm looking for a buyer,' he said.

'Buyer for what?' I asked, confused. Were Sasha and he thinking of moving?

'*The Marker.* I'm broke. If I don't do something, we'll have to sell the house, and the kids will have to move schools in the autumn. I'm going to sell the work I've done to date. I've got a couple of interested parties.'

I've done? *I've* done? Did I hear that right?

It was the look he shot me that killed it all for me. He didn't see me as a partner. I was a silly schoolboy to him.

Wrong, Marc. So very wrong.

I needed a little more time for my plans to come to fruition, so I played along. The plans I'd so carefully crafted – to gather the cash from Pen and Pete, Robbins and Chelsea – to enable us to finance the next stage of the project. The next stage that had involved him. Until that moment when I decided Marc would join the ranks of these scumbags and make a contribution too. I would take this thing to market, alone.

Silly man.

'I've got some good news,' I lied, as confidently as I could for someone who had just been smacked in the face with the club of betrayal. 'I've lined up two backers. One's a dead cert. The other I'm working on for a fairer percentage split.'

'What?' he asked, with that perplexed look he's worn since losing his job. It's now got rather tiresome.

'Yep. Leave it to me. I'm all over it,' I said. 'I'm waiting for them to get back to me with a date for us to meet. Stop stressing. I'm going to get this thing to market if it kills me.'

But alone, Marc. Not with you.

I take another bite of my sandwich as my laptop notifies me of an incoming email. I glance over to take a look. Gasping loudly, I choke on a lump of chicken.

It's from Marc.

I snatch the serviette from my lap and spit my food into its creases, coughing and spluttering. What does he want now? Calmly, I open the email.

One solitary line delivers his message.

'Your time is up. I'm going home.'

I smirk. He can do what he likes. I'll be sipping a sling in a Singapore bar before that happens. I bin the email. I wish I were there to see him explain himself to his family, though. When they've viewed what I plan to send them before I board the plane in the morning. I chug the last of the champagne, feeling quite fuzzy. Time for bed, I think.

The bar area and foyer have grown increasingly busy, and several people join me in the lift. I pay them little attention, as I can feel myself swaying. I focus on my trainers, chuckling at the sensation the alcohol has given me.

When I reach the room, I fumble with my key card. It doesn't work. What's wrong with it? Bloody thing. I laugh out loud when I realise that I'm not slotting it in the right way, unsure why I find this quite so funny. I turn the card around and let myself in. The maids must have been: someone has turned down the bed covers, and a single chocolate sits in the middle of the pillow. The ambient lighting casts a shadow across the room. I fling myself on the bed and unwrap the chocolate.

This is the life!

A few minutes pass, although it could have been longer, when a knock at the door startles me. Who could that be? The maids again? I stagger to the door, swing it open and gasp. 'What the bloody hell are you doing here?'

'I warned you you'd pay.'

I try to close the door in their face, but they push against it.

'You're drunk. Makes this all the easier.'

I laugh out loud. 'You don't have it in you.'

A firm hand in the chest pushes me into the room. I stumble backwards, my arms flailing as I try to regain my balance. I fall against the wall, confused. 'What's your problem?'

'You. You're my fucking problem, Luke Walker.'

I don't notice the knife until it is brandished in my face, threatening to carve out my future. I try to kick out, but miss, and my knee buckles. I start to panic. 'What are…?' I can't get any more words out. Fear clenches my senses with freezing cold hands. The room spins. Get a grip, Luke. A harsh prickling sensation, like an electric shock, shoots through me. What *was* that? Champagne burns my throat. It's so hot – so bloody hot in here. Throbbing pain paralyses me. It's wild, excruciating: a feeling of being thumped and kicked in the stomach. My insides are going to explode. I'm falling. I can't stop myself.

Blood, so much blood.

THIRTY-EIGHT

Snatching a napkin from the metal holder on the sideboard, I enclose the fragments of the Post-it note and slip the evidence in my pocket. I piece together the shreds of orange:

$$M5 \ R10 \ C10 \ P10 \ P20 = 55$$

My fingers drum the table as I stare at the series of numbers and letters, but I'm stumped. What do these mean? I gaze around the room. It's a mess, like this family's life. Above the sideboard, a collage of framed photos dominates the wall, portraying the story of a perfect family holiday in Florida. I've admired these before, several times when we've visited, and I've always been in awe of the perfection of this family.

Even though I should know by now that no family is perfect.

One of the five of them posing in front of the Magic

Kingdom hangs in the centre. Marc's arms are wrapped around Sasha and the kids, their faces expressing such elation. We've got a similar photo at home, taken last year when Jim and I took Joe and Isabella to Disneyland Paris. I had it printed onto a giant canvas, and it takes pride of place in our dining area. What makes the picture so special is that I'm looking at the camera, so are the kids, but Jim is looking down at the three of us with such adoration, it still fills me with warmth every time I catch that look in his eye. In front of the Magic Kingdom, Marc is looking at Sasha with an equal amount of devotion.

I shake my head and return my attention to the scribbles on the orange Post-it. 'Come on, Eva, work it out,' I repeat out loud.

$$M5\ R10\ C10\ P10\ P20 = 55$$

Five minutes crawl by as I try to arrange my muddled thoughts in order. Then it clicks. Sliding my phone across the table towards me, I pull up the photos I took earlier in Luke's room. I clap my hands several times. The sound echoes around the room like a round of applause. I grab another napkin and wrap the orange pieces, slipping them into my pocket to join the green ones.

I march to the office. Sasha is still sitting, staring at the wall, her hands propping up her head. I perch on the desk next to her and tap her arm. She doesn't acknowledge me. 'I need to look at the laptop again,' I say.

She turns to stare at me, defeat saddening her expression. 'What's the point?'

'Why don't you make some coffee and leave me here?' I ease her up out of the chair. She feels lifeless, floppy, like a rag doll, as if she'll collapse if I don't hold her up.

'I used to be such a strong person.' She snivels. 'How do I find the strength to get through this?'

I escort her to the kitchen and make her a cup of coffee. She takes it over to the beanbag Hannah was lying on earlier and slumps down.

'I'll be back in a bit,' I tell her.

I return to the laptop and find the wretched image and compare it to Sasha and Marc's photo on my phone. Blinking, my pulse races. I knew it. How has he done this? There's the error. The point where the patchwork throw meets Luke's body. The alignment is out, and the hue and contrast are awry – only visible to the scrutinising eye when compared with the same point on the image of Marc. This photo has obviously been doctored. It is good, boy, it is good, but it's not entirely perfect. I place two fingers on the touchpad and pinch to zoom in. The pixels enlarge, distorting the clarity of the image. I zoom back out and in again. In out, in out.

Very clever.

But not clever enough.

No more sneaking around, Luke. Your game is over, and you can't hide anymore.

My phone rings. 'Rob, thank God you called.'

'Never knew you cared so much. What's up?'

'I need you to come over to Napier Close. I've found

stuff out. I think we'll find Luke Walker at the Sofitel, Heathrow. Check it out with airport police, can you? And pave the way with reception if I'm right. Give clear instructions for them to wait for us. Then get yourself over here, and I'll fill you in on the rest on the way. He's a nasty piece of work, this one.'

'Sure. But you're on annual leave.'

'And when has that ever stood in the way of police business?'

'Point taken. I'll make the calls and be right there.'

I run down the hallway and into the kitchen. 'Sasha, come here.' I extend an arm and pull her up out of the beanbag. 'Quick.'

Reluctantly, she surrenders to my tugs back to the office. I point to the image. 'It's not real.'

'What do you mean?'

'It's fake.'

She catches her breath, looking from me to the screen.

I zoom into the image when a knock at the front door disturbs our concentration. 'Who's that now?' Sasha huffs. 'It'd better not be that blasted Annie.'

Hannah passes the study door, saying, 'I'll get it.'

Sasha stares at the screen, transfixed. 'Are you sure it's fake?' she asks me.

'Undoubtedly,' I say.

Screams pierce along the hallway. 'Daddy! Daddy!'

Sasha's jaw drops. She stares me in the eyes for a second before bolting out of the office.

I turn from the laptop to see Marc across the hallway, standing on the doormat with his daughter clinging to him like a limpet. He is as white as the painted woodwork, his eyes sunken in his pained face, and it looks as if he hasn't shaved since he left. He looks small, the loss of hope weighing him down. Sasha stands in front of him, trying to gulp in air. Throwing out a hand, he draws her towards him and cocoons her in his arms with Hannah, six shoulders involuntarily shaking. They remain entwined until Sasha pushes him away and cups his head in her hands, pulling his face towards hers. Their noses touch. An intense look only they will understand passes between them, before they hold each other again.

He looks up. His eyes lock onto mine, then down to the laptop. He looks crestfallen, a broken man.

I mouth, 'It's a fake. We know it's fake.' I snap the laptop shut.

His face contorts, and his bottom lip quivers as Harry comes hurtling down the stairs, with George in tow. George pushes past Harry, rushing towards his father. Harry hesitates, momentarily challenging his father. 'Dad! Where have you been?' before joining the dramatic embrace. A family of five reunited at last.

'Daddy, Daddy, tell me, was that you outside school the other day?'

Marc gives the faintest of nods. 'I'm so sorry,' he says between sobs. 'I've been in such a mess. It's all over now, though. It's all sorted. I can explain everything.'

I swallow the lump choking me as I leave the office to locate my bag. In the kitchen, I find it hanging from the back of a chair. Voices crescendo as the five of them hug their way down the hall. I gather my emotions to deal with later and slip my bag's strap over my shoulder. George and Hannah are crying. Tears of joy marvelling at how suddenly desperate circumstances can change. Harry looks stunned.

'Don't go,' Sasha says to me. 'Tell her, Marc.'

Marc's shoulders curve over his chest, a middle-aged man stooped from the course of catastrophic events. He follows his wife's orders and invites me to stay.

Another lump forms in my throat, watering my eyes. I reach out and curl my hand over Sasha's shoulder. 'Not now. You need to be alone.'

'But you're one of us.' Sasha lets out an almighty sob, whimpering like Ralph, who is circling Marc's feet.

'I couldn't see clearly,' says Marc. 'It was like I had been taken over by someone else. I kept hearing these excruciating banging noises and voices telling me to end it all.'

Harry cracks at this point. One sentence too much for his fragile state of mind.

My phone beeps. Rob is on his way to take me to the Sofitel. I give a tight-lipped smile. 'I'll come back tomorrow. I have to be somewhere.'

The roads are empty as we pull on to Balham Hill, a stark contrast to the usual grind of the capital's traffic. The streets at this time of night captivate me. There's something about watching London in its slumber, broken only by the honest folk who go about their nighttime duties and the undercurrent of London's irrepressible darker side.

'Luke Walker was blackmailing more people than just

Robbins and that Chelsea.' I update Rob on the rest as he accelerates through London's streets.

'Who's been a busy girl?' he says, enjoying the drama.

It isn't long until we are on the M4, heading out to Heathrow. As we drive through the car park to the hotel entrance, I notice the same car that swerved in front of me earlier on. 'I think Luke may have been followed here.' I point to the Mini Metro. 'That same car pulled in behind his taxi earlier. It nearly caused an accident.'

'It looks like it belongs in the knacker's yard,' he says.

'That's why I remember it.'

We enter the hotel lobby and charge up to the front desk where two police officers are waiting for us. We produce our warrant cards. One of the officers addresses us. 'We've taken the liberty of getting a key card for you.'

'Great work,' I say and take it from them. I give a cursory nod to the hotel manager, who points in the direction of the lift, and we set off with the two officers in tow.

My senses are racing, as they always are when I'm involved in an arrest. This should be easy. Luke is hardly a threat. Rob knocks on the door. 'Luke Walker. It's Detective Robert Sharpe here. Can you open the door, please?' There is silence. 'Luke. Please, open up.'

I wave the key card, suggesting its use. Rob nods. A beep and a click as I enter the electronic key in the slot. I gently push the door open. Luke is not much more than a boy, so it doesn't seem appropriate to go in all guns blazing. I ease into the room. Rob follows me.

The mess confronting us shocks me to the core. Curled up on the floor in the foetal position, Luke lays in a pool of blood, the deep burgundy staining the cream carpet. I gasp in horror, my insides twisting at seeing Annie's son in such a desperate state.

'We need medics here. NOW!' I shout.

In the corner of the room, a figure sits in an armchair in the semi-darkness, rocking back and forth, murmuring, 'I told him. I told him he'd pay.'

'Who do we have here?' I ask.

'I can tell you that,' Rob says. 'Mr Timothy Robbins.'

THIRTY-NINE

Five months later

Gill pushes a bottle of ginger ale across the table. We are at the Italian restaurant up on the High Street, where the chef is preparing a batch of pesto. The smell of basil is overwhelming. It's doing nothing for the incessant queasiness tormenting me as much as a drawn-out hangover. Except I haven't had a drink for over three months now, not that I'm counting. I take a few sips of the ginger ale. It's the only thing that seems to be working this time. With Joe and Isabella, Fanta had hit the spot.

'It's good to have a proper catch-up, finally,' Gill says.

'You will go away on all these trips,' I say, my tone teasing. She knows I'm her number one supporter of the travelling lifestyle she has adopted since retiring. Having dedicated her life to raising foster kids because she couldn't have children of her own, she deserves it more than most. She has just returned from a three-month Caribbean cruise with Derek, although she remains steadfast that their relationship is purely platonic. Her face radiates a healthy glow.

'So, tell me. I've never had the opportunity to ask. What changed your mind in the end?' Gill asks, nodding at my belly.

'Jim desperately wanted a third as much as Joe and Isabella wanted another brother or sister. I guess I realised they're growing up way too fast, and I don't want to live with any regrets.' I exhale a deep breath. 'It's going to be a challenge.'

'You'll find a way to cope.'

'Don't fancy moving in for a few months, do you? Like you did when Joe and Isabella were born.'

She smiles with the love only a mother can give their daughter. 'I'm sure we can sort something out.

'You'd be closer to Derek,' I tease.

'And the kids are all OK?'

'Doing well. Joe is ticking over. And Isabella has a new bff – Aida, the daughter of that woman over there.' I nod towards Siena serving behind the counter. 'She's a cute kid. They have a lovely friendship.'

'I bet Jim was over the moon when you told him you were pregnant.'

'Ecstatic.'

She raises an eyebrow. 'Tell me you're going to take a decent amount of maternity leave.'

'Jim's insisting I take a year, but we'll have to see how his third book goes.'

'A year minimum, I should think.' She picks up the menu. 'You ready to choose?'

I scan the offerings and opt for a turkey sandwich, but when the waitress appears, I ask her to hold the cranberry and grilled brie, and the butter too.

She smiles her understanding. 'A dry turkey sandwich it is.'

'I wish this damn morning sickness would leave me alone.'

Gill orders then pops to the toilet. I pick up my phone and respond to an email to confirm my presence in court next week and check my messages. A text from Sasha asks how long we'll be. I reply:

Having an early lunch with Gill. I'll pick up Jim and head over. Should be with you within the hour.

'I told Sasha we'll be in there in about an hour,' I say, when Gill returns.

'How are Sasha and Marc? Brief me before we see them. I don't want to put my foot in it. They're off to Devon, you said?'

I nod. 'Sasha's moving her business down there.'

'It all happened very quickly in the end, then.'

'With two other houses for sale in the close, they had to accept an offer below the asking price, but they're so keen to move.' The waitress brings our order.

'And how is Marc after all the drama?'

I exhale a deep breath. 'Getting there. He's in therapy.

They found a great clinic, and he's doing well, Sasha tells me. He's working on his marker pen project. I told you about that, didn't I?'

She nods. 'Getting the right therapy is so important when you're in such a dark place that despair overrides hope. Where was he all that time?'

'He went to Cambridge for a night then came back to London.'

'Why Cambridge?'

'He says he doesn't know. It's all a blur. He can't even remember the train journey. Or seeing me at the station before he left. He was born and spent his youth in Cambridge. Perhaps he thought he'd find some comfort there. Who knows? He returned to London and slept rough for a few nights before a homeless charity picked him up and helped him get his act together.'

'Gosh, poor man.'

I take a bite of the turkey sandwich. It makes me gag. 'You don't have to come over to theirs this afternoon. It's just they are off in two days, and I promised I'd help.'

'I'm happy to come along and help too. Devon, lovely part of the world to move to. You'll miss her.'

'All of them.'

'And what about their dodgy neighbours?'

'Annie and Art are out on bail awaiting trial. They're trying to sell their house to pay for their legal fees.'

'Will they go to prison?'

'There's so much evidence; I can't see even the best defence getting them acquitted.' It transpired that Art had been a low-profile dealer for a number of years – supplying users like Marc – but his insatiable need for more got the better of him and he started messing with the big boys. And you mess with the big boys, you have to know precisely what you are doing. The good to come out of it all was that we managed to nail Shane Baker and JJ Harper. 'Luke's in a young offender institution, awaiting trial, as well.'

'How's his recovery going?'

'Surprisingly well considering the injury he sustained. He was a lucky boy. The knife missed his vital organs. Such a disturbed individual. Incredibly intelligent but so deluded. Delusional disorder, a case of psychosis. Unable to see what's real and what's not. Dangerous when you marry it with his level of intelligence. In his sick mind, he was punishing everyone who had done wrong. He believed they all deserved it.' I shake my head, puffing my cheeks out. 'It can't have helped that he found out about his adoption in the way he did or discovering his parents were drug dealers.'

'You've got to feel sorry for the lad in some ways. He's had a lot to contend with. What a waste, all those brains. Think about the good use he could have put them to.'

My dear friend, you always see the best in people.

'There's still time. He's young. He'll be there for a while, though.'

'How long?'

'It's hard to say. A good few years given the number of victims, planning and malicious intent involved. It wasn't a spur of the moment crime. It was long in the planning and execution.'

'What about Robbins?'

'On remand, awaiting trial. He'll go down for a fair while. What a waste of a life. All for a fling. When he went to the police to confess, he realised the enormity of what he'd done. The affair with the pupil had been going on for over a year. His career was over, all his savings were gone. His wife left him. He snapped. Turned out he was going round to Napier Close to have it out with Luke, but saw him getting into a cab and followed him.'

'And is Sasha OK?' she asks.

'I think it'll take her a while to fully accept everything. She feels guilty that Marc was depressed and taking drugs right under her nose, and she never even noticed. She put his mood swings down to the redundancy and not being able to find another job. I feel a bit guilty myself. I had a sneak in his wardrobe, just after he left, and found a small pouch of coke. Perhaps I should have said something.'

'You were only doing what you thought was best at the time.'

I force another bite of sandwich, but then I have to surrender. Chucking it down, I push the plate away. 'Apparently, he'd been saying for over a year he hated his job and wished he could concentrate on his magic pen project, but Sasha didn't listen. She was too scared of the financial impact of him being out of work for any length of time. They won't have the financial burden after the move. Sasha's found the twins places at a state sixth form, so they'll be rid of school fees and be mortgage-free. It'll release the funds for Marc to further develop his magic pen.'

'A good place to be.'

'You sound like Jim. That's what he keeps saying. If we sell the house and move to Devon, we could buy our next home outright.'

'Tempted?'

'Not at all,' I say, steepling my fingers. 'I love my job and my home and would miss London too much.'

After we pick up Jim, heavy traffic delays us getting to Sasha's, stop and go, stop and go, but I'm OK with that. Since an eight-week emergency scan, due to some blood loss, I've found a coping strategy for the inevitable delays of London's congestion. Usually, I've got an audiobook on the go. I don't get the time to read like I used to, so it's a great way to keep up with my love of literature. Ruth Rendall proves a great distraction. Today Gill and I chat while Jim types away on his phone.

When I park up in Napier Close, and get out, I see Pen, dressed in an autumn jacket, the hood covering her head. She is hurrying into Pen's Parlour with her dog. Pete is re-erecting a FOR SALE board which seems to have been displaced from the ground. I hear Pen call out to him. 'I'm having a salad for lunch. You make your own.' He kicks the board when it falls again.

We climb out of the car to a chilled wind flickering the waxy leaves of the eucalyptus trees; autumn taking a firm hold. I lock the car, thinking of the leaves blanketing our garden, and I make a mental note to remind the kids that this is a job for them from now on.

Sasha greets us, holding open the door 'Watch out, it's chaos in here.'

We step inside, weaving our way through half-packed boxes, metres of bubble wrap and rolls of packing tape. Jim doesn't use his wheelchair as much these days. Only when he is really tired or having a bad day. I found him an exercise specialist in West Norwood from whom he sees great results along with his continued sessions with Sasha. Pain still haunts him on bad days, but such days, I'm relieved to say, are now few and far between.

We follow Sasha into the kitchen. 'Drink?' she asks.

I shake my head and hand her a brown paper bag. 'Here, I've brought you all your favourites from the deli.'

'You angel. I'm starving, and the fridge is bare. I was going to ring for pizza.' She steps out of the room and calls out, 'Kids, lunch.'

'We can only stay until pickup time. What do you want us to do?' I ask.

'I've saved this cupboard of glasses for you to pack. They're light.'

'Where's Marc?' I ask, cutting a piece of bubble wrap and handing it to Gill to parcel a glass.

'He's with Alisha, finalising the intellectual property side of things for his *Magic Marker*.' She glances at her watch. 'He should be back soon.' She slaps her forehead and laughs. 'And there was me thinking those two were having an affair when Annie saw them together in the café that day.'

I laugh too. 'And Pen!'

Sasha glances over at me, still laughing. 'What was I thinking?' She's getting back to her old self, her long hair shining in the afternoon light and her soft dimples prominent in her pretty face.

'I've just seen Pen and Pete. They didn't look too happy.'

'They're getting a divorce. Pen told me yesterday.'

'That's hardly surprising.'

'They're waiting to sell the house to split the proceeds, and, get this,' she raises her eyebrows, trying to stifle a giggle, 'she's moving in with Tom.'

I gasp. 'I thought he'd gone to live in Newcastle with his parents after Alisha kicked him out.'

'He did. But she told me yesterday they're still seeing each other.'

A whirlwind of activity occurs as Marc arrives home, and the teenagers swing into the kitchen, ecstatic at the thought of food. Hannah unwraps the packages, arguing with Harry 'I want this cheese one,' she replies to his demand to hand over the Philadelphia and smoked salmon bagel. 'I'll be glad when you go back to uni,' she says, as Harry swipes it out of her hand. Ralph is yapping around their feet, excited at the prospect of some titbits. At Sasha's request, Harry searches for some kitchen roll to use as serviettes, tripping over a packed box of crockery in the middle of the floor. 'Fill the kettle,' Sasha instructs Hannah. Marc scolds George for biting into a brownie, clipping him playfully around the ear. Sasha tells them all to calm down. 'It was quiet in here a minute ago.' She rolls her eyes and smiles, relishing the chaos of her family life. 'You've got all this to come, especially with double trouble,' she says to Jim and me, giving us a knowing smile.

'I can't wait,' says Jim, nuzzling my neck.

I watch the five of them, as I stroke my belly, already expanding with the two babies who have made a home inside me.

PLEASE LEAVE A REVIEW

As for all authors, reviews are the key to raising awareness of my work. If you have enjoyed this book, please do consider leaving a review on Amazon to help others find it too.

mybook.to/DontComeLooking

All of my books go through a rigorous editing process, but sometimes mistakes do happen. If you have spotted a typo, please contact me, so I can get it corrected straight away.

https://www.ajcampbellauthor.com/contact

Thank you.
AJ

A NOTE FROM AJ

According to the mental health charity MIND, mental health problems affect around one in four people in any given year. Someone you know is suffering. Do look out for them and show your support. Always be kind.

I hope you enjoyed reading my second published book *Don't Come Looking* as much as I adored writing it. If you haven't read my debut novel *Leave Well Alone*, check it out at your local Amazon store. Find out how Eva's story began.

http://mybook.to/LeaveWellAlone

LOVE THRILLER AND MYSTERY BOOKS?

For me, building a relationship with my readers is one of the joys of writing.

I set up the AJ Campbell Readers Club for me to keep in contact with you all.

Sign up today to be the first to hear about my new releases, including free and discounted books, plus the chance to win book-related prizes. You will also receive my free short story *Choices*, exclusive to club members.

http://www.ajcampbellauthor.com/download

BOOK CLUB QUESTIONS
DON'T COME LOOKING

1. *'I switch on the radio. A broadcast about depression and suicide catches my attention. Middle-aged men have the highest rate of suicide in the UK, and the rate for young females is now at its highest rate on record.'* Why do you think this age difference exists?
2. Which character did you relate to the most? Why?
3. Eva indulges in criminal activity to help her friend. What does this say about Eva as a person?
4. Eva struggles with the love of her work and of her family. *'Work versus motherhood, a never-ending tug of war that neither side can effectively win.'* Do you agree with this statement?
5. Do you think Sasha was wrong to lie to her children about what had happened to Marc, or do you think her actions were justified in the circumstances?

6. Luke is a complex character. For a young man of his age, with the right treatment and therapy, do you think there is a chance he can go on to lead a normal life?

7. What did you make of Eva and Rob's relationship?

8. Napier Close has some quirky characters. Did the story make you question how well you know your neighbours, or anyone else?

9. As the story progressed, where did you think Marc had gone and why?

10. What long-term impact do you think the events would have on the O'Sullivan children?

ACKNOWLEDGMENTS

Once again, I owe my gratitude to so many people, without whom I could never have achieved publishing a second novel. Firstly, to those who generously gave their valuable time to read *Don't Come Looking* when it was still a work in progress: Christine, Claire, Karen, John and Maddie. Your input was invaluable in enhancing the story. Thank you also to John Black and Alex Ross for answering police-related questions when I needed help.

Thank you to my talented editor, Louise Walters, who, once again, helped me turn my story into one worthy for publication, and to Tim Barber for another cracking cover. To my ARC team - thank you for your sharp eyes in weeding out those last-minute pesky typos. And thank you to dearest Barbara. How lucky am I to have met you on this adventure? A true friend and master of the written word, you have helped me so much this past year. Keep the GIFs coming!

And to you, my readers. Thank you for reading my

books and making me a bestselling author. For that, I will be forever grateful. I also send my heartfelt thanks to all the people who have supported me with the publishing side of things – all the book bloggers who have joined my book tours and the authors and media folk who have featured me in their newspapers, magazines and radio shows, as well as their blogs and podcasts. And a special thank you to Christine Henderson for your continued support with my writing career.

To my wonderful three sons – boys, I am blessed to be your mother. And finally, to Andy. What a year we've had! Keep strong, partner. We have many miles left to walk together.

ABOUT THE AUTHOR

AJ Campbell is the debut author of the Amazon bestselling novel *Leave Well Alone.* An alumna of the Faber Academy, she writes in the psychological suspense and mystery genres.

AJ draws inspiration for her writing from many facets of everyday life. The human mind and how different people react to each other and interact in society fascinates her. She loves settling down with a good book and enjoys thought-provoking stories that beg the question – what would I have done in that situation?

AJ lives on the Essex / Hertfordshire border with her husband, sons and cocker spaniel, Max. She enjoys walking Max in the local fields to boost her creativity, and cooking oriental food while sipping a good glass of white wine.

Printed in Great Britain
by Amazon